Animal
Fairy Stories

Animal
Fairy Stories

Retold by
Alena Benešová

Translated by
Ruth Shepherd

Illustrations by
Karel Franta

Cathay Books

First published 1982 by
Cathay Books Limited
59 Grosvenor Street
London W1

Retold by Alena Benešová
Translated by Ruth Shepherd
Graphic design by Bohuslav Blažej
This edition © Artia, Prague 1982
Reprinted 1984, 1985
ISBN 0 86178 148 1
Printed in Czechoslovakia by Svoboda
1/20/03/51—04

Contents

How Animals Came into the World

Once upon a time when the world was still young, the Sun was a great chieftain and he lived in a great tent in the sky.

All day long the Sun shone down and warmed the world. He was assisted in his work by the strong and powerful Napi.

One day Napi had finished working a little earlier than the Sun. He sat down by the well, filled his pipe and smoked peacefully. To while away the time he picked up a piece of clay and started to knead it in his hands. Very soon he had between his fingers a little animal. He fashioned another and another until at last he had made all the animals that live on the earth today.

Napi put the clay animals on a flat stone to dry. He then picked up his pipe again and thoughtfully puffed it. After a time he took up in his hand the first clay animal, breathed on it and said. 'Off you go, my son, you will be a bison and you will live in the mountains.'

Then he picked up one clay animal after another, breathed on each of them and soon there was an antelope, a beaver, a deer, a mountain sheep, a badger and all the others. He

gave a name to every animal that lives in the world. And he told each of them where its home was to be.

One piece of clay remained on the flat stone. Napi looked at it thoughtfully and went on smoking. After a time, he picked it up in his hand, breathed on it and said. 'Off you go, my son, you will be man and you will live with the wolves.'

And so animals came into the world and with the animals, man.

When Napi had created all the animals and given each its place on earth, he thought he had done well and that everyone would be satisfied. But it was not so. In a few days' time, Napi came to the well again to rest. Hardly had he sat

down than his animals began to run up to him from all directions. They came to tell him they were not satisfied.

The first to speak to Napi was the bison, who said, 'Napi, you have not arranged things well! We are not happy.'

'And what makes you unhappy?' asked Napi.

'After all I gave each of you his own piece of the earth. I can see no reason for your discontent.'

'That is exactly what is wrong,' said the bison. 'You said I should live in the mountains. But I cannot live there. The slopes are too steep, I cannot walk there, the rocks are too hard and hurt my hoofs, and there is very little grass and I have not enough to eat. So you see, Napi, why I cannot live in the mountains.'

The mountain sheep, on the other hand, said. 'Napi, I cannot live in the lowlands. There is nothing there on which to sharpen my hoofs, there is nothing for me to climb and I have nothing to eat because no moss grows there.'

Napi listened to the bison, he listened to the mountain sheep, he listened to all the other animals — the antelope, the goat, the bear, the puma and the wolf. Then he said. 'I understand, my children. I shall redivide the world among you. You, Bison, will live in the plains and with you all animals who will be happy there. You, Sheep, will live in the mountains and with you all animals who will be happy there. And with you, in one region, man will live.'

And so Napi redivided the world among the animals, and the animals at last were content. Only man was not satisfied. Soon men wandered and settled in every corner of the earth. And in every corner of the earth man will be found today.

Brother Rabbit
and
Brother Fox

Brother Rabbit and Brother Fox were once great friends. They went everywhere together, even when they went courting. For the fox had spotted a pretty vixen in a nearby village and Brother Rabbit used to go with him to visit her. But one day Brother Fox caught a cold and the rabbit went alone to visit the vixen.

In fact, Brother Rabbit was quite envious of Brother Fox. As he and the vixen were talking, Brother Fox was mentioned.

'Oh, that fox,' said Brother Rabbit. 'I know him well. He is my very best horse. When I go anywhere, I saddle him and ride like a gentleman.'

The vixen was much surprised, but Brother Rabbit insisted that the fox was his horse. Then the rabbit thought he had better not boast too much in case he angered the fox.

And indeed the fox was angry. Hardly had he recovered from his cold than he went to visit the vixen and learnt from her what his friend, the rabbit, had been saying about him. Furiously he ran to the rabbit's house, knocked on the door and said. 'Brother Rabbit, come outside!'

Brother Rabbit was waiting for the fox. He squeaked in a thin little voice. 'What do you want, Brother Fox?'

'I want to talk to you,' growled the fox angrily. 'I hear you have been saying that I am your horse.'

'That's not true,' squeaked Brother Rabbit in the same thin little voice. 'I have said nothing of the kind.' Brother Fox was partly satisfied.

'Well, if it's not true, come and tell my friend, the vixen,' he said.

Brother Rabbit started to whine again. 'I'd like to, my friend, but I can't,' he said. 'Yesterday I had a fall and I can scarcely walk. But I could come perhaps if you were willing to carry me there on your back.'

The fox wanted to clear his name with the vixen as quickly as he could, so he growled. 'All right, come on then, I'll carry you there.'

Brother Rabbit came out of his cottage, looked at the fox and then said, in a weak little voice. 'That's no good, Fox. I wouldn't manage to hold on. But perhaps if you had a saddle on your back and a bridle round your head, I should have something to hold on to!'

The fox wanted to get the rabbit to his sweetheart as quickly as possible, so he growled. 'All right, if there is no other way. Put a saddle and bridle on me, but hurry!'

The rabbit did not need to be told twice. He brought a saddle and a bridle and put them on the fox, picked up a whip and hopped into the saddle.

In a short time they were in the village where the vixen lived. The fox stopped and said. 'Come on, Brother, get down. We shall go the rest of the way on foot. I will not carry you any further.'

But Brother Rabbit did not get down from the saddle. He flicked the fox between the ears with his whip so hard that the fox shot off like an arrow and did not stop running till he was in the yard behind the vixen's house. Only then did Brother Rabbit jump down. He then tied the bridle to a post and went into the house.

It was true. There in the yard by the post the fox was jumping up and down. On his back was a saddle and on his head a bridle which was tied to the post. Only when he pulled with all his strength did the bridle break. Thereupon the fox took to his heels and never showed himself in that village again.

That is the story of how Brother Rabbit took

'Now you will see,' he said to the vixen, 'that I wasn't lying and that the fox really is my horse. Just look in the yard!'

a ride on Brother Fox. He taught Brother Fox to be a wilier fox, but since then has kept out of Brother Fox's way. And he still keeps out of his way, because to this day the fox cannot forget the shame he suffered and whenever he gets the chance he hunts the rabbit who was once his friend.

The Crow,
the Fox and
the Cheese

Long ago, when all the animals could still talk, a crow one day found a piece of cheese. A farmer had dropped it on his way to market and the crow carried it off to a tall oak tree to enjoy it in peace.

But hardly had she taken the first bite when a fox appeared under the oak tree. The fox had caught the scent of the cheese from a long way off and was determined to taste it. But how was he going to get hold of it when the crow was holding it in her beak and, at the same time, was perched high up in the oak tree?

But the fox deserved his reputation for wiliness. He sat down under the tree and said. 'My dear sister, you just don't know how beautiful you are. Your feathers gleam like precious stones, your beak shines like gold, your claws glisten like silver! Everything about you is beautiful. There's only one thing wrong with you. What a pity it is that you can't sing as beautifully as you look.'

The crow was delighted with everything the fox said. No one had ever told her before that she was beautiful. Only one thing worried her,

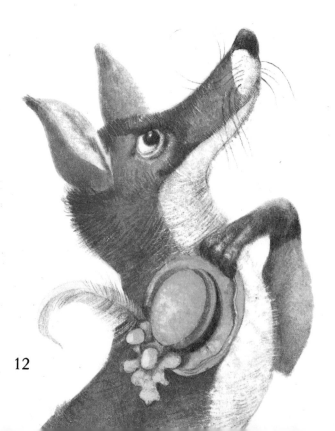

that the fox had not praised her voice too. She forgot that she was holding the piece of cheese in her beak and opening it wide, she let out a tremendous caw. 'Caw, caw, caw! Brother Fox, when I want I can sing well too. Just listen!'

But the fox did not bother to listen to the cawing.

He seized the cheese which the crow had dropped and started to laugh. 'You silly old crow,' he said, 'to believe everything anyone tells you. Your voice is just as ugly as your feathers. The only beautiful thing was that piece of cheese you had in your beak. Now it's mine.'

And off ran the fox with the piece of cheese.

The poor crow learnt that day a lesson that she would remember all her life. Ever since she has never believed flattering words and when she has something in her beak she prefers not to sing.

The Ant and the Dove

Across the blue sky flew a dove. Her outspread wings looked like a fan, gently fluttered by the breeze.

The ant, looking up at the sky, caught sight of the dove and was so delighted by her beauty that his head spun. His knees gave way beneath him, his foot slipped, he tumbled down a bank and fell into the brook at the bottom.

The water flowed fast, tossing the ant hither and thither until he was quite out of breath. On and on it carried him he did not know where.

The dove looked down and saw the drowning ant and her heart was full of pity. She flew down to the brook, and taking a blade of grass in her beak she held it out to the ant and pulled him to safety.

The sun soon dried the ant and as he waved goodbye to the dove he wondered how he could ever repay her for saving his life. His chance soon came.

In the heat of the midday sun, the dove perched on the branch of a tree to rest. In a few minutes she had fallen asleep. The sleeping dove was spied by a boy who happened to be walking by. In his hand he held a catapult. Cautiously he came close to the tree and picked up a stone . . .

The ant saw what was happening and as hard as he could he nipped the boy's leg. The boy gave a shout and dropped his catapult. The boy's cry wakened the dove just in time. She flew off high into the sky, so high that no eye could see her or no hand reach her.

The ant was happy for he had repaid the dove and he set off merrily for home, singing as he went.

13

The Lion
and His
Counsellors

There once lived a powerful lion who had three counsellors, a wolf, a jackal and a raven. The king lion ruled and hunted, his counsellors advised and ate what their lord and master gave them from his table. And they all were content.

One day a camel strayed into the lion's kingdom. The lion had never seen such an animal before and was curious.

'Who are you and what are you seeking here, stranger?' asked the lion.

'I am a camel and I am seeking protection from people,' replied the camel.

The lion took a liking to the camel and said. 'Stay here with me and be my guest. You will be safe with me.'

The camel accepted the invitation with pleasure and from that time on lived with the lion. He was very contented there; he had lush pastures on which to graze, enough water to drink and his life was protected by the powerful ruler, the lion.

But one day the lion suffered a serious defeat. He was overcome in battle by an elephant.

Wounded by the elephant's tusks, the lion lay in his cave unable to move, unable to hunt. And his counsellors who relied on the lion for food went hungry.

'What shall we do?' they asked each other.

'We would never be able to hunt for ourselves,' whined the lazy wolf.

'Let us eat the camel,' the jackal suggested.

'The lion would not allow it,' replied the wolf. 'After all the camel is his guest.'

'I shall persuade him,' said the raven. 'Leave it to me.' And he flew off to the sick lion.

'Most powerful King,' he said to the lion, 'we are worried about you. You are eating nothing and drinking nothing and we fear you may die of weakness. You must eat to regain your strength.'

'You are right, Raven,' replied the lion, 'but what can I do when I am unable to hunt.'

'Why should you go hunting when there is a good meal to be had close by?' croaked the raven.

'Surely you are not thinking of our friend the camel, you traitor,' said the lion angrily. 'Do you want me to break my royal word?'

'Why should you break it, most powerful King,' answered the raven. 'You will see that the camel himself will offer you his meat. Then you can be free to eat him.'

'Very well,' muttered the lion.

The raven flew back to his friends, the counsellors, and told them what they must say and how they must say it. Then all three counsellors asked the camel to accompany them on a visit to the lion.

Having arrived in the King's presence, the raven was the first to speak. 'Most powerful King,' he said, 'I see that you will die of weakness if you eat nothing. But we, your faithful servants, would willingly give up our lives for you. Eat me and become strong again!'

Before the raven had finished speaking, the jackal cried out. 'No, most powerful King, the raven has little flesh on his bones and his meat would harm you. Eat me instead!'

Before the jackal had finished speaking, the wolf cried. 'No, most precious King, the jackal is unclean. His meat will harm you. Eat me!'

But before the wolf stopped speaking, the jackal and the raven began to shriek. 'No, King, wolf's meat would harm you, you must not eat it either!'

The camel listened to them. At last he said to himself. 'Now it is time for me to show my devotion to the King. But the others will not let me be eaten.'

And so he said. 'Most powerful King, if you cannot eat wolf meat or jackal meat or raven meat, then take mine!'

Before he could finish speaking, the raven, the jackal and the wolf cried out with one voice. 'Yes, great King, that is the meat for you!'

And without mercy they flung themselves on the camel and tore him to pieces.

The Wolf and the Lamb

The wolf was hungry, so hungry that he could scarcely crawl for weakness. But nowhere in the woods was there a single living thing to eat. Exhausted, he stopped at a stream in a quiet glade to refresh himself. And what did he see?

Just below him, drinking from the same stream, was a lamb. The wolf sniffed the air in anticipation and his mouth began to water. There was no shepherd in sight, no sheep dog ... only the white lamb down there by the stream.

The wolf raised his head and began to think. He knew he had a bad reputation, that people spoke ill of him, saying that he could not be trusted and was a killer who showed no mercy. He looked at the lamb and knew it could not escape. But before gobbling it up, he wanted to think of a reason for killing it. So he went slowly down the bank so as not to frighten the lamb, took a deep drink of the crystal clear water, then growled at the lamb. 'You are little and you are impolite. Don't you know you have polluted the water that I am drinking?'

The lamb lifted its little muzzle in surprise. 'Excuse me, please, Brother Wolf, but I would never dream of doing that. In any case I could not have polluted the water because you were drinking higher up the stream.'

The wolf was annoyed. The lamb was right, there was no denying it. And so he tried again. 'I have heard on good authority,' he growled, 'that you have been speaking ill of me.'

'When was that?' asked the lamb in surprise. 'How could I have said wicked things about you when I have never set eyes on you before? You must be mistaken, Brother Wolf.'

The wolf found it hard to control his anger. 'If it was not you it must have been one of your brothers. What difference does it make?'

'But I have no brothers, Brother Wolf,' said the lamb.

'If you have no brothers, at least you have a father and I am quite sure he has spoken ill of me,' growled the wolf. 'So I shall waste no more time and punish you.'

And then, before the lamb had time to run away, the wolf jumped on it and in next to no time had gobbled it up.

Poor little lamb, it had been quite right, but what is the use of being right when you are dealing with a wolf.

The Grasshopper and the Ant

It was summer and the grasshopper was as happy as could be. The sun was shining, the meadows smelt sweet and the grasshopper sang and sang. He did not worry at all about what was to come, it was enough for him to sing a song and have the blue sky above him. But summer does not last forever.

One day he woke up stiff with cold, yellow leaves whirling round him, the sky was overcast and it rained and rained. He was hungry too.

'Whatever shall I do? Winter is long and hard, I am sure to starve or freeze to death. What about going to see Brother Ant?' he asked himself. 'Surely he will help me. In summer I had no time to collect food for the winter or to build myself a house. I had to sing all the time. But now it is no fun singing.'

It had begun to snow when, with his heart beating fast, he knocked at the door of the ant's house.

'What do you want?' asked the ant in surprise when he saw the grasshopper at the door.

'I am hungry and I am cold,' said the grasshopper, shaking the snow from his wings and feet and he looked enviously into the cosy little house.

And the ant replied. 'What were you doing in summer when there was plenty of food everywhere and plenty of time to build yourself a house?'

'I sang, I sang all the time.' And the grasshopper glowed when he thought of it.

'And what else?' asked the ant.

'What else? Nothing, I suppose,' admitted the grasshopper.

'You sang, did you? Well, now you can dance!' snapped the ant, banging the door leading to his snug, safe home.

The Little Goat and the Leopard

Long, long ago, when the world was still quite new, all the animals built huts for themselves in the woods. One day a leopard was searching for a suitable place to build his house. He came upon a little clearing among the trees.

'I shall build my house here,' he said to himself, 'but first I must cut down this tall grass.' And he went off to find a sickle.

A little later a little goat came to the same place. He too, was looking for a place to build his hut. He too liked the little clearing among the trees. 'But I must cut this tall grass,' he said to himself. He set to at once and in a short time the grass lay flat. Then the little goat went off to graze.

When, not long afterwards, the leopard came back and saw that the grass had been cut, he was surprised and said to himself. 'It must have been the powerful spirit of the leopards helping me. Tomorrow I must cut the logs to build the house.' And he went off to hunt.

The next day the little goat came to the clearing and cut the logs. He piled them up and went off to graze. Soon afterwards the leopard came back to the clearing. He could scarcely believe his eyes when he saw the pile of logs. 'It must have been the powerful spirit of the leopards helping me again,' he said. 'Tomorrow I must drive these logs into the ground.' And he went off to hunt.

The third day the little goat came to the clearing and drove the logs into the ground. In a short time he had built a strong hut. All that was missing was the roof. Then he went off to graze.

Very soon the leopard returned to the clearing. When he saw that the hut was nearly completed he was amazed. 'Again it was certainly the good spirit of the leopards helping me,' he said. 'Tomorrow I must build the roof and the hut will be finished.' And he ran off to hunt.

The next day the little goat came to the clearing and built a roof of leafy branches. When he had finished he went off to graze. Hardly had he left the clearing when the leopard arrived. Again he was amazed, for now the cottage had a roof.

'Certainly it must have been the powerful spirit of the leopards helping me,' he thought. 'Tomorrow I shall move in.'

When the next day, dawned he went to the clearing and what did he see? The little goat and his wife were moving in.

'What are you doing here?' he roared at them.

'We are moving into our house,' replied the
the little goat.

'Your house?' said the leopard. 'And who
found this clearing?'

'I did,' replied the little goat.

'And who cut the grass?' asked the leopard.

'I did,' replied the little goat.

'And who cut the logs?' growled the leopard.

'I did,' replied the little goat.

'And who built the hut?' roared the leopard.

'I did,' answered the little goat.

'And who made the roof out of leafy
branches?' asked the leopard angrily.

'I did, I did,' replied the little goat fearlessly,
and stood in the doorway.

'Do not quarrel about it,' said the little goat's
wife, trying to make peace between them. 'The
hut is big enough for all of us. The leopard can
live in one half and we in the other.'

The leopard and the little goat agreed to this
arrangement and they began to keep house
together. The leopard went hunting antelope,
the goat brought vegetables and the little
Nanny goat cooked for them all. But one day it
happened that the leopard had not caught
an antelope and in the village he killed a kid.
When he brought it home to the hut and showed
it to the little goat, he knew immediately what
had happened.

'I do not eat this kind of meat!' he said and
immediately began to plan his revenge.

The next morning he stopped a hunter in the
forest and asked him to kill a leopard for him.
The hunter did what the little goat asked and
that evening brought him a dead leopard. The
little goat took it home and showed it to his
neighbour, the leopard. 'Just look at the
antelope I killed today,' he said.

The leopard knew at once what it was and
said. 'I do not eat that kind of meat!' And he was
frightened.

The next day, when the little goat had gone
hunting, the leopard said to the little Nanny
goat. 'Tell me, how did your husband kill that
leopard?' And the little Nanny goat told him, as
her husband had advised her to.

'I shall tell you, but you must keep it secret.
My little goat has the evil eye. When he wants
to, he just looks at someone with that evil eye
and it is the end of him. He falls to the ground
as if shot by an arrow. He has gone hunting
again today. Just wait and see what he brings
back!'

The leopard was very frightened. 'What if
that little goat should be angry with me and
looks at me with that evil eye,' he thought. 'It
would be the end of me. I had better keep out of
his way!' And he ran off into the undergrowth
at the other side of the forest.

Ever since then leopards have never built
huts for themselves but have lived in the
thickets. And neither do goats live with
leopards in the forest, but prefer to make their
homes with people.

The Owl
and
the Ravens

Once upon a time all the birds, except the raven, met in the bird parliament to elect a king. After a long discussion they chose the owl as their ruler. But just as they were going to put the crown on his head, the raven flew in. And so before continuing with the ceremony, they asked the raven for his opinion. The raven did not approve of their choice. 'I have nothing against the owl,' he said, 'but he is not the one to be king. A king should see better than anyone else and the owl is blind in daylight. A king

should be modest and the owl is puffed up. A king should be seen at all times by his subjects and the owl hides himself away.'

The birds agreed that the raven was right. So instead of the owl they elected the eagle as king. But the owl never forgave the raven and since that time owls and ravens have been enemies.

It happened one night that owls attacked a raven's nest, killed some of the young and injured many more. The next day the chief of the ravens called together his advisers and asked their advice. One counsellor advised him to find another home, a second that he should attack the owls and kill them and a third that he should beg the owls for peace. The oldest adviser did not agree with any of these suggestions.

'We cannot buy peace,' he said. 'We cannot defeat the owls. You shall not find a new home. We must use cunning. Pluck out a few of my feathers, leave me lying by your nests, take your families and fly away to the next wood. When the owls come to attack again at night, they will find me here and take me prisoner. I shall

20

behave with great humility and prepare my revenge.'

The ravens took the advice of their wise old colleague. They did what he said and left him — half-plucked of his feathers — beside their nests, and flew off. That night the owls found the ravens' nests empty. Only one old and ragged raven remained. The owls took him prisoner and brought him before their queen.

The owl queen blinked and demanded sharply, 'Speak, Raven, who are you and who has treated you thus?'

'I am the adviser to the chief of the ravens,' the old raven said, 'and my own brothers drove me out because I advised them to make peace with you.'

The owls cried out in disbelief, assuring their queen that he must be a spy. But the owl queen liked his respectful manner and she made him her own chief counsellor. Then the raven gave her advice as to how to punish his brothers.

The queen wanted to follow his counsel. 'But where shall I find them?' she asked.

'Leave that to me, Your Majesty,' answered the old raven. 'I shall find them for you.' And at once he flew off to the wood in search of his brothers. He found them easily. 'Listen,' he told them, 'tomorrow when the owls are asleep, each of you must bring a dry twig to the rocks where they live. Everything else you can leave to me.'

Next day at noon the ravens flew to the rocks and in a few minutes there was a great pile of brushwood beneath the owls' castle. Soon afterwards the old raven arrived too. He carried in his beak a burning branch he had pulled out of a woodman's fire. He dropped the burning branch onto the pile of brushwood and soon the owls' castle was in flames.

Thus the ravens had their revenge. All the owls perished in the fire and the ravens at last had peace. The wise old raven, alas, died in the flames, but his death was not in vain. From that day all the ravens spoke of his wisdom and courage which together had saved them.

The Cat, the Weasel and the Rabbit

One morning, the weasel was walking in the fields when he came upon a little house belonging to the rabbit. Without a second's thought he moved in and waited to see what would happen. The little rabbit who was the owner was nibbling his way through a nearby cabbage patch. After a while he started to run races with the wind, and when he had outrun it he set off for home.

'What's this?' he squeaked, as he peeped through the window of his house and saw the weasel's nose. He came nearer to get a closer view of the intruder.

'Brother, I swear by every cabbage in the patch that you have made a mistake. You are in my house, not yours,' said the rabbit.

'Here I am and here I stay,' snapped the weasel. 'Anyway, can you prove it is your house and not mine?'

'Brother,' said the rabbit angrily, 'get out of my house or I shall set all the mice in the neighbourhood on you and then you will see what happens.'

'I shan't see anything,' snapped the weasel. 'This morning I moved into an empty house and so it's mine and not yours. Until you give me convincing proof that the house is yours, I shall not stir.'

'Right is on my side, Brother,' said the angry rabbit, 'and right declares that a house belongs to the one who moved in first. My grandfather lived here, my father lived here, and according to right, I now live here.'

'Enough is enough,' snarled the weasel, 'I can see that we shall never reach agreement like this. It will be best if we find a judge who is fair and ask him to decide who is in the right.'

'That's a good idea,' said the rabbit. 'Do you know of anyone?'

'Well, there's the old Tom Cat who lives by himself. He has a very good reputation,' replied the weasel. 'You must have heard of him.'

'No, I don't think I have heard of him,' the rabbit answered. 'Is he a judge?'

'Old Tom Cat is a very wise cat and everyone goes to him from far and wide to settle their quarrels.'

The rabbit listened but said nothing.

'He would certainly be the best judge for us,' went on the weasel. 'He can settle even the most difficult cases.'

'All right, do not let us waste time, agreed the rabbit. 'Let us go to him at once.'

So they went and knocked at the Tom Cat's door.

'Come in, come in, what an honour! What fair wind has brought you to my house?' said the old cat, purring with satisfaction and drawing in his sharp claws.

'We should like you to advise us,' piped the weasel.

'We need your help,' added the little rabbit.

'And in what way can I help you?' asked the old cat, leaning forward to listen to them. 'I am old and rather deaf. Come nearer so that I can hear you.'

'We have come to you, sir, to ask your opinion on a difficult matter,' they said, speaking one after the other.

'We just cannot agree about it.'

'I understand everything,' purred the cat, secretly licking his whiskers. 'I'll settle the problem even quicker and more fairly than you had hoped.'

And because the weasel and the rabbit had come within reach of his claws, it was no trouble to treat them both the same. Before they could count three he had pounced and they had no more need of his judgement.

The Jackal and the Sun's Flock of Sheep

Long ago, when the sun still lived with all the animals in one village, they made him shepherd.

Every morning he drove his flock of white sheep and lambs out onto the blue meadow of the sky and every evening he came back with them to the village to sleep.

The animals were fond of the sun because he not only warmed them but also gave them water to drink. For when it was very hot and dry, the sun milked some of his white sheep and it would rain. And so the other animals left the sun's white sheep in peace.

Not even the lion, or the leopard, or the panther, or the jaguar ever attacked any of them, even if they were very hungry and had not been able to hunt anything on the steppes or in the forest.

They knew that if they harmed the sheep the sun would be angry with them.

The jackal knew this as well as all the others. But he was discontented. The less he had of something, the more he wanted it. Everywhere he went he kept wondering how he could steal one of the sun's sheep without being found out.

But one day luck was on his side.

One of the little sheep wandered far away from the herd and onto the steppes. The jackal saw her, ran after her, attacked her and in the thicket ate her up.

Hardly had he finished eating when he became terribly thirsty. He ran to the well and said. 'Well, give me a little water, for I am terribly thirsty.'

And the well said. 'Drink your fill, Jackal. That is what I am here for.'

But hardly had the jackal bent over the well, when the water disappeared and all that was left in the well was a little mud.

The jackal was startled. He became more and more thirsty, so he ran to the river.

'River, give me a little water,' he said. 'I am terribly thirsty.'

And the river answered. 'Drink your fill, Jackal! That is what I am here for.'

But hardly had the jackal bent down to the river, when the water disappeared and all that was left on the river bed was gravel.

The jackal was startled. But his thirst was so great he could hardly bear it. So he ran to the lake.

'Lake, give me a little water,' he said. 'I am very thirsty!'

The lake said. 'Drink your fill, Jackal. That is what I am here for.'

But again the jackal was unable to drink. Hardly had he bent down to the lake when the water disappeared and all that remained in the lake was stones.

The jackal could not bear his thirst any longer. He fell to the ground and wailed. 'Forgive me, sun! Do not burn me and do not torture me with thirst. I shall give you back your little white sheep.'

And the jackal did give back the sun his little white sheep. He spat her out, bit by bit, until she stood before him alive and whole. Joyfully she ran off to join the rest of the flock grazing in the heavens.

The sun took pity on the jackal. He put back the water into the lake, put back the water into the river and into the well. But he did not come back himself in the evening to the village and to the animals.

He stayed up in the heavens for ever and there he grazes his white sheep and lambs from the clouds.

And the jackal to this day prefers to go hunting only when the sun has set.

Johnny and the Tree Frog

There was once a poor widow who owned nothing in the world but an old cottage and a son. His name was Johnny. The cottage stood near a forest where Johnny was completely at home. He went there for firewood which he tied up in bundles and sold to the neighbours. One day Johnny was coming back from the forest with a bundle of firewood when suddenly he heard a cry such as he had never heard in his life before, although he knew the voices of all the animals and birds of the forest.

Anyone else would have been frightened, but Johnny was never afraid. He flung the bundle of wood to the ground and ran quickly in the direction of the cry. He did not have to run far.

A little further on, he saw, lying on the path, a beautiful green tree frog. She was pinned to the ground by a fox. Johnny immediately picked up a stone to threaten the fox. The fox let go his prey, took to his heels and was off like the wind. Thanks to Johnny the tree frog was free. She lay on the ground helpless and scarcely breathing. Johnny lifted her gently, put her inside his shirt, picked up the bundle of firewood and ran home.

At home his mother was waiting for him. 'Where have you been all this time?' she asked Johnny. And Johnny told her.

'I have been in the forest,' he said. 'Just look what I have brought home.' And he showed his mother the little tree frog.

His mother was surprised. 'But that's just an ordinary frog,' she said. 'There are hundreds of them everywhere.'

But Johnny knew what he was talking about. 'It is not an ordinary frog, Mother. It is a tree frog,' he said. 'And I rescued her from a fox.'

And he told his mother what had happened. His mother looked at the little tree frog again.

'You are quite right, Johnny,' she said. 'It is no ordinary frog. I have never seen such a beautiful tree frog before. Since you saved her life, you must keep her and take good care of her.'

Johnny looked after the little frog. He

borrowed a jam jar, put pebbles in it and some moss and water. He put the jar on the window-sill and every morning fed the little frog. And the tree frog grew stronger every day.

When she was well again Johnny took her to the meadow behind the cottage and set her free. But she just jumped back into the jar. This happened several times, but always the frog jumped back into the jar.

And so the beautiful little frog stayed at the cottage for good.

She brought good fortune with her to Johnny and his mother. When the wind blew down a tree in the garden they found among its roots a crock of gold coins. Then they inherited money from a distant relative and the little family prospered.

'Our happiness is all due to our little tree frog,' Johnny's mother told the neighbours, and the neighbours believed it to be true.

The years went by and Johnny grew into a tall, clever young man. Because they already had everything they needed in the cottage and Johnny did not have to worry any more about making a living, he decided one day that he would go to the city to study. And so it came about that he became a scholar, highly thought of and respected by all. But he never forgot his native cottage, his mother and the little tree frog. Whenever he had time he came home to visit them.

Then after a time, Johnny came home for good. How pleased his mother was. Johnny kissed her on both cheeks and unwrapped the presents he had brought for her. Then he hurried to the window to look at his little tree frog. He took the frog out of the jar and put her on the palm of his hand.

'It is all thanks to you, little tree frog,' he said. 'Ever since we have had you, everything has gone well. This evening we shall celebrate and you will sit at the table with us!'

His mother laughed at the idea, but Johnny was serious. When everything was ready for supper, he drew up a third chair to the table, put a cushion on it and on the cushion placed his beautiful little tree frog. Then he and his mother sat down at either side of the table. They wished each other good appetite and Johnny served the soup. The first to be served was the little tree frog. Scarcely had he filled her plate when something amazing happened. Sitting at the table instead of the little frog was a beautiful girl dressed in green. She spoke.

'Don't be frightened, Johnny, don't be frightened, Mother,' and her green eyes shone. 'I am your little tree frog! Years ago Johnny saved my life and I have stayed with you ever since to help you to be happy. But now you no longer need my help and I must go back to my sisters, the woodland fairies.'

When Johnny heard this, he bowed his head sadly and said. 'You want to leave us now? Are you not happy here?'

And the lovely girl replied. 'Yes, I am happy, Johnny. But now you are a man, and soon you will be married. I should only be in the way in the cottage.'

Johnny did not want to hear of getting married. 'I will not marry at all, unless you will have me, my dear. Tell me, would you like me as your husband?'

And the lovely girl answered. 'If you are serious, Johnny, yes, I will be your wife.'

And Johnny assured her. 'Of course, I am serious. The only thing that worries me is that now I am poor again. Everything we had has been spent on my studies!'

But she only smiled and said. 'Do not worry about that. Just look!' And she took from a dish that was on the table a handful of lentils and dropped them one after another onto the floor. As they touched the ground each lentil turned into a glistening gold coin. Never again would they be poor.

In three days a wedding took place. Johnny's bride was a girl with shining green eyes. And her children and her children's children, down to the seventh generation, had the same green eyes. At least that is what they say in this story of Johnny and his little green tree frog.

How the Rabbit Went Hunting with the Wolf

This story tells why the rabbit and the wolf dislike each other. Brother Wolf and Brother Rabbit used to go hunting together. The rabbit acted as beater and roused the game while the wolf killed it and every time they had an excellent bag.

But the rabbit did not get much of the bag for himself. Even though he drove the game as fast as his legs could carry him, the wolf did not give him credit for it. After the hunt, the wolf divided the bag, but kept all the best pieces for himself. When Brother Rabbit complained that it was unfair, the wolf would bare his teeth at him and Brother Rabbit had to be thankful that he had not been gobbled up.

The rabbit got angrier and angrier and

wherever he went he kept wondering how he could pay out the wolf for the injustice. One day he met Brother Dog.

'What's the matter with you, Brother? You look angry,' said the dog.

'How can I be anything but angry, Brother?' said the rabbit, and he told the dog how the wolf had been cheating him of his share of the hunt.

Brother Dog smiled to himself. 'I know the wolf only too well,' he said. 'He has always been like that. But I shall help you. Next time you go hunting take me with you and I shall hide somewhere in the undergrowth nearby. The rest you will see for yourself.'

Brother Rabbit agreed. And Brother Dog hid in the undergrowth near the woods and by the meadow where they always divided the bag. But this time when they got there Brother Wolf suddenly changed. He was like a different creature. He had caught the scent of the dog and was afraid. Brother Rabbit noticed this and said. 'What is the matter, Brother? Go on and divide the spoils.'

'No,' muttered the wolf, 'you do it today.'

'But why, Brother?' the rabbit asked in surprise.

'Because the world has changed,' replied the wolf.

But the rabbit was firm and would not take on the task. So the wolf was forced to do it himself. He chose all the best pieces of game and laid them before the rabbit, saying. 'These are for you, and that and that too.' And he kept scarcely anything for himself. Brother Rabbit could not believe his eyes. 'Since when, Brother Wolf, have you divided the spoils so fairly?'

'Since the time the world has changed,' came the reply. 'Until today the world was unjust, but from today it is just.' And so saying he took his share and hurried off.

The dog came running out of the thicket laughing heartily. 'Now you see, Brother Rabbit, that when he is afraid the wolf is just in his dealings.'

Brother Rabbit thanked the dog for his help and divided the spoils with him. There was plenty for both of them. But he never hunted with the wolf again. Brother Wolf did not invite him again. He did not want to make a just division of the spoils every day. He preferred from that day to hunt by himself.

Brother Rabbit and the Dog

One day Brother Rabbit set out for the market in town. He had to buy some things for his family, but only the most necessary things, because at that time he had little money. He got up early so as to be at the market in good time. He set off quite cheerfully through the woods, but it was not long before he felt less happy. There was still dew on the path and as the rabbit's boots were full of holes, his feet were soon very wet. As he came to a clearing he saw that someone had lit a fire in the night and the embers were still glowing. The rabbit made up the fire and dried his feet. After a time he was joined by Brother Dog. He too was on his way to the market, but he strode along like a lord in fine new boots. When he saw Brother Rabbit, he sat down beside him and started to talk.

'Where are you going, Brother Rabbit?' he asked curiously.

Brother Rabbit looked enviously at Brother Dog's beautiful boots and said. 'To the market. I want to buy new boots just like yours. Will you let me try on one of your boots?'

Brother Dog was proud of his boots and willingly lent one to the rabbit. The rabbit pulled it on, took a few steps and then said. 'Not bad, but a little bit worn. I feel as if I was limping on one leg.'

Brother Dog was offended. 'It is because you are wearing only one boot. Try both of them,' he said. And he lent the rabbit the other boot, too. The rabbit pulled it on and took a few steps.

'Not bad,' he said, 'but I still think, a little bit worn. I feel as if I was always falling on my nose.'

Brother Dog came to the defence of his new boots. 'That is because you are only wearing them on your hind feet. Try having them on all four feet.' And he lent the rabbit both boots for his front paws, too.

Brother Rabbit put them on, took a few steps and then said. 'Fine, Brother Dog. They fit me as if they had been made to measure. It would be hard to find better ones. I shall keep them and bring you the money when I have it.' And before Brother Dog could pull himself together, the rabbit and the new boots were off and away.

Since that time the dog does not wear boots but prefers to go barefoot. And Brother Rabbit has long ago worn out the fine boots and goes barefoot, too. But the dog has never forgotten those stolen boots, and whenever he sees a rabbit he chases him to try to get them back. People think he is barking, but it is not true. He is just shouting. 'Boots, boots, give me back my boots!'

The Hare and the Tortoise

knows that you're the slowest animal in the world.'

'Well, let us have a wager,' insisted the tortoise. 'I assure you I'll reach first whatever winning post you choose.'

'Just as you like,' the hare said with a sigh. 'But you have lost the wager before we even start.'

Then they decided on their course.

'This is perfect for me. This is where I always win my races with the hounds on my heels,' boasted the hare. 'I certainly shall waste no time. But what about you? It's enough for me just to stroll along and I'll be ahead of you.'

One day the tortoise said to the hare. 'Come, let us run a race and see who will win.'

'What an idea!' grinned the hare. 'Everyone

'You talk too much, Brother Hare. What about giving the signal for the start?' said the tortoise.

The hare gave the signal and the race started.

The tortoise set out slowly but surely along the stony path. In the meantime, with a blissful smile, the hare stretched himself out in the grass.

'I'll just take a nap,' he said. 'I have plenty of time. It's only fair to give such a slow opponent a start.'

The tortoise took no notice and went slowly but surely ahead. Later the hare woke up and gazed around him. He stood on his hind legs to see where the tortoise had got to. It was high time for him to start along the track.

In the meantime, the tortoise at her own slow pace had nearly reached the winning post. And indeed she did reach it long before the hare. He had delayed so long that not even his long legs could help him win the race.

The Heron and the Crab

Among the roots at the edge of the fishpond there once lived a crab. Every day a heron used to make her way across the water meadow to the fishpond. She liked to catch fish but the fish were always on the watch and more than once the heron went home hungry.

'This cannot go on,' thought the heron, 'or I shall starve.'

Next morning she went to visit the crab and started to grumble. 'Oh, Crab, things are going badly. I've just heard a fisherman say that they're going to drain our pond. Whatever shall we do?'

The crab was alarmed and passed on the news to the fish. The fish were even more alarmed: the heron could fly away, the crab could creep off, but what about the fish? They could neither fly nor walk. The heron felt quite sorry for them and so she said.

'If you let me, I'll help you. Beyond the woods there is another fishpond. I'll take you there, a few at a time.'

'Yes, yes, do take us,' called the fish and started to push ahead of each other to be first. The heron chose the plumpest of them, seized them in her beak and flew off with them to the other side of the woods. And there in peace and quiet she ate them up until only a few fins and a bone or two remained.

In that way the heron spent the whole week carrying the fish to the new fishpond. Then the crab came and asked for her services. 'Do take me, too,' he said. 'It would be difficult for me to get there on my pincers.'

The heron suddenly developed a taste for crab meat and readily agreed. She took the crab in her beak and carried him beyond the woods. But a crab is not a fish. When he saw the pile of fins and bones he knew at once what had happened. Quickly he seized the heron round her neck with his strong pincers. The heron fell to the ground like a stone and that was the end of her. And the crab slowly made his way back to the fishpond. He never made friends with a heron again.

The Turtle and the Monkey

In a little grove by the sea shore there once lived an old monkey. He was quite happy, he had enough to eat and drink, and just one thing was missing — a friend to talk to. Then one day he found a friend. A turtle came out of the sea to eat the windfalls from the fruit trees that grew there. The old monkey enjoyed his visit, and quite soon they were spending whole days together. At night the turtle went home to a little island in the sea, but sometimes he slept all night in the monkey's grove.

The turtle's wife did not like this at all. For many days she thought of ways of breaking up this friendship and in the end she had an idea.

One day the turtle came home and found his wife lying on the beach breathing heavily.

The turtle was worried. 'What has happened to you, my dear?' he asked. But his wife only sighed and moaned and sighed again. At last she said to him.

'I am ill as you can see. And the doctor has told me that the only thing that can save me is a monkey's heart. You must bring me one, otherwise I shall die.'

The turtle was at a loss. Where could he find a monkey's heart? Eventually he thought of his old friend.

'What shall I do? He is my friend but necessity is more important than friendship.' And at once he set out to find the monkey.

'My dear friend,' he began in a flattering way as soon as the monkey had greeted him. 'For a long time I have wanted to invite you to my home and offer you hospitality. My wife too would like to make your acquaintance.'

The monkey was delighted to be invited.

'I would like to accept your invitation,' he

said, 'but I must refuse. How could I cross the sea to your island when I cannot swim?'

'That's easily settled,' replied the turtle. 'Sit on my back and I'll ferry you across.'

The monkey agreed. He jumped down from the tree, sat on the turtle's shell and in a moment they were surrounded by waves. The turtle swam on and on. Suddenly he stopped. He was wondering if it would not be a good idea to drown the monkey before they got to the island. The monkey realized something was wrong and was afraid.

'What's the matter, my friend? Why have you stopped swimming?' he asked.

'I cannot conceal the truth from you, my dear friend,' said the turtle. 'My wife is ill and the only thing that can cure her is a monkey's heart. That's why I am taking you home with me.'

The monkey knew then that he was in great danger, and that only by guile could he save himself.

'Why didn't you tell me that at once?' he said. 'I could have brought it with me.'

'What! You don't have your heart with you?' the turtle asked in surprise.

'No,' said the monkey. 'Didn't you know that monkeys leave their hearts at home when they travel? But if you like we can go back and I shall give it to you.'

The turtle turned round quickly and made for the grove on the shore. Hardly had they got there when the monkey jumped from the turtle's back. Climbing quickly to the top of the nearest tree he sat there looking very pleased with himself. The turtle was impatient.

'Dear friend, hurry up, and fetch your heart,' he said, 'so that we can set out again.'

But the monkey did not move.

'Where should I fetch it from?' he called down. 'I have my heart in my breast like everyone else. But I am certainly not going to sea any more with a friend like you.'

And so the turtle had to go home without the cure for his wife — and also without a friend.

How Brother Rabbit Did not Want to Dig a Well

There was once a great drought. Rivers and lakes dried up and the animals had nothing to drink. A council of the animals was called and it was decided that together they would dig a deep well. They could then be certain that never again would they be without water. All the animals agreed to dig and at once they set to work — all but the rabbit who did not want to dig. Hard work with a spade was not for him. The other animals were angry.

'Look out, Brother Rabbit,' they said, 'if you do not work there will not be a drop of water for you to drink.'

But the rabbit only laughed and would not dig. 'I shall get a drink in spite of you,' he said.

The animals took no further notice of the rabbit and went on working. In two days they had dug a deep well and on the third day they struck water. They drank their fill and went off to rest after their labours. They all quite forgot about the lazy rabbit. And at dead of night he went to the well and drank his fill.

In the morning when the animals went to the well they saw the rabbit disappearing into the bushes.

'He has been here in the night,' they said. 'But he will not drink again.'

That night they put a guard on the well. It was Brother Bear who was to watch. When the rabbit saw him there he hid in the undergrowth and started to hum a song — the kind of song everyone wants to dance to.

He sang. 'Hey hop, hey hop, step out briskly, don't delay!'

And Brother Bear did not delay. He stood up slowly, very slowly and started to dance. But in the middle of his song the rabbit stopped. The bear was puzzled.

'That was a jolly song,' he said. 'I wonder where it came from. It did not come from the water, nor from the moon. It must have been someone in the woods!' And off he lumbered into the woods in search of the singer.

Brother Rabbit did not wait. As quick as lightning he sped to the well and drank his fill.

In the morning the animals once again saw the rabbit disappear into the bushes. They turned on the bear and accused him of being a bad watchman and gave the job to the monkey.

Brother Monkey did not do much better. Night was falling when the rabbit came to the well and started to sing his song. And Brother Monkey began to dance. But in the middle of his song the rabbit stopped. The monkey was puzzled.

'Who was the singer?' he wondered. 'It wasn't the moon, nor the water. It must have been someone in the woods.' And off he ran into the woods.

So Brother Rabbit drank water from the well a second night.

In the morning when the animals came to the well they again saw the tip of the rabbit's tail disappear into the bushes. And they were angry with the monkey for not keeping guard.

They looked for another watchman. But Brother Fox had a better idea.

'We do not need a watchman,' he said. 'We shall put up a scarecrow in the night and just you wait and see. Brother Rabbit will catch himself!'

The animals let the fox have his way. They made a scarecrow and set it up by the well. Then each went his own way. Night had scarcely fallen when the rabbit came hopping along and started to sing.

'Hey hop! Hey hop! Step out briskly, don't delay!' But the scarecrow did not move. The rabbit was surprised. He crept close and sang more loudly. But still the scarecrow did not move. The rabbit came closer still.

'Why do you not dance to my song?' he cried. 'Are you asleep?' And he patted the scarecrow with a paw. His paw stuck fast to the scarecrow and no matter how he pulled, it still stuck fast.

'Let me go,' he cried, 'or I shall strike you with my other paw.' He struck the scarecrow with his other paw and it too was stuck fast. The cunning fox had smeared the scarecrow with tar and the more the rabbit pulled and pushed, the more firmly was he stuck.

And that is how the other animals found him in the morning. How they laughed at the rabbit's plight.

'And now we shall punish you,' they cried, one after another. 'But how?'

'Do what you like to me!' wailed Brother Rabbit. 'Shoot me, beat me, drown me, but please do not throw me into the bushes.'

The animals ignored his appeal. 'That is just what we will do with you,' they said, 'since you're so afraid of it.' And pulling the rabbit from the scarecrow they hurled him into a patch of thorn bushes.

But a rabbit is always at home among the bushes, for that is where he hides and where he makes his bed. So Brother Rabbit hopped up gaily, stood on his hind legs, looked round once and was off like the wind. But he never came back to drink at the well again. He had learned a lesson which would last him all his life.

The Tortoise, the Stag and the Bird

There were once three friends: a stag, a tortoise and a bird. One night the stag was caught in a net that had been left in the wood by a hunter. He tried to free himself, but soon he knew that neither his antlers nor his hoofs could cut through the strands. He called for help from his friend, the tortoise.

The tortoise crawled to the spot, and when she saw what had happened she at once set to work to chew through the strands of the net.

As the tortoise was still working, dawn broke. The hunter who had set the trap rose, took up his bow and arrows and set out to inspect his net.

When the hunter reached the wood the stag's friend, the bird, was already awake. As the tortoise had not yet finished her work, the bird began to flutter round the hunter, pretending to be wounded. The hunter at once went after the bird. In the meantime, the tortoise at last succeeded in freeing the stag.

When the hunter returned to the net it was torn and empty. Angrily he seized his bow and arrow and took aim at the bird. He was about to shoot when the tortoise bit his toe. The hunter gave a yell of pain, missed his aim and the bird flew free. The tortoise, however, was unable to escape. Next moment she was in the hunter's pouch.

On his way home the hunter felt hungry. He stopped to eat a slice or two of bread which he had brought with him. As he was eating, the stag crept up unseen. Quickly he hooked the hunter's pouch on his antlers and sped off into the forest. There his friend, the bird, was waiting. The bird at once began to peck at the pouch. He pecked and pecked until he had made a hole in it and the tortoise at last was free.

And so it was that the stag, the tortoise and the bird saved each other and lived to be faithful friends for ever.

The Mean Tapir

Long ago when the world was still young, no fruit trees grew. People did not know what bananas were, or kasavas, or yams. But they did know what hunger was. And so did the animals.

People often went hungry, the animals too. All but the tapir grew thin from lack of food. Every morning the tapir went off and every evening he came back looking well fed and satisfied. The people and the animals watched and wondered. Then one day they said. 'The tapir has found a place where there is plenty to eat. Let us have him followed. It will be best that the mouse should go. She is small and clever. The tapir won't even notice her.'

The next day the mouse followed the tapir. They travelled a long way until at last the tapir stopped in the middle of a dense forest. A little hill rose there and at the top of the hill there grew a miraculous tree. On its branches were all the fruits of the earth; bananas and pineapples, kasavas and yams, sweet corn and sugar cane too.

The tapir sat down under the tree and began to eat the fruit that had fallen from its branches.

He ate his fill, then lay down and went to sleep. He did not hear the mouse running to the tree, nor did he hear her begin to nibble at the fruit. The mouse too ate her fill, but did not lie down to sleep. She ran quickly back to the people and the animals. They praised her and next day they all set out for the forest, led by the mouse.

They followed her until she stopped in the middle of the dense forest under the tall tree, the tree which stood on a small hill. And they looked in amazement at its branches which were heavy with all the fruits of the earth. The people and the animals ate their fill of the ripe fruit which lay on the ground. Then they tried to climb the tree. Each of them wanted to break off one branch and take it back to plant in their village. But the tree was too tall, its trunk was too thick and too smooth. Neither people nor animals could climb it. So the people and the animals said.

'We shall have to cut down the tree with hatchets.'

For ten days the people and the animals hacked at the tree without success. For twenty days they hacked, but still it stood. For thirty

39

days the people and the animals hacked and at last the miraculous tree fell. Each one took a branch of the fruit he liked best. One took pineapple, another banana. One took kasava, another yam. One took sweet corn, another sugar beet and another melon. And what they took they carried off to their village and planted in fertile ground.

And that is how all the different fruits came to grow on the earth.

The Lion, the Wolf and the Fox

Once the lion — the King of Beasts — was very ill and all the animals hurried to his aid. The old wolf, too, set out for the lion's royal seat. On the way he stopped to call on the fox and said. 'Fox, you must go to the King, he is ill and needs our help.'

But the fox was not willing to do so and interrupted the wolf.

'What is the King to me. Go there yourself,' he said. 'You can both die for all I care!'

The wolf was offended. That was not going to do the fox any good, he thought. He went on his way and at last reached the lion's royal lair.

'Good day, Your Majesty. How are you feeling today?' he asked.

The lion only sighed. 'Badly, badly, Wolf,' he said. 'Nothing seems to help me!'

'The fox could certainly help you, Your Majesty,' said the wolf. 'That is why I visited him on my way here. But do you know what he told me? He said that we could both die for all he cared!'

The lion was angry. 'I shall punish him for that!' he said.

But meantime the fox had guessed that the wolf would report him to the King. So he hurried to the royal court where he arrived quite breathless.

'Good day, Your Majesty! How are you feeling today?' he asked. 'This is the fourth day I have been running hither and thither, trying to find a cure for you.'

The lion forgot his anger and said. 'And have you found anything?'

The fox answered. 'Not yet, but I have heard of a cure. If you are to get better, you must wrap yourself in the skin of a live wolf.'

The old wolf was alarmed and said. 'But my skin would not be of any use. I am too old.'

'How old are you?' asked the fox.

'I am seven,' the wolf replied.

'Seven? That is when the skin is best!' said the fox cunningly.

And before the wolf could take to his heels, the lion's servants fell upon him and skinned him alive.

That is what happens to people who try to trick each other: one digs a pit for another and falls into it himself.

The Proud Jaguar

A proud jaguar once lived in the depths of the forest. When he went hunting all fled before him. When be roared everyone was afraid. He himself fled from no one. He was afraid of no one. But there came a day when he too learned what fear was.

The jaguar was returning from hunting, when on the path through the forest, he suddenly saw a round little man carrying a dead tapir over one shoulder and a small club over the other. The jaguar had never seen him before and was amazed that the little man did not flee from him in terror.

He hid in the thicket, and when the round little man was only a few steps away, he jumped onto the path in front of him with a roar. The round little man stopped in his tracks. 'You did startle me, Brother,' he said.

The jaguar began to boast. 'You would be still more startled if I showed you my full strength!'

'All right, show me, Brother!' the round little man said.

The jaguar did not need to be asked twice. He bared his teeth, stretched out his claws and started to tear up the ground. Grass and soil flew in all directions, and the little man narrowly escaped being buried. The jaguar shouted proudly. 'Did you see my strength, Brother?'

The round little man replied. 'I did, Brother.'

'But that's nothing,' boasted the jaguar. And he started to tear up the thicket. Leaves and branches flew in all directions, and the little man again narrowly escaped being buried.

'Did you see my strength, Brother?' asked the jaguar proudly.

'I did, Brother,' said the little man.

'But that's nothing,' boasted the jaguar for a third time.

'Just watch!' And he bared his teeth, stretched out his claws and began to tear at a tree. Roots and twigs went flying in all directions. And the little man again narrowly escaped being buried.

'Did you see my strength, Brother?' asked the jaguar proudly.

The round little man replied. 'I did, Brother. But what of it?'

'What of it?' gasped the jaguar. 'You show me how strong you are, Brother, or I shall eat you up!'

The round little man shrugged his shoulders. 'Maybe I am not as strong as you, Brother. But if I must, I shall let you see how strong I am.' And he laid the tapir on the ground and took hold of his small club. As he swung it round, lightning flashed over the jaguar's head and there was a clap of thunder. For the round little man was himself Thunder.

'You see, Brother?' he said modestly.

The thunder startled the jaguar. He leapt into a tree and roared. 'Yes, I saw all right, Brother. But you must stop now!'

But the round little man did not stop. He swung his club round again. Over the trees lightning flashed and the thunder roared still louder. The tree split down the middle and the jaguar fell to the ground like a ripe pineapple.

And the round little man said. 'You saw that, Brother?'

The angry jaguar had shrunk into a hole in the rocks, and from there he roared. 'Yes, I saw it, Brother, but you must stop now.'

But the round little man did not stop. He swung his little club round his head for the third time. Over the rock there was a flash of lightning and a clap of thunder which split the rock into a thousand pieces. The jaguar narrowly escaped being buried. The jaguar took to his heels, and the round little man called out after him. 'You saw that, Brother?'

The jaguar, still running, roared. 'I did indeed, Brother, but I beg you to have mercy on me!'

The round little man relented. 'All right, Brother,' he called. 'I will take pity on you, but next time do not boast so much and do not be so proud of your strength. You know now that there are others on the earth stronger than you are.'

Since that day the jaguar has not boasted too much and is not so proud, they say. And when he hears thunder he hides in the deepest hole in the rocks. And he trembles with fear and sees again that round little man with a club over his shoulder.

The Fox
and
the Lion
Cub

The King of Beasts was old and no longer had the strength to go hunting. He did not want to die of hunger, so he thought of a clever plan. He lay down in his den as if he was mortally ill, and his moans were enough to break any heart.

It did not take long for the news to spread throughout the animal kingdom that the King of Beasts was dying. One by one the animals went to the sick king to pay their respects. The lion, in a feeble voice, begged them to come in.

'Do not be afraid, my friend,' he would say. 'Come in so that I can talk to you for the last time.'

But scarcely had the animal entered the den than the lion hit out at him with his paw and enjoyed a good meal.

This went on for a long time. Visitors came, one after another, but none of them went away. And the lion ate well, even better than in his hunting days.

The fox replied politely. 'Yes, I trust you, Lion, but I believe my own eyes still more!'

The lion was surprised. 'And what do your eyes tell you?' he asked.

The clever fox answered. 'They tell me that many tracks lead to your den, but none lead out of it. So, if I may, I will stay where I am.'

He once more wished the lion good health, and ran off.

One day the fox came to pay his last respects to the King of Beasts. He bowed courteously and asked after the lion's health. But he did not go into the den. The lion called out in a feeble voice. 'Come in, come in! Do not be afraid. Or do you not trust me?'

The Monkey Who Was Too Clever

Two friends, the monkey and the tortoise, were arguing one day about which was worse — a wound or a lie. The monkey said. 'A wound is worse. A wound hurts, a lie does not hurt.'

But the tortoise insisted. 'A lie is worse. A wound can be healed with herbs or ointment, but nothing can heal a lie.'

'Let us put it to the test,' said the monkey.

'Very well,' agreed the tortoise. 'You begin!'

And the monkey began. He took a knife and pricked the tortoise until he bled. But the tortoise did not care about the pain. He put some herbs on the wound and by the next day it had healed without leaving the smallest scar.

Then it was the turn of the tortoise. Secretly he went and bought some good meat, cut it in pieces, roasted them, seasoned them and hung them on the branches of a tree as if they were growing there. This done, he went in search of the monkey.

'I have found a tree with roast meat growing on it,' he told him.

'What sort of tree can it be which has meat growing on it?' asked the curious monkey.

'I don't know. But if you like I'll show it to you,' lied the tortoise and took the monkey to the tree where the pieces of meat were hanging. The monkey could smell the meat from a distance. He climbed the tree and set to work on the meat. He did not notice that the tortoise had left him and was hurrying as fast as he could to the village.

At the first hut he stopped to talk to a dog. 'I have found a tree,' he said to him, 'on which roast meat grows.'

'What sort of tree is it?' asked the curious dog.

'I don't know, but if you like I'll show it to you.' And the tortoise led the dog to the tree where the monkey was feasting.

The dog could smell the meat from a distance. He ran quickly to the tree, but when he saw the monkey there, he started to bark furiously. The monkey, frightened at the sight of the dog, lost interest in eating the meat. Instead he began to throw down pieces to the dog who hungrily gobbled them up. But he would not leave the tree. This went on for three days and three nights. The dog kept barking and eating while the monkey went hungry and shook with fear, as he threw down all the meat to the dog.

But on the fourth day a leopard appeared. He passed close to the tree and when the dog caught the leopard's scent, he fled back to the village.

But the monkey was no better off. Instead of the dog, it was the leopard who lay in wait. At last the tortoise arrived at the tree.

'Leave the monkey in peace, Leopard,' he said. 'Can't you see that thanks to hunger and fear he is nothing but skin and bone? What sort of meal would he make for you?'

'You're quite right, Tortoise,' growled the leopard and ran off to hunt elsewhere.

Only then could the monkey come down from the tree. And the tortoise said.

'Now you have had proof that a lie is worse than a wound. The wound you gave me healed in a day, but the lie I told made you miserable for three days and three nights. And that's still not the end of it.'

And the tortoise was right. For the monkey was so hungry and frightened that it was more than a month before he recovered.

How
Brother Rabbit
Fought a Duel
with
the Elephant

One day Brother Rabbit was sitting at home when all at once his cottage started to quiver and shake. Frightened, he ran outside. And what did he see? Brother Elephant was picking plums in his garden and propping his hindquarters against the wall of the rabbit's cottage. It was a wonder he had not brought the whole place down.

'You're as stupid as you're big, Brother Elephant!' cried Brother Rabbit. 'If you must come stealing my plums, at least take care not to knock down my cottage!'

And Brother Rabbit went on shouting and complaining at the top of his voice. In next to no time all his neighbours came out to see what was going on. The elephant did not quite know what to do.

'Be quiet, Brother, be quiet,' said the elephant, trying to calm the rabbit. 'You've done me enough damage in the past, haven't you?'

'But I've never brought your house down about your ears, have I,' cried the rabbit. 'You'll have to pay for this!'

The elephant was annoyed. 'Don't threaten me, Brother!' he said. 'I am not one to be frightened, certainly not by you. If I wanted, I could flatten you like a raspberry!'

'You're not going to do any flattening,' shouted the rabbit. 'You may be bigger than I am, but you're not stronger. I'll show you! I challenge you to a duel. Then we'll see who'll run away from whom!'

Brother Elephant only laughed. 'We'll see, Brother. But it won't be me!'

And so the duel between Brother Rabbit and the elephant was arranged. When they met in the morning in the village, the village green was already full of curious onlookers. There was just enough room in the middle of the green for the two who were to fight. The eagle owl was chosen to preside over the duel since he was the oldest and the wisest.

According to their agreement each of them had the right to strike three blows. Whoever dodged a blow or retreated would be the loser. Brother Rabbit was to start.

'I am ready, Brother Owl!' said the rabbit, and prepared to deal the first blow. But before he did so, he said to the elephant. 'Don't be afraid, Brother, I am not even going to scratch you. I'll just give you a light blow on the trunk, like this. Just look!'

And he pulled from his pocket a mouse, a live mouse, and threw it at the elephant.

Elephants are strong fellows as everyone knows, but one thing that strikes terror into all of them is a mouse. When Brother Elephant felt a mouse running up and down his trunk, he began to trumpet and retreat as if in the face of fire. But Brother Rabbit did not let him off.

'Wait a minute, Brother,' he said. 'I've the right to deal you two more blows, you know. Here is the second!'

And he threw a second mouse at the elephant. The mouse took a bite at the elephant's ear. This was too much for the elephant. He raised his trunk, flapped his ears, swished his tail and fled. He did not even wait for Brother Rabbit's third blow.

The duel was over. Brother Eagle Owl had no difficulty in announcing the winner. Brother Rabbit was the undoubted winner, and to his dying day the elephant left him in peace. He never again dared to steal the rabbit's plums.

The Goat, the Kids and Brother Wolf

Once upon a time in the forest there stood a cottage, and in the cottage lived a goat and her seven kids. When she went to graze the goat told her kids. 'Children, you must not open the door to anyone! The hungry wolf of the forest might come and eat you all up.'

The wolf was hiding under the window and heard what she said. As soon as the mother goat had gone, the wolf knocked at the door and growled.

'Little kids, little kids, open the door. I have brought milk for you and water to drink, and there is grass on my horns for you to eat.'

'You are not our mother! Our mother has a thin little voice,' said the kids. 'You are the wicked wolf!'

And they would not open the door.

The wolf ran off to the blacksmith's forge and cried. 'Blacksmith, blacksmith, file down my tongue so that I may have a thin little voice.'

The blacksmith filed down the wolf's tongue and again the wolf knocked at the door.

'Little kids, little kids, open the door. I have brought milk for you and water to drink, and there is grass on my horns for you to eat.'

'That is our mother's voice,' said the kids, and ran to open the door. But the smallest kid said.

'First show us your hoof!'

And the wolf pushed his black paw through the window and the kids said.

'You are not our mother. You are the wicked wolf. Our mother has feet as white as goose feathers.' And they would not open the door.

The wolf ran to the baker's and said.

'Baker, baker, sprinkle my paws with flour, so that they are as white as goose feathers.'

And the baker sprinkled the wolf's paws with flour and the wolf knocked for a third time at the cottage door.

'Little kids, little kids, open the door. I have brought milk for you and water to drink, and there is grass on my horns for you to eat.'

And he pushed through the window his paw sprinkled with flour.

'That is our mother's voice, her thin little voice,' said the kids, 'and her little paw as white as goose feathers.' And they wanted to open the door. But the smallest one said. 'Show us your tail!'

The wolf showed them his bushy tail, and the kids at once cried.

'You are not our mother. You are the wicked wolf. Our mother has a tiny tail like an ear of wheat.'

The wolf ran to the carpenter and said. 'Carpenter, carpenter, saw off my tail, so that I shall have a tiny little tail like an ear of wheat.'

And the carpenter sawed off the wolf's tail. Once more the wolf knocked at the cottage door.

'Little kids, little kids, open the door. I have brought milk and water to drink, and there is grass on my horns for you eat.'

And the wolf pushed through the window his floury paw and his tiny tail.

'That is our mother's thin little voice, her paw as white as goose feathers and her tiny tail, like an ear of wheat,' said the kids. And they opened the door.

The wolf leapt into the cottage and swallowed the kids — all but the smallest one who had quickly hidden in the stove.

When the wolf had swallowed them, he went to the stream to drink. Then he lay down and fell fast asleep.

The mother goat came home and saw that the door was open and that her kids were nowhere to be seen. She searched for them bleating, 'Little kids, little kids, where are you? I have milk for you and water to drink, and there is grass on my horns for you to eat.'

At that the smallest kid jumped out of the stove and told her mother all that had happened.

When the mother goat had heard her tale, she ran quickly to the stream. There the wolf lay, still fast asleep. She leapt on him and next moment had slit open the wolf with a sharp horn. All the little kids tumbled out, and the mother goat and her little kids lived safely and happily ever after.

Sister Python and Brother Rabbit

Brother Rabbit was terrified. Not far from his burrow Sister Python made her home, and several times he had barely escaped her fangs.

'This must not continue,' Brother Rabbit said to himself. 'I must think of a way of getting rid of Sister Python.'

For a long time he could think of nothing, and he became more and more fearful. But at last he had an idea. He took up a large sack made of rough canvas and a piece of cord. He would wait for Sister Python to eat her fill and slither back to her lair. This was in an old hollow tree above the water.

Brother Rabbit hurried to the tree with the sack and the piece of cord and called out as if he was arguing with someone. 'She'll go in!'

And then in a different voice. 'No, she won't.'

And in his own voice. 'But she will!'

And in the other voice. 'But she won't!'

'Let's bet on it. I'll bet my head!'

Sister Python was dozing after her dinner, but these shouts disturbed her. She stuck her head out. 'What are you arguing about?' she asked.

Brother Rabbit dropped the sack and ran to the snake's lair.

'Don't be angry with us, Sister Python, but my cousin declares that you couldn't get into this sack.' And he pointed behind him as if someone was really there. 'He says you're too big and also that you're too fat. But I say that it's not true and you would go in. We have made a bet on it.'

Sister Python was in a good mood after her dinner. She would prove that she was not as fat as the rabbit's cousin said.

'Just show me the sack!' said Sister Python to the rabbit. 'Then perhaps you will stop shouting and let me sleep.'

Brother Rabbit opened the sack and Sister Python wriggled into it.

'You see,' she said proudly. 'I am in the sack.'

'You are, Sister Python,' said Brother Rabbit, very pleased with himself. 'And I was afraid I would lose my head.'

Quickly he took the cord and tied the top of the sack with three strong knots, and flung Sister Python far into the water.

The hares one day called a council meeting to discuss the injustices of their lives.

'It is unfair that no one is afraid of us, and that we must flee from everyone,' they cried, one after another. 'Such a life is not worth living.'

After a long discussion they all agreed that their life was not worth living and the best thing to do was to put an end to it themselves.

'We will go and drown ourselves,' they decided, and rushed off to the pond.

In the meadow by the pond the frogs saw the hares racing towards them. Terrified, they leapt away, and croaking loudly, one after the other they jumped head first into the water.

When the hares saw this they laughed.

'Just look, there is someone after all who is afraid of us and runs away.'

And the hares laughed and laughed till they all split their lips. Ever since then hares do not think of jumping into ponds, but to this day, they all have split lips.

The Hares and the Frogs

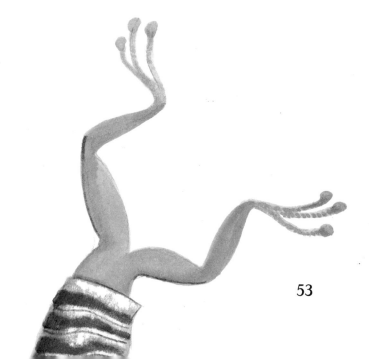

The Crab
and
the Monkey

The crab had a little field in which he grew rice. When he was harvesting the rice his neighbour, the monkey, paid him a visit. Unlike the crab, the monkey was lazy. Nevertheless he wanted to taste some of his neighbour's rice.

'Listen, Crab, if you like I shall make you a nice rice purée,' he said.

The crab had never eaten rice purée and thought he would like to try it. 'I should be glad if you made some for me,' he replied.

The monkey put a pan of water on the fire, boiled the rice and turned it into a bowl.

'And now we must beat the rice well,' he said. 'But it can't be done here. We must take it to the top of the hill.'

The crab was surprised but obediently set out after the monkey who was carrying the bowl of rice. When they were about half way up the hill, the tired crab asked.

'Can't we beat the rice here?'

'No, we must go up higher,' snapped the monkey and went on.

At last they reached the top of the hill. The crab was so tired he could scarcely breathe. But the monkey began happily to beat the rice in the bowl. He was looking forward to a tasty meal.

'But there will only be enough for me,' he said to himself.

When he had beaten the rice thoroughly the bowl suddenly slipped to the ground and went rolling down the hill. In a flash the monkey was after it. The hungry crab watched sadly and slowly shuffled after him.

'There will be no rice purée for me,' he muttered hungrily. But suddenly his heart leapt. Halfway down the hill lay a heap of rice purée. As the bowl rolled down the hill the rice had fallen out and was lying in the grass. The crab did not hesitate but fell on it hungrily.

In the meantime, at the bottom of the hill, the monkey had overtaken the bowl and found it empty. Angrily he ran up the hill again and, half

way up, found the crab happily eating the last mouthful.

'Leave a little for me, Crab,' called the monkey.

'You can have what's left in the bowl!' snapped the crab.

'There's nothing left in it!' cried the monkey.

'So there's nothing for you,' said the crab happily.

'Just you wait. I'll pay you out,' said the furious monkey.

'I'll call out all the monkeys who live around here and not even your shell will save you. We'll pull you out of it alive!' And off he ran.

The crab was frightened. It shuffled home moaning. 'Oh dear, oh dear! Whatever will become of me?'

'What are you moaning about, Crab?' asked a round chestnut, lying in the grass nearby.

'I have good reason to moan,' answered the crab. 'The monkeys are going to pull me out of my shell alive.'

'Don't be afraid,' said the chestnut. 'I shall help you!' And the chestnut went along with the crab. But the crab would not be consoled. Sadly he shuffled home, moaning.

'Oh dear, oh dear, whatever will become of me?'

'What are you moaning about, Crab?' asked a passing wasp.

'I have good reason to moan,' replied the crab. 'The monkeys are going to pull me out of my shell alive.'

'Don't be afraid,' said the wasp. 'I shall help you!' And the wasp went along with the crab and the chestnut.

But the crab was still frightened. He shuffled sadly on, moaning all the way. 'Oh dear, oh dear! Whatever will become of me?'

'Oh, whatever are you moaning about, Crab?' asked a cow pat, lying on the path.

'I have good reason to moan,' replied the crab. 'The monkeys are going to pull me out of my shell alive.'

'Don't be afraid,' said the cow pat, 'I shall help you!' And it went along with the crab, the chestnut and the wasp. But the crab would not be consoled. Sadly it shuffled on moaning.

'Oh dear, oh dear, whatever will become of me?'

'What are you moaning about, Crab?' asked the bowl and the wooden spoon.

'I have good reason to moan,' replied the crab. 'The monkeys are going to pull me out of my shell alive.'

'Don't be afraid and stop moaning,' said the bowl and the wooden spoon. 'We shall help you.' And they went along with the crab, the chestnut, the wasp and the cow pat.

At last the crab felt more cheerful as he hurried home with his friends. When they got there, they each settled down comfortably in their own ways: the crab slid into a tub of water, the chestnut lay down in the cinders under the fireplace, the wasp settled on the window, the cow pat in the doorway and the bowl and the wooden spoon on the roof. And they waited quietly for the monkeys.

In a little while the monkey arrived with a band of his friends. Leaving his friends outside, he crept into the house alone. Hardly had he stepped into the room when he began to shiver with cold.

'Hm, I'd better warm the room up a bit!' he said, and started to rake the cinders in the fireplace. But as soon as he started to rake them, the chestnut popped out and burned him.

'Oo!' cried the monkey, and jumped into the tub of water to cool his burn. The crab was waiting for him and he nipped the monkey's finger with his pincers.

'Oo!' cried the monkey, and leapt in fright towards the window. There the wasp was waiting for him and it stung the monkey's nose.

'Oo!' cried the monkey, running to the door to get out of the house as quickly as he could. In the doorway the cow pat was waiting for him. The monkey slipped on it and fell flat on the floor.

'Oo!' cried the monkey, trying to get up and out into the yard as quickly as he could. But on the roof the bowl and the wooden spoon were waiting for him. Down they rolled on top of him, hitting the monkey's head so hard that two large lumps appeared. With a yell of pain and fright he ran off into the hills with the rest of the monkeys after him.

Ever since then the crab has lived in peace in his little house with his friends. And he prefers always to cook his own rice.

The Jackal,
the Panther,
the Lion
and
the Brave Kid

One day a kid decided to make a pilgrimage to holy places. He threw a haversack on his back, balanced a jug of sweet honey on his head and set out.

It was a long way to the holy places. The kid walked and walked and walked until he was suddenly overtaken by a storm. The only thing to do was to find shelter. The kid looked around to see if there was anywhere a place he could hide from the rain.

But for ten miles around there was no sign of human habitation. But just a little way from the path lay a fallen baobab tree. Under its roots was a deep hole.

'I'll shelter there,' said the kid.

So without delay, he hopped into the hole. But to his horror he found it was already occupied. Crouching there were a lion, a panther and a jackal.

The kid was terrified. 'What now?' he said to himself. 'If I don't think of something quickly, it will be the end of me.' Carefully he set down in front of him the jug of sweet honey.

The old jackal was the first to raise his head. 'Where are you going to, Kid, all by yourself?' he asked.

The kid did not want to show that he was frightened. He replied boldly. 'I am on a pilgrimage to holy places.'

At this the panther raised his head too and asked. 'What have you got in that jug?'

The kid replied boldly. 'I am taking medicine with me in case I fall ill on the way.'

Then the lion raised his head too. 'And what is the medicine for, Kid?' he wanted to know.

The kid replied boldly. 'For everything, Lion. It cures every ache and pain and every illness!'

'That's just what I need, Kid,' growled the lion. 'I've got a pain in my side. Give me a little of your medicine.'

The kid replied boldly. 'With pleasure, Brother Lion. Only I would need a piece of skin to dip in the medicine.'

'What sort of skin?' growled the lion.

'Jackal skin would be best,' the kid replied.

'Jackal,' growled the lion, 'give the kid a piece of your skin.'

What could the jackal do? Whether he liked it or not — and he did not like it at all — he had to give the kid a piece of his tail. The kid took the skin, dipped it in the honey and said. 'Shut your eyes and open your mouth, Lion!'

The lion shut his eyes, opened his mouth and the kid put on his tongue a bit of jackal skin dipped in honey. The lion swallowed it and growled. 'That's good medicine, Kid! I feel better already. Give me a little more.'

'With pleasure, Lion,' he said, 'but I shall need another piece of jackal skin.'

What could the jackal do? Whether he liked it or not — and he did not like it at all — he had to give the kid another piece of his tail. The kid took the skin, dipped it in the honey and put it on the lion's tongue.

The lion swallowed the skin and the honey and growled. 'That really is good medicine, Kid. I feel even better now. Give me a third dose for luck!'

'With pleasure, Lion,' said the kid. 'Only I shall need another piece of jackal skin — a little bigger this time.'

'You hear that, Jackal,' growled the lion. 'Give the kid another piece of your skin, but a good-sized piece this time or I shall flay you alive!'

The jackal realized the danger he was in. If this went on the lion would indeed skin him completely. And he did not mean that to happen. So he jumped up, leapt out of the hole and was off like the wind.

'Just wait, Jackal,' roared the lion. 'You won't get away with it. Running off like that when I want a piece of your skin.' And off he went after the jackal.

The kid was left alone in the hole with the panther. He did not show that he was afraid, and said boldly. 'You ought to be grateful to me, Panther.'

The panther was surprised. 'What do you mean, Kid?' he asked.

'I have saved your life,' the kid replied. 'I said that jackal skin is best. But that is not true. Panther skin is much better. It would have helped the lion's pain still more.'

At this the panther jumped to his feet. He did not wait for the lion to come back, but leapt out of the hole and was off like the wind.

So the kid saved himself by his own cleverness. He waited for the storm to pass over, then he flung his haversack over his back, balanced the jug of sweet honey on his head and set out once more on his pilgrimage to holy places.

Why the Chameleon Changes Colour

Once a long time ago, the Good Spirit of the Heavens called all living creatures to him and said. 'I want to give each of you your place on earth where you will live. Tell me now where each of you would like to live.'

The first to speak was man. 'I would like to live in a village,' he said, 'with fields round it.'

Then each of the animals spoke.

'I would like to live on the steppes!'

'And I in the thickets!'

'And I in the forests!'

They all spoke in turn — except the chameleon. He said nothing.

'And what about you, Chameleon?' asked the Good Spirit.

'I would like to be at home everywhere!' answered the chameleon softly.

'Very well,' said the Good Spirit. 'All of you shall have what you desire.'

And ever since then man has lived in a village, the animals have had their homes on the steppes, in the thicket or in the forest — and the chameleon is at home everywhere, for he can change his colour to suit the place where he is.

The Fox and the Stork

The fox was an artful creature. No one except the stork had yet been able to equal him in wiliness. It angered the fox that so far he had not succeeded in outwitting the stork.

One day the fox invited the stork to dinner, and at the appointed time the stork arrived at the fox's home.

'Please sit down,' said the fox with a smile. 'I have made excellent soup in your honour, from the tenderest of veal.' And into large shallow soup plates he poured some for his guest and some for himself. 'I am sure it will be to your liking,' he said.

In a few seconds the fox had lapped up every drop of soup from his plate.

Out of the corner of his eye he watched the stork trying in vain to sup the soup with his long beak.

'I am sorry the soup is not to your liking after all,' said the fox, removing the stork's plate and finishing it off himself behind the kitchen door.

The embarrassed and hungry stork stayed no longer, but went quickly home vowing vengeance.

A few days later the stork invited the fox to dinner. 'I wanted to repay your hospitality,' he said, as he led the fox to the table.

The fox licked his lips as his nose caught the delicious smell which wafted from the stork's kitchen.

But what a shock was in store for him. The stork served dinner in tall narrow jars. No matter how he tried the fox could not reach the food. The stork, thanks to his long beak, enjoyed every mouthful.

'I am sorry the dinner is not to your liking,' said the stork, as he watched the fox struggling to force his muzzle into the narrow jar.

'Please do not force yourself to eat it. Next time I shall cook something better,' declared the stork, taking away the fox's jar and supping its contents behind the kitchen door. Then he followed the fox to the edge of the meadow.

Thereupon the fox ran off as fast as his legs would carry him, glad that he met no one on the way who might ask what the stork had given him for dinner.

The Bear and the Grasshopper

One day a bear was running along a path. He was not looking where he was going, so he did not notice when he trampled on the nest of a tiny grasshopper. The grasshopper was angry.

'Just you wait, Bear,' he chirped, 'I shall get even with you!'

'What's that, little grasshopper,' laughed the bear, 'you do not mean that you want to test your strength against mine?'

'And why not indeed?' asked the grasshopper. 'I challenge you tonight. Call your seconds and I shall call mine. We shall meet tomorrow in the meadow. Then we shall see who is stronger.'

'Very well,' rumbled the bear. 'Tomorrow it shall be.' And he called, as his seconds, a pack of wolves, a pair of badgers, a family of foxes and several horses. The grasshopper meantime summoned to his side a nest of hornets, a swarm of wasps, a hive of bees and a cloud of mosquitoes.

When the bear rallied his forces the meadow was full of them. The grasshopper's troops were nowhere to be seen.

'Where are your troops?' the bear asked. 'Have they fled before the battle?'

'No, they have not fled,' said the grasshopper. 'Here they are.'

And he signed to the hornets, wasps, bees and mosquitoes to take off.

Before the bear's troops knew what had happened they were surrounded by hornets, wasps, bees and mosquitoes. With a great buzzing they were upon them like a shower of hail pricking, nipping, stinging.

'Go to it!' cried the grasshopper, 'we are seven to their one!'

And indeed for every four-legged creature there were seven of the grasshopper's troops.

Worst off of them all was the bear himself, for the hornets had chosen him as their target. When he could not stand their stings any longer he sounded the retreat. 'Back, comrades, to the river!'

And the bear's entire army flung themselves into the nearby river to protect themselves from their terrible enemies.

The bear himself was nearly drowned. And from that time on he took care to look where he was going and never again to get involved in a fight with a grasshopper.

The Three Little Pigs
and
the Wolf

There was once a sow who had three little piglets. Because she had nothing to give them to eat, she sent them out into the world to seek their fortunes.

The first little pig walked on and on and on, until he met a man carrying bales of straw.

'Good man,' said the little pig, 'may I have a little straw to build myself a house?'

The good man gave the little pig some straw and he at once built himself a house with it. In a little while a wolf came by. He knocked at the door and said. 'Little pig, little pig, open the door and let me come in.'

But the little pig replied. 'I won't and I won't, by the bristles that grow on my chin!'

To which the wolf replied. 'Then I'll puff and I'll huff and I'll blow your house down!'

And he puffed and he huffed and he blew the house down. And he gobbled up the little pig.

In the meantime, the second little pig walked on and on and on, until he met a man carrying bundles of faggots.

'Good man,' said the little pig, 'may I have a few of your faggots to build myself a house?'

And the good man gave the little pig some faggots. And the little pig built himself a house. In a little while the wolf came by. He knocked at the door and said. 'Little pig, little pig, open the door and let me come in.'

But the little pig replied. 'I won't and I won't, by the bristles that grow on my chin!'

To which the wolf replied. 'Then I'll puff and I'll huff and I'll blow your house down!'

And he puffed and he huffed and he blew the house down. And he gobbled up the little pig.

In the meantime, the third little pig walked on and on and on, until he met a man with a cartload of bricks.

'Good man,' said the little pig, 'may I have a few of your bricks to build myself a house?'

The good man gave the little pig a few bricks and the little pig built himself a house with them. In a little while, the wolf came by, knocked at the door and said. 'Little pig, little pig, open the door and let me come in!'

But the little pig replied. 'I won't and I won't, by the bristles that grow on my chin!'

To which the wolf said. 'I'll puff and I'll huff and I'll blow your house down!'

And he puffed and he huffed, but puff and huff as he might, the house did not blow down. So the wolf said to himself. 'I shall have to trick the little pig.' So he said. 'By the way, little pig, do you know a place where fine turnips grow?'

'Where?' asked the little pig.

'In a garden behind the forge,' said the wolf. 'If you like I'll come and fetch you in the morning and take you there. Then we shall have a fine dinner.'

'Of course I should like to,' replied the little pig. 'At what time am I to be ready for you?'

'At six o'clock,' the wolf said. But the little pig did not wait for the wolf. He got up at five and by the time the wolf came for him he was home with the turnips. The wolf arrived at six and called. 'Little pig, little pig, are you coming?'

'Why ever should I?' answered the little pig, 'when I've already been there and back. I have brought home the turnips and, in a little while I shall have a very fine dinner.'

The wolf was very angry. But he did not show it. He said. 'By the way, little pig, do you know a place where fine apples are ripening?'

'Where is that?' asked the little pig.

'In the orchard on top of the hill,' said the wolf, 'and if you like, I shall come for you tomorrow at five o'clock in the morning and we shall go there together.'

Of course the little pig did not wait for the wolf.

He had just picked enough apples and was about to come down from the tree, when the wolf appeared beneath the tree and said. 'Little pig, you have come early again, haven't you? And what do you think of the apples?'

'Oh, they are beautiful,' said the little pig bravely, although he wasn't feeling very brave. 'I'll throw one down to you and you can try it for yourself.' And he threw down a beautiful red apple. But the apple went rolling down the hill and before the wolf caught up with it, the little pig had jumped down from the tree and run home.

The next day the wolf came to the house of the third little pig once more and said. 'Do you know, little pig, that there will be a market in the town tomorrow afternoon?'

'Yes, I know,' replied the little pig. 'I shall be going. When will you go?'

'At three,' answered the wolf. Of course the little pig did not wait for the wolf. He got to the market earlier and bought a milk churn. Then he set out for home with the churn. But when he got to the top of the hill, he saw the wolf coming towards him.

'Whatever shall I do now?' said the little pig to himself. He was terrified and he did not know where to hide. But an idea came to him just in time. He hid himself in the milk churn and went spinning down the hill towards the wolf. When the wolf saw what was rolling down the hill towards him, he was frightened and at once took to his heels.

Next day the wolf came to the little pig's house and complained about the shock he had had the day before. The little pig only laughed and said. 'But you know it was only me. I had been to the market and bought a milk churn and when I saw you coming up the path, I hid in it and rolled all the way home.'

The wolf was really angry and vowed that he would gobble up the little pig come what may. He waited till it was getting dark, then he scrambled onto the roof of the little pig's house and started to crawl down the chimney.

But the little pig heard him and wasted no time. He hung a cauldron of water beneath the chimney and lit a fire under it. When the wolf jumped down the chimney, the little pig lifted the lid. The wolf fell straight into the boiling water. Quickly the little pig put the lid on the cauldron again and left the wolf to boil until he was quite tender. Then he ate him for supper.

After that he went on living happily and peacefully in his little brick house.

The Jackal and His Gratitude

One day a flock of hens were pecking around on the other side of a river. The crafty jackal's mouth began to water. He remembered that he had seen a camel grazing a little way off. He ran up to him and said. 'Listen, Camel, would you not like to have a little wheat?'

The camel raised his head from the dry grass and replied. 'Of course, I would. But where can I find it?'

The jackal said. 'There, on the other side of the river I have a whole field of wheat. If you take me across you can eat your fill.'

The camel looked and sure enough, on the other side of the river was a field of wheat.

'Jump on my back,' he told the jackal. 'I shall take you across the river.'

On the other side, the camel made straight for the field of wheat and the jackal pounced on a nice fat hen. He gobbled it up as if he had not eaten for many weeks. Then, satisfied, he thought he would have some fun. While the camel was grazing peacefully in the wheat field, he ran to the village and started to shout. 'Listen everybody! There is a camel grazing in your wheat field!'

The villagers gathered quickly and seizing sticks, they ran to the field. The poor camel was beaten from the wheat field and made his way painfully back to the river. On the bank the jackal was waiting for him. He at once jumped on the camel's back and asked to be taken back across the river. But the camel only moaned.

'I have scarcely the strength to take myself across,' he said.

The jackal started to laugh. 'How so?' he asked.

The camel answered. 'The people chased me and beat me with sticks.'

The jackal laughed all the more. 'And did it hurt much?' he asked.

The camel moaned again. 'Of course, it hurt. It is a wonder I got away with my life!'

The jackal nearly laughed his head off. 'And do you know that I set those people on you?' he asked.

The camel said nothing. For a little while he swam quietly, then suddenly he started to sink. The jackal was startled.

'What are you doing?' he cried. 'I shall be drowned!'

It was the camel's turn to laugh. 'Nothing can be done about it. That is what I'm like!' he said.

And he sank right under the water. And the jackal was carried away by the current.

The camel was surprised. 'But why?' he asked. 'After all I carried you across the river to the other bank, didn't I?'

The jackal told him. 'Nothing can be done about it. That is what I'm like!'

The Fox
and
the Horse

Brother Fox made so much mischief among the animals that he was unpopular with all. Not even the monkey liked him and whenever she had a moment to spare she thought about ways of punishing the fox for all the trouble he caused.

All this thinking made her wrinkle her forehead and those wrinkles she has to this day.

One day the monkey saw a horse with a beautiful, long tail resting in a meadow near the woods. He was sleeping peacefully in the grass and the monkey stopped to admire his beautiful tail. Suddenly she had an idea.

She hurried from the meadow and went to wake the hare who was sleeping in a nearby thicket.

'Get up, Hare, and come with me!' she said. 'We are going to punish Brother Fox.'

Then she told him what she had planned, and the hare liked the idea.

'Come on, Monkey!' he said. 'We shall teach him a lesson this time.'

And so they set out together for the fox's hole.

'Do you know, Brother Fox,' the monkey said, 'what is the best kind of meat in the world?'

'I'm afraid I don't,' admitted the fox. And his eyes sparkled. 'What is it? Tell me!'

'What is it?' the monkey said. 'Horsemeat, from the leg of a horse. There is only one problem. It is very difficult to get hold of. The best thing to do is to tie your tail to the tail of a horse.'

But this was not to the fox's liking. 'Why should I tie myself to him?' he asked.

'Because otherwise the horse would shake you off, and you would not be able to bite even the tiniest mouthful,' the monkey explained.

'That is true,' the fox admitted.

'All right, I shall think it over.' And he ran off as if he had no interest in tasting a mouthful of horse's leg. But it was not true. As soon as he got to the nearest thicket, he turned back and ran to the meadow where the horse was sleeping.

The monkey and the hare ran after him, keeping themselves hidden, so as not to miss anything. And indeed it was worth their while. The fox could not wait to taste horsemeat. He crept quietly up to the sleeping horse, carefully tied his own tail to that of the horse and took a quick bite of the horse's rump.

He did not have much chance to enjoy it. The horse at once awoke, jumped up on all fours, kicked out with his hind legs and raced off. The fox, tied to the horse's tail, went bumping along after him.

The monkey looked down on it all from a tree and laughed so much that she fell out of the tree and landed on her behind. Since then monkeys have had red bottoms. As for the hare — he laughed so much that he split his lip and since then all hares have had split lips.

But the one who came off worst was Brother Fox. Before he managed to untie the knot in his tail he was half dead. That was the last time he ever tied himself to a horse's tail.

And the horse, since that time, does not like lying down in the grass. Even when he is tired he prefers to sleep standing up.

The Spider
and
the Lion

One day a spider thought he would like to eat fish. He wove a fine web to use as a net, went to the river and spent the whole morning fishing. By noon he had a whole basketful of fish. 'And now let's taste some of them,' he said to himself. And he made a fire on the bank and started to cook the fish.

The baking fish could be smelled far and near and the scent was soon picked up by a lion. He trotted up to the fire.

'What are you cooking, Spider?' he asked.

The spider realized that he was in great danger. So he said humbly. 'I caught a few fish in the river, Lion, and now I am cooking them. But there are hardly enough for one.'

The lion laughed. 'That's all right, Spider, I should just like to have a taste. Show me how you have been cooking them.'

The spider had no choice but to let the lion taste his fish. He ate one, he ate a second and went on until he had eaten every one. There was not a morsel left for the spider. He had to make do with the smell. Tears of anger came to his eyes. The lion noticed this and asked. 'Why are you crying, Spider?'

The spider did not want to admit why he was crying, so he said. 'Oh, it's nothing, Lion. It's just the smoke from the fire stinging my eyes.' And in his heart he swore revenge on the lion.

Just at that moment, a wild guinea fowl ran past. She was so beautifully speckled that it was a joy to look at her. When she saw the spider she wanted to stop and have a few words with him. Then she saw the lion and was frightened. Without a word of greeting she ran on.

The spider watched her, then sadly shook his head as if something was worrying him.

'You see, Lion, how one's good deeds are repaid! When that guinea fowl wanted me to make her beautiful speckled feathers, she could not have been more friendly. She only had to see me to run and welcome me. She was happy to greet me at any moment of the day. But now that she has her speckled feathers, she passes by without a word.'

'I did not know, Spider,' said the lion, 'that you could make such beautiful things. I thought them quite wonderful.'

68

'Oh, that's nothing,' said the spider modestly. 'It is an art my father taught me. If you like, I could make you a speckled coat like that. Only it would hurt a bit.'

'That wouldn't worry me, Spider,' said the lion. 'I can stand the pain, if only you will make me a coat such as no one else has. Make it for me straight away.'

And the spider said. 'Well, Brother Lion, first you must hunt and skin a buffalo. I shall need his skin.'

The lion was surprised. 'Why should you want the skin of a buffalo, Spider?' he asked.

'For straps, Lion,' said the spider.

'And why do you want straps, Spider?'

'You will soon see, Lion, when we have them,' was the reply. 'Just hurry and find a buffalo.'

Above all things the lion wanted to have a speckled coat so he set off at once to hunt for a buffalo. In a very short time he came back dragging a dead buffalo. He cooked it on the spider's fire, skinned it and cut the skin into long strips. In the meantime, the spider enjoyed a meal of roast buffalo. It was much better than a whole basketful of fish. By the time he had eaten his fill, the straps were ready.

The spider took the straps, led the lion to a sturdy baobab tree and said. 'Now, Brother Lion, try if you can to uproot this baobab tree.'

The lion pushed the tree with all his strength, but he could not move it.

'It is no good, Brother Spider,' said the lion. 'The tree's too strong.'

The spider nodded. 'Do as I say, Brother Lion. Grasp the tree with all four legs and I shall tie you to it.'

The lion was suspicious. 'Why should I do that, Spider?' he asked.

The spider answered. 'There's no other way of doing it, Lion. If you were not tied to the tree, you would lose some of your fur and then you would not have your beautiful speckled coat.'

The lion growled and grumbled but said. 'All right, Spider, if it has to be, it has to be. Tie me to the tree.' And he grasped the baobab tree with all four legs.

The spider took the straps and quickly started to bind the lion to the tree. When he had tied the last knot, he said. 'Try now, Brother Lion, to break the straps.'

The lion tried with all his strength, but he could not break the straps. 'It is no good, Spider. You have tied them too tight,' he said.

The spider was pleased. 'Good. Now I must make that speckled coat you want so much.'

And he pulled a burning branch from the fire and drew it across the lion's back. The lion roared with pain. The spider said, as if surprised. 'What is the matter, Brother Lion? Did you not say you wanted a speckled coat? Now you shall have one. That's in return for the first of my fish that you ate!'

Then he drew the burning branch across the lion's back a second time. The lion again roared with pain. Again the spider said, as if surprised. 'Why do you roar, Lion? That's for the second fish you ate.'

Then he drew the burning branch across the lion's back a third, a fourth, and a fifth time, counting off the number of fish the lion had eaten. At last he stopped and said. 'And now your coat is as speckled as a guinea fowl's feathers. You have got what you deserved, Lion. Never again will you eat fish you have neither caught nor cooked.'

And the spider ran happily home, taking with him as much of the buffalo as he could carry.

The lion remained tied to the baobab tree, roaring with pain and anger. At last termites set him free by eating their way through the straps.

Never again did the lion steal fish from the spider. And the spider never went fishing again. Instead of fish he preferred to catch flies in his web, for lions do not eat flies.

The Tiger and the Fox Cub

Once upon a time a fox cub met a tiger. There was not time to either hide or run away. 'Only cleverness can help me,' she said to herself, and boldly faced the tiger. 'Tiger!' she said, 'listen to me.'

The tiger was surprised. Never before had he been addressed in such a way, or by such a little animal.

'Why should I listen to you?' he growled.

'Because I could tear you to pieces,' said the fox cub.

'You tear me to pieces?' said the tiger, even more surprised.

'Yes, I could,' said the fox cub. 'Because I am more terrifying than you. Perhaps a mouse may be afraid of you, or a hare, but even a man is afraid of me.'

'I do not believe it,' growled the tiger.

'If you do not believe it, just come with me and see for yourself,' said the fox cub. And she ran through the long grass to the path leading from the village to the town. The tiger ran after her. The fox cub could not be seen in the long grass whereas people noticed the big tiger at once and ran from him in terror. Soon the path to the town was completely deserted.

The fox cub stuck her head out of the long grass and said. 'Do you believe me now, Tiger? I went first and hardly had people caught sight of me when they took to their heels and ran away as fast as their legs could carry them. Nobody took the slightest notice of you.'

The big tiger had to admit that the fox cub was right. She had gone first and people had indeed fled before her. Suddenly he too was afraid of the fox cub. He put his tail between his legs and ran off as quickly as he could. The fox cub, on the other hand, stopped being frightened. She realized that strength lay not only in large teeth and powerful claws, but also in a clever head. And since that time she has not been frightened of tigers.

71

The Donkey Who Was King of the Lions

Once upon a time a donkey thought he would like to see the world. So he shook himself free of his halter, trotted out of his yard and set off for the mountains. The grass grew high, the water in the streams was clean and cold and the donkey, far away from his master, felt happier than he had ever been in his life. Out of sheer joy he started to bray as loud as he could.

His braying was heard by a lion who had never heard such a noise before. Stealthily he crept through the long grass to have a look at this strange unknown animal. When he saw the donkey he could scarcely believe his eyes.

He approached the large, long-eared creature and greeted it politely. 'Good day, Brother. From where have you come and what is your name?'

'I have come from afar and my name is Arch Lion,' replied the donkey.

'Arch Lion?' said the lion. 'Does that mean that you are ruler of all the lions?'

'That is true. There is no animal in the world who can compare with me!' brayed the donkey.

'If that is the case, Arch Lion, let us join forces and together we shall be the strongest of all animals,' said the lion. And he invited the donkey to go hunting with him.

On the way they came to a river. The lion was on the other side in one jump, but the donkey slid cautiously into the water, and so strong was the current, he was nearly swept away. It was only with greatest difficulty that he was able to scramble out on the other side.

'That's strange,' said the lion to himself. 'This creature who calls himself Arch Lion cannot even ford a river. Can't you swim?' he asked the donkey.

'Certainly,' said the donkey. 'I can swim like a fish.'

'Then why were you so long in the water?' the lion asked.

'Did you not see the huge fish I caught with my tail? It nearly pulled me down to the bed of the river,' said the donkey.

The lion was amazed that Arch Lion was so strong, and shaking his mane, he ran on. On the way they came to a high wall. The lion leapt up and in one bound was over the wall. The donkey, on the other hand, took at least half an hour to scramble to the top of the wall. When he finally succeeded he could neither go forward nor back.

'What are you doing up there?' the lion asked.

'Can't you see? I'm weighing myself,' said the donkey. 'I want to know which is heavier — my front or my rear.' And he jumped down.

'I have a feeling that you have been deceiving me,' said the lion, 'and that you are not as strong a fellow as you make out.'

'What's that? Let us make a wager as to which of us will knock the wall down first!' said the donkey.

The lion hurled himself at the wall with his paws and his head. He was covered in blood, but the wall still stood. But when the donkey turned his back to the wall and started to kick out with his hoofs, it was down in less than no time.

'Now you can see that I am stronger than you,' said the donkey. 'But that is not all I can do. Look at these thistles. They would scratch you to death. But I am so strong I can eat them up.'

And the donkey set to work on the thistles, and in a few minutes they had vanished down his throat.

The lion was greatly impressed and said. 'I can see that you really are stronger and more powerful than I. You deserve to be King of all the lions.'

The next day the lion summoned a parliament of all the lions in the country and there the donkey Arch Lion was elected King of all the animals.

From that day on the donkey lived as a king. He was a king loved by all, because he harmed no one and demanded no taxes. He was quite satisfied with grass ot thistles, and there was no shortage of either.

It was a pity that such a good king could not live for ever. One day the lions found him lying dead in the meadow. They arranged a royal funeral for him and mourned him for a long, long time.

Even today when they remember their good king they roar so loudly that all other animals flee in fright.

The Wolf, the Fox and Snowy the Goat

There were once three good friends, a cock, a cat and a goat called Snowy. They lived together on a farm not far from a forest. The cock scratched around on the dung heap and crowed, the cat warmed himself in the sun and purred, and the goat, Snowy, nibbled the grass behind the house and bleated. She did not like being tied up with a rope. All the time she jerked at it and gnawed at it and longed to reach the forest on the hillside. She told her friends. 'The grass there is much sweeter.'

'It is not sweeter,' said the cock, Cockadoodle, 'and it is quite likely that a fox lurks there!'

'Or a wolf,' warned the cat, Tom.

But little Snowy would not believe them. 'It is not true,' she said.

'It is true, Snowy,' insisted the cock once more.

'Do not think of going there,' repeated the cat.

But Snowy the goat did not believe her friends. 'They only talk like that to frighten me,' she thought, and quietly went on gnawing the rope that held her, until one evening she gnawed it right through. Hardly was she free when she was pushing her way through the fence and running straight for the forest.

While it was still light she enjoyed every minute of her freedom. She ran here and there, nibbled a little grass even though it was dry and yellow, she chewed up some leaves although they were beginning to rot, and she was very happy. But when darkness began to fall, Snowy felt homesick and longed for her friends at the farm. She started to run downhill. Suddenly she stopped as if she had been turned to stone.

In the twilight two green lights gleamed. 'A fox,' thought Snowy, and she was afraid. She was right. On the path before her stood Sister Fox. Snowy turned quickly. But she had not taken more than three steps when she stopped again as if turned to stone.

In the twilight two yellow lights gleamed. 'A

wolf,' she thought, and was afraid. She was right. On the path, in front of her was Brother Wolf. Snowy the goat was trapped.

Sister Fox was licking her lips. 'Look who is here,' she said. 'The little goat, Snowy, from the farm. What a good meal we will have, Brother Wolf!'

Brother Wolf bared his teeth. 'We will indeed, Sister Fox! What do you say to gobbling her up at once?'

But Sister Fox was a dainty eater. 'Not yet. Let us take her to your house and cook her slowly.'

Brother Wolf agreed. 'You are right, Sister Fox. Besides I have never tasted stewed goat.'

He put the rope Snowy had bitten through into her mouth and led her to his house. The fox followed behind. She wanted to make sure that Snowy did not run away or that the wolf did not keep Snowy for himself.

In Brother Wolf's cottage, Sister Fox prepared to cook. She raked the fire but found she had not enough firewood.

'I shall go into the forest to fetch some!' offered Snowy, the goat, in a soft little voice.

'Oh no, you will not,' laughed Brother Wolf in his gruff voice. 'To make sure you do not run away, I shall go for the wood myself.' In a few minutes he was back with a bundle of firewood. Sister Fox threw the wood on the fire, put a tripod over it and a three-legged cauldron. But she did not have enough water.

'I shall go to the well for water!' said the little goat, Snowy, in a soft little voice.

'Oh no, you will not,' laughed Brother Wolf in his gruff voice. 'To make sure you do not run away, I shall go for the water myself.' A few minutes later he was back with a pail of water. Sister Fox poured the water into the cauldron and sprinkled salt and herbs into it. But she did not have enough herbs.

'I will slip out to the shop for them,' said Snowy, the little goat, in her soft little voice.

'Oh, no, you will not,' laughed Brother Wolf in

his gruff voice. 'To make sure you do not run away, I shall go to the shop myself.' And he ran off to the village shop.

It was quite a long way to the shop and some time passed before Brother Wolf returned.

'What has happened to Brother Wolf?' grumbled Sister Fox. 'Before he gets back all the water will have boiled away. Little goat, have a look in the pot and see if there is still enough water!'

But the little goat, Snowy, replied. 'You look, Sister Fox! I am afraid I might fall in.'

Sister Fox laughed. 'Why ever should you fall in. It is easy. Just stand on the stool, lift the lid and look in.'

And Sister Fox climbed onto the stool, lifted the lid and leaned over the cauldron. That was just what Snowy, the goat, was waiting for. The moment the fox leaned over the cauldron, she jumped up and with all her strength pushed Sister Fox into the cauldron. All Snowy had to do then was put on the lid.

Just then, Snowy heard Brother Wolf returning to the cottage. Quickly Snowy ran to the door and bolted it. The wolf banged on the door.

'Sister Fox,' he called. 'Open the door! I have brought the herbs.'

The little goat, Snowy, called to the wolf. 'Sister Fox is not here. She locked the door and took the key with her. She went to get some cream. She said you could come in by the chimney!'

Brother Wolf was surprised. 'Down the chimney,' he said. 'Then you will have to take away the cauldron of water. I do not want to be scalded!'

'Very well,' said the little goat. But she left the cauldron where it was and just lifted the lid. There was a crackling and a rustling in the chimney and Brother Wolf came tumbling down straight into the boiling water. Snowy replaced the lid.

What happened to Brother Wolf and Sister Fox under that lid nobody knows. But the little goat, Snowy, sped home to her friends on the farm, and since then she has never wanted to escape again.

The Fox and the Grapes

A hungry fox wandered into a vineyard, and there he saw a vine weighed down with large ripe grapes. They looked so tempting in the morning sunshine and he had not eaten for so long.

'What a fine breakfast these would make,' he said, 'if only I could get at them.'

The grapes were just out of reach. The fox jumped up once, he jumped up twice, he jumped up a third time, but all in vain. Each time he fell back to the ground with a heavy thud. Exhausted, he realized he was not going to have those grapes for breakfast. He looked up at them once more, then he turned up his nose and said. 'It doesn't matter. They are sure to be sour. I shall go and find something better for breakfast.'

And he ran proudly, but still hungry, out of the vineyard.

The Cock
and the Centipede

When the Jasper Emperor still ruled the heavens, the cock did not look as he does today. On his head he had beautiful antlers like a stag's and he was very proud of them. All the beasts envied him these antlers, especially the dragon who lived in a deep pool. The dragon had a head shaped like a camel's, eyes like the devil's, ears like a buffalo's, a neck like a snake's, talons like a vulture's and pads like a tiger's. What made him unhappy was the fact that his camel-shaped head was quite bald.

One day the Jasper Emperor invited all the animals to a banquet at the Celestial Palace. All the animals looked forward to this banquet. Only the dragon was unhappy. He wondered how he could cover his bald head. He was still wondering when the cock came strutting past the dragon's pool. He carried himself like a lord and on his head were his beautiful antlers.

The dragon said to him. 'Tomorrow, Cock, I am invited to the Celestial Palace to the banquet, and I have nothing to wear on my head. Will you lend me your antlers?'

'I cannot, Dragon,' replied the cock. 'I too am invited to the Celestial Palace.'

'But even without your antlers you look quite handsome,' the dragon said in a flattering way. 'You have such beautiful feathers, a splendid tail and such fine spurs. I would even say those antlers detract from your beauty!'

At that moment the centipede went past. When she heard what the dragon said, she immediately joined in the conversation.

'The dragon is quite right, Brother Cock,' she said. 'You are beautiful even without those antlers. Take my advice and lend them to the dragon. If you like, I shall guarantee their safety.'

And so, in the end, the cock allowed himself to be persuaded.

'I shall lend them to you for one day, Dragon,' he promised. 'After the banquet you must give them back to me.'

The dragon promised to return the antlers immediately after the banquet. Happily he put

them on his head and set out for the Celestial Palace.

The Jasper Emperor welcomed all the animals and bade them be seated. The dragon he placed next to himself. The cock was displeased.

'It is because I lent my antlers to the dragon,' he complained.

Next day he went to the pool. 'Dragon,' he called, 'give me back my antlers!' But the dragon had forgotten his promise. He liked the antlers and had no intention of giving them back.

'What use are they to you, Brother Cock?' he said. 'You are good looking enough without them, while I must have something on my head.'

The cock was angry. 'It is my business whether I am good looking or not,' he said. 'Give me back what you borrowed!'

The dragon took no notice of the cock's cries.

'Don't be angry, Brother Cock. I have other things to do than argue with you. We shall talk about it another time,' he said, and dived, with the antlers, to the bottom of the pool.

The cock set up a cry. 'Dragon, give me back my antlers! Dragon, give me back my antlers!'

But he cried in vain. The dragon, at the bottom of the pool, could not hear him. But the centipede heard him and she came running to ask what was happening.

'The dragon will not give me back my antlers,' cried the cock. 'And you are a witness to his promise.'

'That is true,' said the centipede, 'but what can I do when the dragon has gone into hiding at the bottom of the pool?'

'What's that to me?' he said. 'You should not have guaranteed for him.'

The centipede snapped back. 'And you should not have lent him your antlers. It is all your own fault.'

The cock was beside himself. 'It's your fault!' he shrieked, opened his beak, pecked at the centipede and pecked her right in half.

Ever since then, the cock and the centipede have been enemies. A cock has only to catch sight of a centipede and he is after it at once to kill and eat it. And the cock has not forgotten the dragon, either. When he wakes up in the morning he shouts. 'Cockadoodle-doo!' which in cock language means. 'Dragon, give me back my antlers!'

But to this day the dragon has not given them back, as you can see for yourselves.

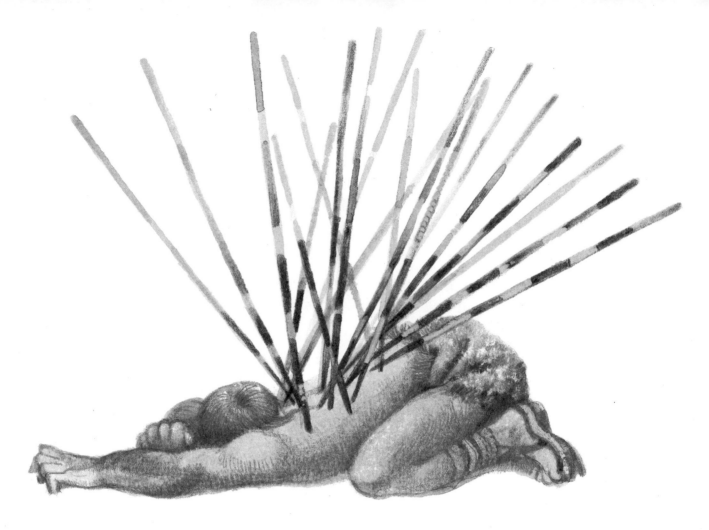

How the Porcupine Came into the World

When the world was still young and everything was different, there once lived a hunter. He lived by himself in a lonely hut and never did he go out hunting with the other men. He always waited until the men came back from their hunting expeditions. Then he would kill one of them, take his share of the game and so have enough to eat.

He went on doing this until the other hunters realized who was killing their comrades and decided they must punish the solitary hunter. One morning they took their spears and surrounded the hut where the hunter lived. He was still asleep, lying face downwards on a mat and heard and saw nothing. He did not wake even when the twigs crackled under the feet of the hunters.

'It will be some animal in the undergrowth,' he thought in his dreams, and slept on.

Then the grass rustled, but even then he did not open his eyes. 'It will be some kind of beetle,' he said to himself, and slept on.

Finally the spears rattled. But even then the hunter did not raise his head. 'It will be some kind of bird,' he told himself, and slept on.

But it was not an animal, it was not a beetle, nor was it a bird. It was the hunters with raised spears. They hurled them with all their strength into the hunter's back. When he did not move they supposed him to be dead and went away believing they had avenged their friends.

But the hunter was not dead. He was still alive and when they went away, he crept on all fours to a hole he had dug under the hut. He stayed there until his wounds healed. But he could not pull the spears out of his back. They grew into his body and remained there to this day. And to this day that solitary hunter has walked on all fours, and when a branch crackles, the grass rustles or an enemy approaches, he quickly crawls into a hole in the ground.

People call him the porcupine.

Why the Crocodile Lives in the Water

When the world was still young and everything was different, the crocodile and the dog were great friends and lived together in the same house on the banks of a wide river.

In those days the crocodile still had small jaws and a small mouth and could only eat little morsels and drink tiny sips. That he should bite anything was quite impossible. The dog too found it just as difficult to eat and drink.

One day the dog became so impatient that he found a knife, gave it to the crocodile and said.

'Help me, Crocodile. Cut my mouth with this knife so that it will be a little bit bigger and I shall be able to bite properly.'

The crocodile agreed. 'With pleasure, Dog,' he said, 'but then you must do the same for me.'

The dog promised he would do this.

The crocodile went to work at once. He took the knife and slit the dog's mouth so that he could open it wider. He was very careful and the result was most successful.

The dog was satisfied. But when he took the knife to cut the mouth of the crocodile he did not take care, and the knife went so deep that it was a wonder he did not cut the crocodile's head in two.

The crocodile was very angry. 'Just look what you have done to me,' he said. 'How can I appear before the world like this? Everyone will laugh at me. Rather than be such a laughing stock, I shall go and hide under the water. But I will not forgive you. If you come anywhere near the river, I will pull you into the water and eat you up.'

And ever since then the crocodile has had an enormous mouth and has lived in the water. And if by chance he catches a dog on the river bank, he snaps him up without mercy.

The Goat
with
the Silver Bell

A little Nanny goat was once given a silver bell by her master. She was very proud of it and boasted about it wherever she went. She ran and jumped and her bell rang merrily until one day the bell was caught fast on a thorn bush. The little goat begged the thorn bush. 'Please, thorn bush, give me back my bell.'

But the thorn bush ignored the little goat's request. 'You hung it on me, you must get it back yourself,' it said.

The goat was angry. 'Just you wait,' she said. 'I'll pay you out!' And she ran to an old saw. 'Saw!' she cried, 'help me! The thorn bush has taken my silver bell and doesn't want to give it back to me. Cut down that thorn bush!'

But the saw did not want to. 'I am old and my teeth are blunt,' it said. 'I will not cut down that thorn bush.'

The goat was angry. 'Just wait,' she said. 'I'll pay you out!' And she ran to the fire. 'Fire, help me!' she said. 'The thorn bush has taken my silver bell and doesn't want to give it back to me. I went to the saw and asked it to cut down the thorn bush, but it will not. It says it is old and its teeth are blunt. Burn that saw!'

But the fire would not give in to the little goat. 'Why should I burn the saw?' it said. 'It is true that its teeth are blunt. I will not burn it.'

The goat was angry. 'Just you wait,' she said. 'I'll pay you out!' And she ran to the water. 'Water, help me,' she cried. 'The thorn bush has taken my silver bell and doesn't want to give it back to me. I went to the saw and asked it to cut down the thorn bush, but it will not. It says it is old and its teeth are blunt. I went to the fire and asked it to burn the saw, but it would not, but agreed that the saw was old. Water, put out the fire!'

But the water would not put out the fire. 'Why should I?' it said. 'The fire is right that the saw is old. I won't put it out!'

The goat was even angrier. 'Just wait,' she said. 'I'll pay you out!' And she ran to the oxen. 'Oxen, help me!' she cried. 'The thorn bush has taken my silver bell and will not give it back to me. I went to the saw and asked it to cut down the thorn bush, but it will not. It says it is old

and its teeth are blunt. I went to the fire and asked it to burn the saw but it would not, but

agreed that the saw was old. I went to the water and asked it to put out the fire, but the water would not put out the fire. Oxen, drink up that water!'

But the oxen did not drink up the water. 'Why should we drink it up?' they said, 'when it is right.'

The goat was furious. 'Just wait,' she cried. 'I'll pay you out!' And she ran to the wolf. 'Wolf, help me!' she cried. 'The thorn bush has taken my silver bell and will not give it back to me. I went to the saw and asked it to cut down the thorn bush, but it would not. It says it is old and its teeth are blunt. I went to the fire and asked it to burn the saw but it would not, but agreed that the saw was old. I went to the water and asked it to put out the fire, but the water would not. I went to the oxen and asked them to drink up the water, but the oxen said they would not and that the water was right. Eat up those oxen!'

But the wolf did not eat them up. 'I am not hungry,' he said, 'and I do not want to go near the oxen. They might toss me with their horns.

You had better run away or I might eat *you*!'

The goat was angrier than ever. 'Just wait,' she said. 'I'll pay you out!' And she ran to the gun. 'Little gun, help me!' she said. 'The thorn bush has taken my silver bell and will not give it back to me. I went to the saw and asked it to cut down the thorn bush, but it would not. It said it was old and its teeth were blunt. I went to the fire and asked it to burn the saw, but it would not. It agreed that the saw was old. I went to the water and asked it to put out the fire, but the water would not. I went to the oxen and asked them to drink up the water, but the oxen said they would not, and that the water was right. I went to the wolf and asked him to eat up the oxen, but the wolf did not want to and said he was not hungry. Shoot the wolf.'

But the gun did not shoot the wolf. 'I cannot. I am not loaded,' it said.

The goat was angrier than ever. 'Just wait,' she cried. 'I'll pay you out!' And she ran to the mice. 'Little mice, help me!' she said. 'The thorn bush has taken my silver bell and will not give it

back to me. I went to the saw and asked it to cut down the thorn bush, but it would not. It says it is old and its teeth are blunt. I went to the fire and asked it to burn the saw but it would not, and agreed that the saw was old. I went to the water and asked it to put out the fire, but the water would not. I went to the oxen and asked them to drink up the water, but the oxen said they would not and that the water was right. I went to the wolf and asked him to eat the oxen, but the wolf would not and said he was not hungry. I went to the gun and asked it to shoot the wolf, but it said it was not loaded. Gnaw through that gun!'

But the mice did not want to gnaw through the gun. 'It is made of iron,' they said, 'and it would break our teeth.'

The goat was angry again. 'Just wait,' she said. 'I'll pay you out!' And she ran to the cat. 'Cat, help me,' she said. 'The thorn bush has taken my silver bell and will not give it back to me. I went to the saw and asked it to cut down the thorn bush, but it would not, saying it was old and its teeth were blunt. I went to the fire and asked it to burn the saw, but it would not, and agreed that the saw was old. I went to the water and asked it to put out the fire. But the water would not. I went to the oxen and asked them to drink up the water, but the oxen said they would not and that the water was right. I went to the wolf and asked him to eat up the oxen, but the wolf would not, and said he was not hungry. I went to the gun and asked it to shoot the wolf, but it would not, and said it was not loaded. I went to the mice and asked them to gnaw through the gun, but the mice would not, and said it would break their teeth. Catch those mice!'

But the cat did not catch the mice. 'I would not stir a claw for you,' the cat said. 'How many times have you nearly tossed me on your horns? Get the silver bell yourself!'

The goat was furious. 'Just wait. I'll pay you out!' she said. And she ran to the farmer. 'Master, help me!' she cried. 'The thorn bush has taken my silver bell and will not give it back to me. I went to the saw and asked it to cut down the thorn bush, but it would not. It said it was old and its teeth were blunt. I went to the fire and asked it to burn the saw, but it would not, and agreed the saw was old. I went to the water and asked it to put out the fire, but the water would not. I went to the oxen and asked them to drink up the water, but they said they would not, and that the water was right. I went to the wolf and asked him to eat up the oxen, but the wolf would not, and said he was not hungry. I went to the gun and asked it to shoot the wolf, but it would not, and said it was not loaded. I went to the mice and asked them to gnaw through the gun, but the mice would not, and said it would break their teeth. I went to the cat and asked her to catch the mice, but she would not, and said she would not stir a claw for me. Thrash that cat!'

But the farmer only laughed. 'Why should I thrash the cat, you stupid goat?' he asked. 'Come along with me and I shall get your bell down from the thorn bush. It is all your own fault that the bell was caught in the thorn bush. No one did anything to you, but you have been blaming and slandering everyone. And so as a punishment I shall not give you back the bell.'

And the farmer hung it on the stable door so that whenever the door was opened the bell rang. And no matter how much the goat kicked up her heels and tossed her head, the bell never hung round her neck again.

The Lion
and
the Carpenter

There was once an island in the middle of the sea where no man had ever set foot. On this island lived all the animals that are in the world today. They were happy and free among the flowers of the meadows and the trees weighed down with fruit, and where sparkling streams flowed.

One of these animals was a duck who swam happily in the streams and fed on sweet water plants. But one night the duck had a strange dream. In her dream she saw a beautiful land, a land more beautiful than her native island. When she awoke she yearned to leave home and find this beautiful land of her dream.

She knew she would have to swim across vast seas but she was not afraid, and for many days and many nights she swam, until at last she reached the unknown land. She was so tired when she reached the shore that she at once fell asleep.

While she slept she heard a voice saying, 'Poor little duck, you have at last found the land of your dream. It is beautiful and rich, but do not forget that man lives here. I advise you to be

wary of him for he is capable of every kind of deceit.'

The duck opened her eyes. She did not at first know which way to go. But in the distance she saw mountains and she set out towards them. At last she reached a cave surrounded by rocks. At the mouth of the cave, a young lion basked in the sun. The little duck looked at him curiously, and the lion looked at the duck in wonder too. 'What is your name, you strange creature, and to what family of creatures do you belong?' he asked.

'I am called a duck and I belong to the family of birds,' the duck replied.

'Have you travelled far?' asked the lion in surprise.

The duck told him her story, and the lion listened.

Then he said. 'I too had a dream last night like yours. In my dream I too heard a voice giving me the same advice.'

The duck was frightened. 'But you are strong,' she said. 'You are the son of the king of beasts.

Could you not kill man? Then no one could threaten us any more and we should live happily in this beautiful land.'

The lion stretched himself, yawned and bared his teeth.

He said. 'Tomorrow I shall go out hunting and kill man. If you like, you can come with me and no harm will befall you.'

Upon hearing this, the duck felt better. She bowed courteously to the lion and sat down on the bank of a stream to rest. The next day she set out with the lion. They crossed a desert, they crossed a plain, but not a trace of a man did they find. But suddenly in the distance they saw a cloud of dust. When they came closer, they saw an animal with huge ears.

'Who are you and where do you come from?' asked the lion.

'I am a donkey,' replied the animal, 'and I am running away from man.'

'Come with us,' said the lion, 'nothing will harm you. We are looking for man too and I mean to kill him.'

And so the three of them continued their journey. Suddenly they saw in the distance another cloud of dust. When they came close to the cloud, they saw a beautiful animal with strong hoofs.

'Noble beast,' said the lion. 'Who are you and why are you racing across this desert?'

'I am a horse and I am running away from man,' was the reply.

'You too are running away from man?' said the lion in surprise. 'Come along with us and do not be afraid.'

And so they continued their journey together

until once more they saw approaching on the horizon a cloud of dust. This time it was a camel who was also running away from man.

'I shall deal with him,' growled the lion threateningly. The camel joined them and they continued their journey.

It was not long before they met a man. On his head he carried planks of wood and in his hand a bag of carpenter's tools. The animals halted and very uncertainly inspected the man.

Then the lion approached him and asked. 'Who are you and why do you tremble?'

'I am a carpenter,' said the old man, 'and I tremble because I am afraid of man.'

The lion roared. 'I shall find man and kill him. Follow us, but tell me first where you are going.'

'I am on the way to the panther who is the vizier at the court of the king — your father,' replied the old man. 'He summoned me as soon as news reached him that man had come to this region. He asked me to build him a house which no man could enter. As you can see I am carrying planks and tools with me.'

The young lion growled, because secretly he envied the panther. He said. 'All right, carpenter, but first you must build a house for me. After that the panther can have *his* house.'

'I cannot do what you ask, son of the king,' said the carpenter. 'I must first build a house for the panther as I promised.'

The lion roared menacingly and struck at the carpenter with his paw. The man fell to the ground. 'How strong you are, Lion,' he said.

'And you are weak,' roared the lion in reply. 'Build a house for me at once.'

So the carpenter laid the planks on the ground, took tools out of his bag and set to work. In a short time he had made a crate with no lid.

'Here is your house, Lion,' said the carpenter. 'Step in and I shall make a roof for you.'

The lion jumped into the crate and the carpenter quickly put on the lid and secured it with long, strong nails.

'Carpenter, open my house!' roared the lion. 'I cannot breathe.'

'With pleasure, my friend,' laughed the carpenter. 'I shall open it as soon as I have made a cage for you so that you cannot escape.'

'What do you mean?' roared the lion.

'I mean that you have fallen into my trap,' laughed the carpenter.

'Then you are a man, carpenter?' asked the lion.

'You have guessed right, son of the king. And my cleverness is greater than your strength,' said the carpenter. In vain the lion roared with anger, for nothing could help him.

The camel, the horse and the donkey saw that they could not escape their master, man, and without a struggle they followed him.

Only the duck flew off unnoticed. She reached the sea shore at last, and after swimming many days and many nights, she came again to the island where no man had set foot. There she lived happily for the rest of her life.

The Hedgehog, the Fox and His Seventy-Seven Brains

One day a fox met a hedgehog and they stopped to talk. And as the fox liked to boast, he said. 'Listen, Hedgehog, how many brains have you got?'

The hedgehog was surprised. 'How many brains have I got? Just one, of course. And what about you?'

'I have seventy-seven,' said the fox. 'That is why everyone has such respect for me.'

The hedgehog decided to punish the fox for his boastfulness. 'Seventy-seven brains,' he said. 'I do not believe you. You would have to swear it is true at some sacred place.'

The fox agreed. 'I shall swear to it wherever you like,' he said. And the hedgehog took the fox to a place where a hunter had laid a trap. 'This is a sacred place,' he said. 'Now swear to it.'

The fox stood on the trap. It snapped shut and the fox's foot was caught in it. He started to moan with pain. 'Help me, Hedgehog. Please help me!'

The hedgehog could not help. 'I wish I could help you, Fox,' he said, 'but how can I? I have only one brain, as you know, while you have seventy-seven. You should be able to think of something yourself.'

The fox went on moaning. 'I see, Hedgehog, that this sacred place wants to punish me for being boastful. If you cannot help me, at least give me some advice.'

So the hedgehog advised the fox. 'When the hunter comes to the trap, pretend to be dead. Do not move even if he prods you with a stick. The hunter will open the trap and lay you beside it. Then you can easily escape.'

The fox did as the hedgehog suggested. When he heard the hunter in the woods, he shut his eyes, stretched out his legs and pretended to be dead. The hunter poked him with a stick, and when he did not move, he opened the trap and laid the fox on the ground. This was what the fox was waiting for. He at once jumped to his feet and was off. But since that day he has never boasted that he has seventy-seven brains.

The Crocodile and the Hen

Once upon a time a hen came to the river to drink. A hungry crocodile saw her and thought what a nice, plump hen she was.

'I shall have a good dinner,' said the crocodile happily, and grabbed the hen by the tail. But the hen began to shriek. 'Let me go, Crocodile, let me go, dear brother!'

The crocodile was amazed. 'Why does the hen call me brother?' he wondered. And he let her go.

The next day the hen came to the river again. The hungry crocodile was waiting for her and grabbed her by the wing. But again the hen let out a great shriek. 'Let me go, Crocodile, let me go, dear brother.'

Unwillingly the crocodile let her go. But after all he was not going to eat his sister. He kept turning the matter over in his mind, however, and at last he went to his friend the lizard for advice.

'Listen to what happened to me, Lizard,' he said. 'I caught a hen by the river, but when I wanted to eat her she started shrieking that I should let her go, and she called me her dear brother. Am I the brother of a hen?'

The lizard began to laugh. 'The hen was telling the truth, Crocodile. Don't you know that hens are hatched out of eggs, just as crocodiles are?'

The crocodile nodded. 'You are quite right, Lizard, I had never thought about it before. If you look at it that way the hen really is my sister, or at least my niece.'

And ever afterwards the crocodile left hens in peace.

The Old Dog and the Wolf

A shepherd once had a dog that had grown very old. He had one lame leg, was blind in one eye and his teeth were falling out. Nevertheless he served his master faithfully and well. When he was guarding the sheep, wolves kept well away from the flock. But the shepherd at last thought to himself. 'Of what use is such an old dog. I shall get a younger one.' And he drove the old dog out.

The old dog did not go far. He crept into the undergrowth close to the fold, and there cold and hungry, he fell asleep. When a wolf came in the night and carried off a sheep from the field, he had not the strength to bark. And the young dog did not bark either, for he had a full stomach and slept so soundly that he did not even hear the wolf.

In the morning, when the shepherd discovered that a sheep was missing, he began to regret that he had driven the old dog out. 'He was old, he was lame and half blind, but he was faithful,' he said. 'He would not have let a sheep be carried off.' And he called to the old dog. He gave him food and water, and the old dog went back to guarding the flock.

When the wolf came in the night, the dog went for him, growling. 'What do you want here, Wolf?'

'I want a sheep,' answered the wolf, 'like the one I had last night.'

'You will not have one,' said the old dog. 'Last night you stole one because I was hungry and had not the strength to chase you away. But today my master has fed me and I am quite able to protect the whole flock.'

'We shall see about that,' said the wolf. 'If you are so strong we shall fight it out. Come to the clearing in the woods tomorrow. Bring your friends with you and I shall bring mine. Then we shall see which of us is the stronger.' And he ran off.

The next day the old dog and his friends set out for the woods. He took as his seconds a tomcat and a sow.

At the clearing the wolf was waiting for them. He had brought as his seconds a bear and a fox. As they waited, the wolf, the bear and the fox boasted about what they would do to the dog. But when they saw him approaching with the cat and the sow, they were afraid. The old dog was limping in one leg, and the bear whispered fearfully.

'Just look, friends, how the dog moves sideways at every step. He must be picking up stones to throw at us.'

The tomcat thrashed his tail as he approached and the fox was afraid.

'Look, friends,' she said, 'the cat is swinging a sabre.' The sow was grunting happily as she came along, pleased to be in the woods once more. This sound frightened the wolf.

'Just listen, friends. That is their leader and that is their battle cry! We had better hide!' And he jumped behind a big stone. The fox quickly crept into the undergrowth and the bear climbed a tree.

When the old dog and his friends arrived at the clearing there was no sign of the wolf and his seconds. Suddenly the cat caught sight of a mouse in the undergrowth and sprang after it. The fox, thinking he was after her, instantly took flight. At the same time the sow had seen some acorns under the tree, and with a contented grunt, she set to work on them. But the bear thought she was going to gnaw through the tree in which he was hiding. So he slid down quickly from the tree, and he too fled.

The wolf watched it all from his hiding place behind the stone. When he saw that his allies had fled, he waited no longer, but was off as fast as his legs could carry him.

So the old dog was rid of the wolf for ever, and thanks to his faithful service the shepherd kept him until the day he died.

The Lion and the Jackal

The King of Beasts, the lion, was a harsh ruler. When he went hunting, all the other animals shook with fear, wondering which one of them he was about to tear to pieces. One day all the animals decided to approach their ruler and make him an offer. Instead of the lion hunting for himself, they said, they would send him game. The lion agreed, and from then on, once a week, they drew lots as to which of them would be the lion's victim.

Eventually it was the turn of an old and clever jackal. He accepted his fate calmly, but on the way to the King of Beasts, he said to the animals who accompanied him. 'Let me go, brothers, I'll make my own way to the King. Just wait and see how I'll free you from his cruel rule.'

Then he set off on his journey to the King. He did not hurry and arrived at last about midday. The King of Beasts was extremely hungry and greeted the jackal with a snarl.

'Where have you been all this time, you good-for-nothing? You should have been here hours ago!'

The jackal was not at all perturbed. 'Excuse me, Your Majesty,' he said, 'but it really wasn't my fault. I was bringing you a nice hare for your dinner, but on the way I was attacked by another lion who took the hare from me. I told him it was for you, but he took no notice!'

'"I am ruler here,"' said the lion. '"Go and tell

your so-called king that he'd better leave the jungle at once or I shall tear him to pieces.'"

The Lion King couldn't believe his ears and his mane stood on end in anger. 'What's that? Not King of the Beasts! Just show me where this upstart lives. I'll settle with him!'

The old jackal wasted no time. He bowed deeply to his ruler and led him to an old well. When they stood directly over the well, he pointed down to the water. 'There is the lion, Your Majesty,' he said. 'Look for yourself!'

The lion leaned over to look and indeed at the bottom of the well he could see a lion. Of course, it was his own reflection, but he was so angry that he did not recognize himself. With a great roar he leapt into the well, and there he stayed, drowned like a mouse. And since that time all the animals lived there in peace.

The Mouse and the Cat

At the edge of a wood there grew a sturdy oak tree. High in its branches an owl had its nest and in its hollow trunk there lived a weasel. Among the roots a wild cat had her lair and deep in the ground a little mouse had made her hole. But one day hunters came to the tree and set a snare. And in the night the wild cat was caught. In the morning the mouse found her there.

At first she was delighted, for after all, the cat was her worst enemy. But she soon felt less happy. In the branches above her lurked the owl and the path to her hole was blocked by the weasel.

'What should I do?' she thought. 'If I don't fall victim to the owl's talons, the weasel's claws will get me! The only thing to do is to make peace with the cat.'

And so she said to the cat. 'Listen, Cat, it will be all up with you when the hunter returns. I too shall be no better off. Only a pact between us can save both our lives. If I nibble through your snare, then you must protect me from the owl and the weasel.'

The wild cat agreed. 'You are right. I need you

as much as you need me. Don't be afraid and come close to me.'

So the mouse crept up close to the cat.

When the weasel and the owl saw this they knew that neither of them could catch the mouse and would have to go hunting elsewhere.

In the meantime, the mouse began to nibble through the snare, but she did not work very quickly. The cat was puzzled.

'Why are you taking so long, Mouse? Surely you don't mean to leave me in the snare?'

'No, Cat,' the mouse replied. 'I won't leave you here in the snare. But I'm afraid of what will happen to me when you are free. That's why I'm in no hurry.'

In the meantime, dawn had broken and a hunter appeared in the wood. This was just what the mouse was waiting for. She nibbled through the last strand of the snare and the cat was free. She only had time to leap into the thicket without even saying 'thank you' to the mouse. But that didn't worry the mouse. The cat had gone and she was alive to scuttle safely into her hole once more.

The Leopard, the Frogs and the Gazelles

Long, long ago, when gazelles were still the servants of the frogs, a frog borrowed money from a leopard. She promised to return it soon. But time passed and she still could not repay the money. The leopard waited, then one day he decided to visit the frog and remind her of her debt.

After dinner, he set out for the marsh where the frog lived with her friends. Close to the marsh he was greeted by loud croaking. The frogs had settled down after their meal — as was always their custom — and were singing at the top of their voices. But it did not sound like singing to the leopard. He thought the frogs were mourning someone.

'Who are you mourning?' he asked the frog who owed him money.

'My grandmother has died,' she answered. 'Do not be cross, Leopard, that I cannot pay you today. I am in mourning. Come another day.'

Three days later the leopard came again. But again by the marsh he was greeted by loud croaking. The frogs croaked so loudly that the leopard was almost deafened.

'Are you again in mourning?' the leopard said to the frog who owed him money.

'My sister has died,' answered the frog. 'I am in deep mourning. Come another day for the money!'

And the leopard went again two days later. At the marsh he was greeted once again with mournful croaking.

'My little brother has died,' said the frog, when he asked her for the money. 'Come another time, Leopard!'

Far from pleased, the leopard was on his way home when he met a gazelle.

'What is the matter, Leopard?' asked the gazelle, when she saw his frown.

'Three times I have been to collect a debt from one of the frogs, and three times I have failed,' said the leopard. 'Always they are mourning someone. Just listen!'

And indeed, from the distant marsh the mournful croaking of the frogs could still be heard. But the gazelle laughed.

'You have been hoodwinked, Leopard,' she said. 'Don't you know that frogs croak like that every day? I know because we gazelles are in their service.'

The leopard was angry and went back to the marsh. 'Frog,' he said, 'give me back my money at once!'

The Deer and His Banquet

One day a deer decided to hold a large banquet. To this banquet he invited all the animals. Only the tiger was not invited, for he was the deer's greatest enemy.

The deer was not the only animal to fear the tiger, and if he had been invited to the banquet, none of the other animals would have come. One by one the guests arrived and sat down happily at the table. The deer was only worried about one thing — who was to sit at the head of the table?

'I am the oldest,' declared an old crow who wanted the honour. And he cawed in such a deep voice that he must have been at least a hundred years old.

At that, the toad demanded the honour. 'I am still older!' he croaked in a still deeper voice than the crow. The animals acknowledged that the toad must be the oldest and seated him at the head of the table. The banquet could now begin.

The festivities were at their height when a roar was heard in the distance. The tiger had discovered that the deer had not invited him to the banquet and he was roaring with anger.

'I will have my revenge on all the animals,' they heard him vow. The animals were afraid and no longer enjoyed the merry feast. Everyone was looking around to see in which direction he could escape most quickly. The host, the deer, turned to the fox.

'Listen, Fox,' he said. 'You are the cleverest of us. Go to the tiger and pacify him somehow, so that we can continue our celebrations.'

It took some time to persuade the fox to go, but in the end he agreed. He ran off in search of the tiger and when he found him he greeted him respectfully.

'Why are you so angry, Tiger?' he asked.

The tiger growled. 'Why was I not invited to the banquet?'

'Excuse us, Brother Tiger,' apologized the fox. 'How could we invite you to such a banquet at which only herbs and roots are being eaten and where the only drink is pure water? And are

The frog made excuses. 'But I told you,' the frog replied, 'I have not time today. We are mourning my little brother.'

'That is not true,' growled the leopard. I know because the gazelle told me.'

The frog was angry.

'If the gazelle said that, she slandered me. She is my servant and you may have her instead of money. My debt will then be paid.'

But the leopard would not hear of such a thing. 'The gazelle has sharp teeth and will bite me,' he said.

'You need not be afraid,' the frog assured him. 'The gazelle has blunt teeth. Give her this nut and you will see if she can bite it or not.'

And the frog jumped into the water.

The leopard took the nut 'and went off to find the gazelle.

'I have brought you a nut, Gazelle. I hear you like them,' he said.

But the gazelle did not want the nut.

'Thank you, Leopard,' she said, 'but my teeth are too blunt for nuts.'

When the leopard heard this he did not hesitate. He leapt, and seizing the gazelle by the neck, carried her off to his den.

Since then leopards have eaten gazelles and thus collected their debts from the frogs.

you not the ruler of the mountains and we only your servants? How could such servants invite their master?'

The fox's flattering words pacified the tiger.

'You are right,' he muttered. And he went off to hunt.

The fox returned happily to the banquet. But when he got there no one was to be seen. All the animals, fearing the fox would not succeed in his mission, had gone into hiding. It took a long time for the fox to persuade them to return to the forest.

But the toad did not take his place at the head of the table. He was so frightened of the tiger that he had crept to the bottom of his pool. To this day he may still be hiding there.

The Silver Hare
and the Three Rulers
of the Animals

There was once an old count who had three beautiful daughters. The daughters had just grown up, when one day a great black cloud passed over the castle garden, and the girls vanished no one knew where. The old count died of a broken heart, leaving quite alone in the castle his only son.

For a long time the young man mourned his father and his lost sisters. For a whole year he did not leave the castle, not even venturing into the castle garden, far less the forest where once he had loved to hunt.

But one day, after a year had passed, he did go hunting and a strange thing happened to him. In a clearing he suddenly caught sight of a beautiful silver hare. The hare sat in the grass, gazing at the young man and staying quite still as if not at all frightened of the hunter.

The young man tried to catch it. Running up to it, he reached out his hand, but when it was almost within his grasp, the hare jumped up, ran a short way off and sat down again. The young man tried again, but again failed to catch it. And so it went on until evening. At last the young man, tired and out of temper, sighed.

'I have wasted the whole day,' he thought. 'I have caught nothing, and now I shall have to spend the night under the open sky.'

But at that moment the silver hare spoke. 'If you follow this little path,' it said, 'you will come to the castle where your eldest sister lives.' Then the hare vanished as if the earth had swallowed it up.

The young man set off along the little path

and soon arrived at an old castle. He knocked loudly, and inside the castle he heard the voice of his eldest sister call out. 'Who is there?'

The young man answered. 'It is I, sister, your brother!'

His eldest sister opened the door joyfully, welcomed her brother warmly and led him in.

But after supper she said. 'I should like you to stay longer, but I am afraid for you. My husband is a giant, the king of all the horned beasts, and if he finds you here this evening he might eat you. He eats half a dozen oxen for supper every night.'

But the young man was not afraid. 'I shall stay, sister,' he said. 'Show me where I can hide so that I may have a look at this husband of yours. In the morning I shall leave.'

The eldest sister told her brother to hide behind a barrel at the far end of the room. Hardly had he done so when the giant returned from hunting. He flung on the table half a dozen dead oxen and said. 'Here is my supper.'

Then he threw from his shoulders a cloak which must have weighed at least half a ton, draped it over the barrel and sat down at the table. 'Get me something to drink, woman,' he growled.

The eldest sister took a bucket, filled it from the barrel of wine and set it before her husband. The giant seized the bucket with both hands. He was about to drink when he gave a sudden roar.

'This wine smells of a human being. Who have you got here, woman? Where is he? Let me see him or it will be the worse for him!'

The eldest sister was frightened. 'Do not be angry, husband,' she said. 'It is only my brother, who has called to see me. Do not, I beg you, do him any harm!'

The giant calmed down. 'If it is your brother,' he said, 'nothing will happen to him. Just show him to me!'

The eldest sister went over to the barrel, took her brother by the hand and led him before the giant.

The giant took an immediate liking to the young man.

'Sit down, brother-in-law,' he said. 'Have a drink with me and tell me how long you have spent hunting that silver hare?'

'The whole day,' the young man replied.

That made the giant laugh. 'My dear boy,' he said, 'I have been hunting it for five hundred years but I still do not know where it goes when it vanishes from sight. You would do better to stay here peacefully with us and stop thinking about that silver hare.'

But the young man did not want to give up. 'No, brother-in-law,' he said. 'I shall try once more.'

At this the giant said. 'Very well! In that case I shall help you. Take this ivory horn, and when you need help blow on it.'

The young man took the horn, thanked the giant and went to lie down.

Next day they both set out early, the giant to go hunting, the young man to seek the silver hare. He found it, as before, in the clearing in the forest and chased after it until evening. Every now and then he thought he was about to catch it, but at the last minute the hare always escaped his grasp.

By evening the young man was again tired and out of temper.

'Night is falling and I have again caught nothing,' he said. 'I fear I shall have to spend the night under the open sky.'

But at that moment the silver hare spoke for a second time. 'If you follow this path,' it said, 'you will come to the castle where your second sister lives.' And then it vanished.

The young man set off along the path and quite soon he did arrive at an old castle. He knocked loudly, and inside the castle he heard the voice of his second sister call out. 'Who is there?'

The young man answered. 'It is I, sister, your brother!'

The second sister opened the door joyfully, welcomed her brother warmly and led him in.

But after supper his sister said. 'I should like you to stay longer, but it might cost you your life. My husband is a giant, the king of all the birds, and if he finds you here this evening he might eat you. He eats a dozen oxen for supper every night.'

But the young man was not discouraged. 'I shall stay, sister,' he said. 'Show me where I can hide so that I may take a look at this husband of yours. In the morning I shall be off.'

The second sister told her brother to hide behind a barrel at the far end of the room. Hardly had he done so when the giant returned from hunting. He flung on the table a dozen dead oxen and said. 'Here is my supper!'

Then he threw from his shoulders his cloak which must have weighed at least three-quarters of ton, laid it on the barrel and sat down at the table. 'Get me something to drink, woman!' he cried.

The second sister took a tub, filled it from the barrel of wine and set it before her husband. The giant seized the tub with both hands. He was about to drink when he gave a sudden roar.

'This wine smells of a human being. Who have you got here? Where is he? Let me see him or it will be the worse for him.'

The second sister was frightened. 'Do not be angry, husband,' she said. 'It is only my brother, who has called to see me. Do not, I beg you, do him any harm!'

The giant calmed down. 'If it is your brother,' he said, 'nothing will happen to him. Just show him to me!'

The second sister went over to the barrel, took her brother by the hand and led him before the giant. The giant took an immediate liking to the young man.

'Sit down, brother-in-law,' he said, 'have a drink with me and tell me how long you have spent hunting that silver hare?'

'Two whole days,' the young man replied.

That made the giant laugh. 'My dear boy,' he said, 'I have been hunting it for seven hundred years, but I still do not know to this day where it hides. You would do better to stay here with us and stop thinking about the silver hare.'

But the young man did not want to give up. 'No, brother-in-law,' he said. 'I shall try once more.'

To this the giant replied. 'Very well! In that case I will help you. Take this bird's beak and if you need help, blow on it and help will come.'

The young man took the bird's beak, thanked the giant and went to bed.

The next morning they both set out early, the giant to go hunting and the young man to seek the silver hare. He found it as usual in the clearing and chased it as before until the evening. But it was in vain.

Then the young man, tired and out of temper, sat down under a tree.

'It will soon be night,' he said, 'and I shall have to sleep under the open sky.'

But the silver hare spoke to him for the third time. 'If you follow this path,' it said, 'you will come to the castle where your third and youngest sister lives.' And then it vanished.

The young man set off along the path and soon arrived at an old castle. He knocked on the door and inside the castle he heard the voice of his youngest sister.

'Who is there?' she called.

The young man answered. 'It is I, sister, your brother!'

His youngest sister opened the door, and joyfully led her brother into the castle.

When he had eaten, she said. 'I should like you to stay longer, but my husband is a giant — the king of all the furry animals, and if he finds you here this evening he might eat you. He eats three dozen oxen for his supper every night.'

But the young man was not discouraged. 'I shall stay, sister,' he said. 'Show me where I can hide so that I may take a look at this husband of yours. In the morning I shall be off.'

The youngest sister told her brother to hide behind a barrel at the far end of the room. Hardly had he done so when the giant returned from hunting. He flung on the table three dozen dead oxen and said. 'Here is my supper!'

Then he threw from his shoulders a cloak that must have weighed a ton and laid it on the barrel. Then he sat down at the table. 'Get me something to drink, woman!' he cried.

The youngest sister took a cask and filled it with wine from the barrel and set it before her husband. He was about to drink when he let out a sudden cry.

'This wine smells of a human being! Who have you here? Where is he? Let me see him or it will be the worse for him!'

The youngest sister was frightened. 'Do not be angry, husband,' she said. 'It is only my brother, who has come to visit me. Do not, I beg you, do him any harm!'

The giant calmed down. 'If it is your brother,' he said, 'nothing will happen to him. Just show him to me.'

The youngest sister went over to the barrel, and taking her brother by the hand, led him before the giant. The giant took an immediate liking to the young man.

'Sit down, brother-in-law,' he said. 'Have a drink with me and tell me how long you have been hunting that silver hare.'

'For nearly a week,' replied the young man.

That made the giant laugh. 'My dear boy,' he said, 'I have been hunting it for a thousand years, but I still do not know to this day where it hides. You would do better to stay here with us and forget about the silver hare.'

But the young man did not want to give up. 'No, brother-in-law,' he said. 'I shall try once more for the last time.'

To this the giant replied. 'Very well. In that case I will help you. Take this lock of golden hair and whenever you need help just shake it and help will arrive.'

The young man took the lock of golden hair, thanked the giant and went to bed.

Next morning they both set out early. The giant to go hunting and the young man to seek the silver hare. He found it, as usual, in the clearing.

All day he chased it through the forest until at last the trees thinned and he found himself on

the sea-shore. The silver hare leapt into the sea and ran across the water as if it were on dry land. The young man could not follow.

Quickly he looked round and saw a poor hut standing between two rocks. The door of the hut was wide open and he went in. In the hut lived an old cobbler.

The young man greeted him. 'Tell me, good man,' he said, 'did you see a silver hare run past?'

The old cobbler put his finger to his lips. 'Hush, young man,' he said, 'that is no hare. She is a princess — the daughter of the King of Persia. I am her cobbler and every day I make for her a new pair of slippers and take them myself to her palace.'

The young man thought for a moment. 'Could I go there with you?' he asked.

'You could,' replied the cobbler. 'But you must tell no one that I have taken you there. We shall go there on my flying cloak as soon as I have finished another pair of slippers for the princess. And so that you will not be found in the castle, I shall give you another cloak. As soon as you throw it over your shoulders you will be invisible.'

When the old man had finished making the slippers for the Persian princess, he gave the young man the cloak which would make him invisible, threw the other over his own shoulders and told the young man to climb on his back. Like the wind they flew across the sea to the castle of the Persian King.

'Follow me,' said the old man, when they had landed in the castle courtyard. 'Do not be afraid. As long as you have my cloak on your shoulders, no one can see you!"

And the young man and the cobbler walked through the castle to the princess's room where the old man left the slippers for the princess and went away, leaving the young man to watch and wait.

After a time the princess herself appeared. She was as lovely as the day was long, but her face was sad.

As she reached the doorway, she said to her lady-in-waiting. 'I spent the whole day running through the woods, but today my sweetheart was not there. I am worried. Why did he not come today?'

The lady-in-waiting tried to reassure the princess. 'Do not be alarmed, dear lady, you will certainly see him again. Eat now and drink,' she said, 'so that you will have strength for tomorrow and everything will be all right!'

The princess ate and drank, but she did not

101

enjoy her meal. Sad at heart, she retired to her chamber.

Unseen, the young man had watched and heard everything. And now that the princess was alone, he took courage and spoke.

'You have eaten and drunk, lovely princess, but I am hungry and no one has offered me food.'

The princess was startled. 'Who are you?' she said, 'and where are you? I can hear you, but I cannot see you.'

'Do not be afraid. It is I. Look!' And the young man threw the old man's cloak from his shoulders. The princess, full of joy, flung her arms round his neck. Then she called her lady-in-waiting and told her to bring food and wine for her sweetheart.

The next day the princess went to her father, the King of Persia, and said. 'Father, it is time for me to be married.'

'And who do you want to marry, my daughter?' her father asked. 'No one has come to ask me for your hand.'

And the princess replied. 'Father, I have chosen a husband for myself. I shall bring him to you at once.'

She hurried to her chamber, took the young man by the hand and brought him to her father. 'This is the man of my choice,' she said.

The old king took an immediate liking to the young man, and ordered immediate preparations to be made for the marriage of his daughter next day.

It was a magnificent wedding and afterwards the happy young man lived with his beautiful princess in great splendour at the castle of the Persian King.

Only one thing worried him. Although they were husband and wife, the princess continued to leave the castle every morning and run in the forest in the shape of a silver hare.

And every morning, before leaving, she would give her husband the keys to all the rooms in the castle. The young man could go wherever he liked except one little room that was forbidden to him.

'If you open the door of that room,' the princess warned him, 'it will be the end of our happiness. But if you wait for a year and a day all will be well, and I shall never go to the forest again.'

Time passed slowly for the young man alone in the castle without the princess. He walked in the gardens, he inspected the castle chambers and everywhere he saw such wonderful things and such treasures that his eyes were dazzled.

But he became more and more curious to know what the forbidden room contained. In the end he could not resist the temptation to look inside. But hardly had he opened the door of the forbidden room when out leapt the devil.

'Thank you, young man,' he shrieked. 'Now your wife is mine forever. You will never see her again.'

The young man was frightened. 'That is a fine reward for freeing you,' he said. 'In return, let me say goodbye to her for the last time. Come for her tomorrow.'

'Very well,' replied the devil, 'but tomorrow at noon I shall carry her off and show no mercy.' And he vanished as if he had been swallowed up by the earth.

When the princess returned in the evening, the young man greeted her sorrowfully.

'I know why you look so sad,' said the princess. 'You have opened the door of the forbidden room and now I belong to the devil who was imprisoned there.'

'Yes, my princess,' said the young man. 'I have

done a terrible thing. But do not fear. I shall save you from this devil.'

Next day at noon the devil came to carry off the princess. But the young man was unafraid.

'I shall give her to you,' he said, 'but go first to the meadow in front of the castle.'

The devil hurried to the meadow in front of

and again demanded the princess. Instead of answering him, the young man drew from his pocket the lock of golden hair given to him by his third brother-in-law and shook it vigorously. Scarcely had he done so than furry animals came running from all directions and attacked the devil with their teeth and claws. It was a long battle, but in the end the devil was overcome by their superior strength. Then the castle servants seized and bound him and threw him onto a bonfire burning in the middle of the meadow.

It is true that the devil did not perish in the flames, but he suffered agonies before he was at last forced to withdraw his demand for the Persian princess.

The young man to ensure his future happiness then forced the devil to confirm his withdrawal in writing. Only then did he allow him to go free. Instantly the devil vanished as if he had been swallowed up by the earth.

And now the Persian princess was quite free. No longer did she have to go running in the forest all day in the shape of a silver hare, no longer did the young man have to wander through the castle and its chambers by himself.

From that time on his beautiful wife never left his side and they lived together happily till the end of their days.

the castle, and in a few minutes he was followed there by the young man and the princess. But instead of giving the princess to the devil, her husband put to his lips the ivory horn that had been given to him by his first brother-in-law. He blew it with all his strength.

Scarcely had he done so than horned animals came running from all directions and attacked the devil with their horns. It was not long before the devil begged for a truce to last until the next day. The young man granted him his request.

Next day exactly at noon, the devil appeared in the meadow in front of the castle and demanded that the princess should be handed over to him. But the young man put to his lips the bird's beak given to him by his second brother-in-law and blew with all his strength.

Scarcely had he done so than birds came flying from all directions and attacked the devil with their beaks. It was not long before the devil begged for a truce to last until the next day.

'Very well,' said the young man, 'but tomorrow you will come for the last time!'

The third day exactly at noon, the devil appeared in the meadow in front of the castle

The Two Frogs
and the Pot
of Cream

One day, two frogs were lapping cream from a pot. They went on lapping it up until suddenly they fell in and could not get out. The pot had smooth, slippery sides and there was nothing for their feet to grip. The frogs knew they were trapped.

At first they both swam round and round, then one of them stopped swimming.

'What is the use of swimming any longer,' he said. 'I cannot save myself whatever I do.'

So he folded up his feet, sank to the bottom of the pot and was drowned in sweet cream.

The other frog did not give up so easily. He went on swimming, stamping into the cream with his feet. He stamped so hard and so long that he churned the cream into a big pat of butter. Then he was able to stand on the pat of butter and after that it was easy to jump out of the pot.

Since then there has been a saying, 'Things are never so bad that you can't churn cream into butter!'

The Cat,
the Ram
and
the Wolves

Once upon a time there lived in a cottage near the woods an old man and his wife. And with them lived a cat and a ram. The cat used to catch mice, the ram grazed on the green slopes and the old man and his wife kept the cottage neat and tidy. They lived happily there for many long years.

But one day the old lady left a jug of cream on the table and the cat lapped up all the cream. Not only that, he knocked over the jug and it broke. The old lady was angry. She complained to her husband.

'That cat is becoming an awful thief. He has lapped up our cream and broken the jug into the bargain. We shall have to have him destroyed.'

But the cat was behind the stove and heard everything. He jumped out of the window and ran straight to the ram.

'Things are bad, my friend. Our master and mistress want to have me destroyed — and you too.'

The ram was frightened. 'Whatever shall we do, my friend? Have you any ideas?'

The cat was ready with his advice. 'We shall run away into the woods,' he said.

It was easier said than done. The ram was shut up in a pen. He could not open the door and did not know how to jump over the fence like the cat. But the cat helped him. He jumped up onto the door, lifted the latch with his paw and let the ram out.

It was not far to the woods. The cat and the ram ran along the path and in a little while vanished into the thicket. They went on and on and on, until in the middle of the path they suddenly came upon a wolf's head. At first they were frightened, but then they became bolder. The cat said. 'Let us take the head with us; it might be useful.'

And it was indeed useful.

It was already evening and it was getting dark in the woods. The cat and the ram

wondered where they were going to spend the night. Then they saw a gleam of light. They ran happily towards it, but their happiness did not last long. The light came from a fire burning in the middle of a clearing and round the fire sat twelve wolves.

The cat and the ram would have liked to turn tail and flee, but they could not. Fear had turned their legs to stone. At last they plucked up courage and went up to the fire. 'Good evening, Wolves,' they said.

'Good evening, Cat, good evening, Ram,' answered the wolves. They were already licking their lips at the thought of the good supper that had come to them of its own accord.

The cat noticed this, but bravely he turned to the ram and said. 'Ram, we ought to give the wolves hospitality. Go and fetch the game we caught.'

The ram understood immediately. He got up, left the fire and went into the thicket where

they had left the wolf's head, and brought it to the cat.

The wolves could not believe their eyes. The ram had brought them a wolf's head for supper.

But the cat was not satisfied. 'I do not want that one,' he said. 'Go and choose a bigger one!'

The ram did not have to be told twice. He went back with the head into the thicket, rustled round among the undergrowth as if he was looking for something, then came back again with the same head.

But again the cat was not satisfied. 'I do not want that one,' he said. 'Bring me the biggest!'

The ram went back once more into the thicket and came back for the third time with the same head.

This time the cat was satisfied. 'Good,' he said to the ram. 'That one will do. Put it onto the fire to roast.'

The wolves were terrified. What if the cat and the ram turned on them and cut off their heads? They began to think how they could get away unnoticed.

After a time four of them got up and said. 'Let us go and fetch some firewood, friends. We have not enough to put on the fire.'

The cat and the ram agreed that this was a good idea. 'But come back soon,' they said.

The wolves had no intention of coming back. As soon as they were beyond the first thicket, they took to their heels and were off like the wind. When they did not come back, four more wolves got up and said they would go and look for their friends.

The cat and the ram agreed. 'But come back soon,' they said.

But the wolves did not come back. As soon as they were beyond the first thicket, they took to their heels and were off like the wind.

A long time passed and they did not come back. Then the last four wolves got up and said they would also go and look for their friends.

The cat and the ram agreed. 'But come back soon,' they said, 'or we shall have to come and fetch you ourselves.'

But these wolves did not come back either. Beyond the first thicket they too took to their heels and were off like the wind.

In the depths of the woods they met the rest of the wolves. Breathlessly they threw themselves on the ground. Just then a big bear came lumbering towards them.

'What is the matter, Wolves?' he asked. 'Why are you so out of breath?'

'You too would be out of breath,' they said, 'if you had been running away from the cat and the ram.' And they told the bear what had happened to them and how the cat and the ram had frightened them with the wolves' heads.

The bear started to laugh. 'You really are stupid,' he said. 'Whoever heard of a cat and a ram hunting wolves. You should have gobbled them up instead of running away. Come with me and I shall show you how to deal with them.'

The wolves did not need to be told twice. They set out with the bear towards the fire in the clearing in the woods.

When the cat and the ram saw them coming, they were afraid. The cat leapt into the nearest tree. But the ram did not know how to climb trees. He just managed to scramble up to the first branch and hung there.

The bear and the wolves came hurrying up to the fire, but the cat and the ram were nowhere to be seen.

'They have gone,' muttered the bear, 'but never mind. Let us just sit down here under this tree and think where they can have got to.'

And so the wolves sat down round the bear and thought and thought. It took them a very long time, and the poor ram could scarcely hold on to the branch.

'Help me, Cat!' he whispered. 'I cannot hold on any longer.'

And the cat whispered back. 'Hang on for just a moment longer. Hang on!'

The ram did hold on, but the branch suddenly gave way. With a great crack it broke, and the ram fell straight onto the bear's back. When the cat saw this, he began to shout. 'Hang on to him, Ram, we shall have him for breakfast!'

The bear took fright. Shaking off the ram, he took to his heels, closely followed by the wolves. Once again they ran off into the depths of the woods and the cat and the ram were safe. But they quite gave up the idea of journeying into the wide world.

Early next morning they set out for home, to the cottage by the woods. When they appeared at the gate, the old man and his wife welcomed them joyfully. They had missed their cat and their ram. And so all four went on living together happily. The old man and his wife kept the cottage neat and tidy, the ram grazed on the green slopes and the cat caught mice. And if sometimes he did lap up the cream, he took good care never again to break the jug.

Brother Rabbit, the Elephant and the Hippopotamus

Once upon a time Brother Rabbit decided that he would raise cattle. 'I shall buy a cow,' he said. 'The cow will have a calf, the calf will grow and will also have a calf. In two years, from one cow I shall have four, in three years, eight and in four years, a whole herd. Then I shall be rich.'

Brother Rabbit jumped for joy. 'I shall go straightaway to the market and buy a cow.' Then he remembered that he had no money. He scratched his ears for a moment, and then he thought. 'If I cannot buy that cow, at least I can borrow one.'

And the very same day he went to visit the elephant. 'Elephant,' he said, 'lend me a cow. I shall give it back to you soon.'

The elephant was very good-hearted and lent Brother Rabbit a cow. 'Here it is,' he said, 'but as soon as I want it you must give it back or pay for it.'

'I shall give it back to you, or I shall pay for it,' promised Brother Rabbit, and he led the cow home. But he did not take it out to graze. Before

it could have a calf, Brother Rabbit killed it, roasted it and ate it. Only then did he remember that he had to give it back to the elephant. He scratched his ears and then he thought. 'If I can borrow one cow I can borrow another.'

And the very same day he went to visit the hippopotamus. 'Hippopotamus,' he said, 'lend me a cow. I shall give it back to you soon.'

The hippopotamus was also good-hearted

and lent Brother Rabbit a cow. 'But as soon as I want it back you must give it to me or pay for it,' he said.

'I shall give it back to you, or I shall pay for it,' promised Brother Rabbit. But again he did not keep his promise. Before it could have a calf, he killed it, roasted it and ate it.

The very next day he met the elephant. He asked for his cow. 'Give it back to me or pay for it,' said the elephant.

Brother Rabbit saw that things were going badly. 'I shall give it back, Elephant,' he said, 'but just wait a day or two.' The elephant agreed to wait for a day or two.

The next day as luck would have it, Brother Rabbit met the hippopotamus. And the hippopotamus also wanted his cow. Brother Rabbit saw that things were going very badly. 'I shall

give it back, Hippopotamus,' he said, 'but just wait a day or two.' The hippopotamus agreed that a few days more would make no difference.

Brother Rabbit was at his wits' end. He

scratched his ears for a moment, then told himself that only guile could help him. He borrowed a long rope from his neighbour, and holding one end of it, he went to find the elephant in the pasture. 'Elephant,' he cried, 'I am bringing you your cow. But I have let her eat so much that I cannot pull her along by myself. Here is the rope. I shall go and chase her up. When I call, you start to pull. And then between us we shall get her here.'

The elephant was glad he was about to get back his cow and well fed into the bargain. So he took the end of the rope and waited.

In the meantime, Brother Rabbit took the other end of the rope and ran with it to the hippopotamus by the river. 'Hippopotamus, I am bringing you your cow,' he said. 'But I have fed her too well and I cannot pull her along by myself. Here is the rope. I shall go and chase her up. When I call, you start to pull.'

The hippopotamus was also glad he was about to get back his cow and that she was well fed. So he took the end of the rope and waited. The rabbit hid between the meadow and the river and started to shout. 'Pull, pull!'

The elephant started to pull, so did the hippopotamus but neither of them could make any progress. The rope did not move.

'That cow is well fed,' muttered the elephant at one end of the rope and the hippopotamus at the other. They pulled and pulled for nearly half a day, but still no cow appeared.

The elephant at last said. 'I must go and look at that cow.' And the hippopotamus said the same. Both of them followed the rope and in the middle of the path they met.

The elephant was surprised.

'It is you, Hippopotamus?' he said.

The hippopotamus was surprised, too.

'It is you, Elephant?' he said.

So then they knew that the rabbit had tricked them.

The elephant was very angry. 'Just wait, Brother Rabbit,' he said. 'As soon as you show yourself in the meadow, I shall settle with you!'

The hippopotamus was angry too. 'Just wait, Brother Rabbit,' he said. 'As soon as you come to the river to drink, I shall get even with you!'

Brother Rabbit laughed at the tug-of-war till he nearly split his sides. But when he heard the elephant and the hippopotamus vowing vengeance, he stopped laughing.

Since that day he keeps well away from the river. And when he is in the meadow, he does not have a moment's peace. As soon as something rustles in the grass he takes to his heels and runs like the wind.

The Jackal, the Hyena and the Fishes

One day a jackal was looking for something to eat. He was in luck that day, for on the road from the sea he saw a cart full of fish. A fisherman was taking them to the market in the town. The jackal smacked his lips at the sight. But how was he to get at them when the fish were in the cart and the fisherman was sitting on the goat that was pulling it? The fisherman certainly would not give him any.

The jackal thought for a time, and then he had an idea. He ran ahead of the cart, lay down in the middle of the road and pretended to be dead. The fisherman stopped when he came to the jackal, jumped off the goat and said.

'Fancy that, a dead jackal. And what a beautiful skin he has. It will make a fine coat for me.' And he picked up the jackal and threw him into the cart among the fish.

That was just what the jackal wanted. Quietly he took one fish after another and threw them out of the cart onto the road. At last he jumped out himself and quickly picked up the fish. The fisherman suspected nothing.

That evening the jackal had a fine supper of baked fish. He ate and he ate until he was quite full.

The smell of the fish soon attracted his neighbour the hyena. The jackal welcomed him and gave him some fish to taste. But it was not enough for the hyena who wanted more.

This annoyed the jackal. 'If you want any more,' he said, 'go fishing yourself, or do as I did. Lie down on the road along which fishermen come with their catch. But do not move, just pretend to be dead. The fisherman will throw you into the cart with the fish, and you can help yourself to all you want.'

The hyena did not stop to thank the jackal for his good advice, but ran off towards the sea. When he saw a cart loaded with fish coming near, he lay down in the road and pretended to be dead. The fisherman stopped, jumped down from the cart and said.

'Fancy that, a dead hyena! But what a miserable beast, there is not a decent piece of skin on him.' And he beat the hyena few times with a stick and threw him into the ditch before continuing his journey.

The hyena narrowly escaped death. Not only had he got no fish, but he also had had a good beating.

And that is the way of the world: two people can do the same thing, but the results are not always the same!

The Cock and the Fox

A hungry fox once thought he would like a nice fat cock for supper. The cock knew this and was on the alert. He also knew he had a powerful beak and sharp spurs to protect himself.

'Strength is not going to help me,' said the fox. 'I shall have to use guile.' He stole into the yard, waited till the cock was alone there, then said to him.

'I am very glad to see you, Cock. For a long time I have been wanting to tell you how much I like the way you crow. There is only one thing I cannot quite understand. Someone once told me that you can only crow with your eyes open. When you shut your eyes they say you just chirp like a chicken.'

The cock was angry. 'That is quite untrue. I can crow just as well with my eyes shut. Just listen.'

At which he shut his eyes and opened his beak to crow. But no sound came, for the fox had him between his teeth and was running out of the farmyard.

At that moment the farmer came into the yard. When he saw the fox carrying off the cock, he grasped a stick and ran after him. The cock seized his chance. He screeched. 'Fox, look out, or the farmer will kill us both. Tell him I am going with you of my own free will.'

Of course this was just what the wily fox should not have done. Hardly had he opened his mouth when the cock flapped his wings and was perched on the fence.

Since then the fox has never shouted to the farmer when he is carrying a cock. And the cock, since that time, has never crowed with his eyes shut, especially when a wicked fox is near.

The Musicians of Bremen

A farmer had a donkey which served him well and faithfully for many long years. While he was able he carried sacks of grain to the mill and from the mill brought back sacks of flour. However, as time passed, the donkey grew old and weak and the farmer decided to sell him to the knacker. This grieved the old donkey, who had not expected such a reward for his faithful service. He decided to run away from his master and find another job. 'I shall go to Bremen,' he thought, 'and be a town musician.'

And so the donkey set off into the world. He went on and on until he saw by the wayside an old dog. 'What are you doing here, Dog?' he said.

'What do you think,' replied the dog, 'I am having a rest. My master has driven me out because I am no longer strong enough to go hunting with him.'

'Come along with me,' said the donkey. 'I also am looking for a new job. I am going to be a town musician in Bremen. Perhaps they would take you too.'

The dog did not need to be asked twice. He got up and went with the donkey.

In a little while, they saw, sitting on a milestone beside the road, a cat. He looked thoroughly miserable.

'What are you doing here, Cat?' asked the donkey.

'What do you think I am doing?' said the cat. 'I am having a little rest. My mistress has turned me out because I am old and cannot catch mice any more.'

'Come along with me,' said the donkey. 'I am also going out into the world. I am going to be a town musician in Bremen. Perhaps they will take you too.' And so the cat went along with the donkey and the dog. In a little while, they reached a village. Sitting on top of a gate they saw a cock. He was crowing at the top of his voice as if someone had stuck a knife into him.

'What are you doing, Cock?' asked the donkey.

'What do you think I am doing?' answered the cock. 'I am crowing while I can. Tomorrow visitors will be coming and Mistress said she would cut my throat to have something for the guests to eat. That is what I get for my faithful service!'

'Come along with me,' said the donkey. 'I am also going out into the world. I am going to be a musician in Bremen. Perhaps they will take you too.'

So all of them — the dog, the cat and the cock, went along with the donkey on the road to Bremen. They went on and on and on until they came to a deep wood. The sun was setting and Bremen was still a long way off, so the musicians decided to spend the night under a big oak tree. The donkey leant against the trunk, the dog and the cat lay down in the moss at the foot of the tree and the cock perched on a branch.

Hardly had it got dark when the cock, sitting on his perch, saw a light shining close by. 'There is a cottage over there, friends,' he called. 'Let us go and have a look. Perhaps we will find something good to eat.'

The donkey, the dog and the cat all agreed that a little hay or a piece of meat would not come amiss after their long journey. So they set out in the direction of the light.

They went on until they reached the cottage. The donkey went right up to the window and looked in.

'What can you see there, Donkey?' asked the inquisitive cock.

'What can I see?' said the donkey. 'A table spread with food and drinks and round the table seven robbers.'

'That sounds all right for us,' said the cock. 'But how are we going to get rid of those robbers? The best thing we can do is make music for them.'

And that is just what they did. The donkey put his front feet on the window sill, the dog sat on the donkey's back, the cat sat on the dog and the cock perched on the cat's head. And then

they made music. The donkey brayed with all his strength, the dog barked, the cat mewed and the cock crowed. They performed with such energy that the window flew open. The cock went flying into the cottage. After him jumped the cat. After the cat the dog, and last of all the donkey went tumbling into the room. The robbers were so startled by the musicians that they dropped everything, took to their heels and were off as fast as they could run.

The donkey and his friends sat down at the table and ate and drank their fill. Soon the table was cleared, they put out the light and happily went to sleep — the donkey on the straw in the yard, the dog at the door, the cat on top of the stove and the cock on a perch above the stove. In a little while there was not a sound to be heard.

The robbers in the wood were not asleep. They were watching and waiting at a distance. When everything was quiet and the light went out, they grew bolder. The chieftain sent one of the robbers to see what was happening in the cottage. Nothing moved anywhere as he slipped through the open window. Only under the stove something shone.

The robber thought it must be some glowing embers. But it was not; it was the cat's eyes. When the robber bent down to blow on them, the cat jumped up and scratched his nose with his claws. The robber took fright and ran to the door. He had just reached the doorway when the dog woke up and bit him as hard as he could in the calf. The robber ran through the doorway, but in the yard the donkey was waiting for him. He kicked the villain so hard with both hind legs that he flew right over the fence. At which the cock from his perch crowed, 'Cockadoodle doo!'

The robber was glad to get back alive to his fellows in the wood. Breathlessly he told them. 'There's a witch living in our cottage — just look how she scratched my nose! At the door is her assistant — a servant with a knife — just look how he stabbed my leg. And in the yard there is another servant — a giant with feet like great hooves. Just look how he has beaten me. But worst of all is that screaming creature on the perch who kept telling the others to attack me.'

The robbers saw that they would never be able to go back to their cottage again, and they retreated to another forest far away.

The donkey, the dog, the cat and the cock never saw or heard of them again. And because they liked the robber's cottage, they stayed in it together till the end of their days. And together they played like real musicians, although they never did get to Bremen.

How the Jackal Got His Scorched Back

While the world was still young and everything was different, the jackal did not have the dark skin on his back he has today. In those days the sun was not in the sky, but lived on earth among the animals. But he did not like being on earth and the animals were unhappy too. Wherever the sun went it was hot and it was a wonder everything did not burn up under its glare. To help the animals he would settle down in some out of the way place in the sand of the desert. But he wished he was somewhere else, if possible high up in the heavens. But how was he to get there?

In those days the sun had one friend — the jackal. When the jackal saw the sun's distress and learned what he longed for, he promised to help him.

'If you want to be in the heavens,' he said, 'I shall take you there. Just sit on my back.'

The sun thanked the jackal and at once jumped on his back. The jackal started to run, but even for his fast legs the heavens were a long way off. Also the sun was beginning to burn his back. At last he could bear it no longer. He stopped. 'Do please get down, sun, even for just a little while,' he said. 'You are burning me so fiercely.'

But the sun did not get down. He was afraid that the jackal would not take him any further. He hung onto his coat and would not let go, and the jackal was forced to start up again. At last they reached the land where the heavens begin. There the sun jumped from the jackal's back and landed on a cloud.

Since that time the sun has only walked in the heavens, and since that time the jackal has had a dark back which looks as if it had been burnt.

115

Aunty Vixen and Naughty Tommy

In a cottage in the woods lived a grand-mother and a grandfather and their little grand-son, Tommy.

During the day Grandfather used to go to the forest to gather wood, Grandmother picked strawberries, raspberries or mushrooms, while Tommy stayed at home to take care of the cottage. When Grandfather and Grandmother went off in the morning they used to say to him.

'Guard the house well, Tommy, and do not open the door to anyone. What if a wolf came, or Aunty Vixen? They could carry you off and we would never see you again.'

Tommy always promised that he would guard the house well and not open the door to anyone, and for a long time he kept his promise. But one day, as he was eating porridge at the window, Aunty Vixen ran up. When she saw Tommy eating porridge at the window she thought how nice it would be to have some too. She knocked on the window and called.

'Tommy! Leave a little porridge for me. And I shall take you for a ride on my tail.'

Tommy had eaten enough porridge and would have liked to leave some for the vixen. And even more he would have liked to go for a ride on her tail. But he remembered what Grandfather and Grandmother had told him. He said. 'I'd like to leave you a little porridge but I cannot. Grandfather and Grandmother told me to open the door to no one.

Aunty Vixen at once had the right answer. 'That is quite right, Tommy,' she said. 'Why should you open the door? It is enough to open the window!'

Tommy was easily convinced. He opened the window and Aunty Vixen jumped into the cottage, ate up the porridge and then said. 'In return for the porridge, I shall take you for a ride. Just sit on my tail.' Tommy sat on the vixen's tail and she started to give him a ride, first onto the bench, then round the cottage, and finally out of the window and into the woods. Before Tommy could look round they were by the old oak tree among whose roots the vixen had her burrow. Tommy was a little

scared. 'That's enough, Aunty,' he said. 'Now take me home.' But the vixen did not want to.

'Don't be afraid, Tommy,' she said. 'I have two little fox cubs at home. You can play with them.' And she jumped down her hole with Tommy on her back.

It was true. There really were two little cubs in the hole. Tommy played with them all day and he almost forgot Grandfather and Grand-mother. But when evening came he remembered

has happened to Tommy?' they cried. 'Who has carried him off?'

At that very moment a magpie flew past and repeated after them. 'Who has carried off Tommy? Why, Aunty Vixen! She carried him on her tail to her den beneath the oak tree.'

Grandfather and Grandmother wasted no time. 'If that is where he is,' they said, 'we must go and rescue Tommy.' And they set out for the vixen's den. Grandfather took his fiddle and a sack, Grandmother took a little drum and a piece of string, and they hurried to the old oak tree. By the foxhole, Grandfather started to play on his fiddle and Grandmother began to beat her drum. 'Fiddle, fiddle, on my fiddle, tum, tumty tum on my drum. Down the hole are three little foxes and the fourth is Tommy.'

The vixen didn't like their music at all. When they started to play the tune for the third time, she sent one of the cubs to give the musicians a penny and send them away. The fox cub ran out of the hole, but before he could give the musicians the penny, Grandfather had popped him into the sack and Grandmother had tied it up. They went on playing. 'Fiddle, fiddle, on my fiddle, tum, tumty tum on my drum, down the hole are two foxes and the third is Tommy.'

The vixen had had enough of the music. She sent a second cub to give the musicians a penny and send them away. The fox cub ran out of the hole, but before he could give the musicians the penny, Grandfather had popped him into the sack. Grandmother had tied it up. They went on playing. 'Fiddle, fiddle, on my fiddle, tum, tumty tum on my drum, down the hole is one little fox and the second is Tommy.'

The vixen was getting angrier. She ran out of the hole herself to give the musicians a penny and send them away. But she had only shown her head when Grandfather had grabbed her, and she was in the sack and Grandmother tied up the sack and they played for the last time. 'Fiddle, fiddle, on my fiddle, tum, tumty tum on my drum, in the hole are no more foxes, only our Tommy.'

And Grandfather shouted. 'Come out, Tommy, it is us, your Grandfather and Grandmother.'

Tommy heard them. He scrambled quickly out of the hole and jumped into their arms. Then all three went happily home to the cottage near the woods.

And what about the foxes? By the cottage Grandfather let them out of the sack and set them free, but first he gave Aunty Vixen a good thrashing for having run off with Tommy. Tommy too got his share for his disobedience.

them and wanted to go home. But the vixen would not let him go.

'I cannot go with you now and you would get lost on your own,' she said. 'Wait until morning.'

Poor little Tommy started to cry. He wanted so much to go home, but the vixen and the cubs would not let him.

Meanwhile Grandfather and Grandmother had come home from the woods and found the cottage empty. They were alarmed. 'Whatever

The Old Woman,
the Hen and the Dog

Once an old woman, a hen and a dog lived together in a cottage. The old woman cooked, the hen laid eggs and the dog guarded the cottage. They were very happy until one day the hen stopped laying eggs. The old woman had nothing to eat and neither had the dog. The dog crept into his kennel and the old woman sat in front of the cottage and cried.

A passing monk stopped at the door and asked. 'Why are you crying, Grandmother?'

The old woman replied. 'I have good reason to cry! I have a nice fat hen who used to lay an egg every day. But for three days she has laid none, and the dog and I have nothing to eat.'

The monk said. 'Do not cry. I shall help you. I shall come for her this evening, keep her for three days and you will see how I shall teach her to lay again.' And he went away.

Grandmother ran into the house happily and told the dog.

'Dog, everything is going to be all right again! There was a monk here and he promised me he would teach our hen to lay again.'

The dog ran to the front of the house and sniffed. 'That was no monk, Grandmother,' he said. 'It was a fox dressed up in a monk's habit. Just wait till the evening. If he is a monk, he will not be afraid of me, but if he is a fox, he will take to his heels.'

When it grew dark, there was a knock at the door. 'Who is there?' asked the old woman.

'It is me, the monk,' was the reply from the other side of the door. 'I have come for your hen.'

'Come in,' said the old woman, and opened the door. The monk went in. At that moment the dog ran up and started to bark. That was enough. Next moment the monk was off through the open door and into the woods, so fast he nearly left his habit behind. The dog had been right. It was indeed a fox.

'But what now?' cried the old woman.

'Let us sleep on it,' said the dog. And that is just what they did.

But the next day the hen still did not lay an egg. The dog crept into his kennel behind the cottage, the old woman sat at the cottage door and wept bitterly.

Out of nowhere came a rag and bone man with a sack on his back. 'Why are you crying, Grandmother?' he asked.

The old woman replied. 'I have good reason to cry. I have a nice fat hen who used to lay an egg every day. But for four days she has laid none and the dog and I have nothing to eat.'

'Don't cry,' said the rag and bone man. 'I shall help you. This evening I will come for her, keep her for three days and you will see how I teach her to lay again.' And he went away.

The old woman ran to tell the dog.

'Dog, everything is going to be all right again! There was a rag and bone man here and he promised to teach our hen to lay again.'

The dog ran to the front of the house and sniffed. 'That was no rag and bone man,' he said. 'It was a marten in a rag and bone man's coat. Just wait till the evening. If he is a rag and bone man, he will throw a stone at me, if he is a marten he will run away!'

When it got dark, someone knocked at the door. 'Who is there?' asked the old woman.

'It is me, the rag and bone man,' came the answer. 'I have come for your hen.'

'Come in,' said the old woman and opened the door. The rag and bone man came in with his sack of rags and bones on his back. At that the dog dashed up to him and barked. That was enough. The rag and bone man ran through the open door and made for the woods so fast he nearly dropped his sack. The dog had been right. It was indeed a marten.

'But what now?' cried the old woman. 'Let us sleep on it,' said the dog. And that is just what they did. But the next day the hen still did not lay an egg. The dog crept into his kennel behind the cottage, the old woman sat at the cottage door and wept bitterly.

Suddenly a pedlar appeared with a basket of nuts on his back. 'Why are you crying, Grandmother?' he asked.

The old woman replied. 'I have good reason to cry. I have a nice fat hen who used to lay an egg every day. But for five days she has laid none and the dog and I have nothing to eat.'

'Don't cry,' said the pedlar. 'I shall help you. In the evening I shall come for her, keep her for three days and you will see how I teach her to lay again.' And he went away.

The old woman ran to the dog and told him.

'Dog, everything is going to be all right again.' There was a pedlar here and he promised to teach our hen to lay again.'

The dog ran to the gate and sniffed. 'That was no pedlar,' he said. 'It was a wolf with a basket on his back. Just wait till the evening. If he is a pedlar he will chase me off with a stick, if he is a wolf he will run away.'

When it got dark, someone knocked at the door. 'Who is there?' asked the old woman.

'It is me, the pedlar,' came the answer from the other side of the door. 'I have come for your hen!'

'Come in,' said the old woman, and opened the door. The pedlar came in with his basket of nuts on his back. At that the dog dashed up to him and barked. That was enough. The pedlar was off through the open door and into the woods, leaving behind his bag from which all the nuts came pouring out. The dog had been right again. It was indeed a wolf.

'But what now?' cried the old woman.

'First let us tell the hen to peck up all those nuts,' said the dog. And he chased the hen to the patch outside the door.

The hen pecked till her crop was full and what she did not peck up that evening, she pecked up next day, and what she did not peck up next day, she ate up on the third day.

All week she had plenty to eat, and all week she laid eggs. And this time she did not stop laying.

And so all three in the cottage were happy — the old woman, the hen and the dog. The old woman cooked, the hen laid eggs and the dog guarded them all.

As for the fox, the marten and the wolf, they never showed themselves at the cottage again.

The Wolf, the Fox and the Otter

A wolf, a fox and an otter once lived together. They kept a pig which they fed on anything they could find to eat — potatoes, beet, fallen apples and pears and looked forward to the feast they would have when it was fat enough to be killed. The wolf was already licking his lips in anticipation.

'How I am looking forward to my pig!' he would say.

The fox was angry. 'Why do you keep saying my pig when it is ours.' And the otter laughed at both of them.

'Just wait and see whose pig it is,' he said.

When the pig was fat enough, the wolf, the fox and the otter slaughtered it.

Hardly had the pig been killed when the wolf wanted to set to and eat it. The fox was also sharpening his teeth.

But the otter would not allow them to start.

'Surely you are not going to eat such a dirty, unwashed pig?' he said. 'Just look at its ears! Come, the pond is only a few steps away, let us wash it there. It will be all the tastier, you'll see!'

The wolf and the fox admitted that the otter was right. Together they dragged the dead pig to the pond. The wolf held it by its hind legs, the fox by the front legs and the otter dived into the water.

'Hold it firmly,' he said, 'and I'll wash it myself.'

But instead of washing it, the otter pulled with all his strength and dragged it into the water.

'Wait a minute or I'll slip,' cried the fox to the wolf. 'I too!' cried the wolf to the fox. And he let go of the pig. The fox tripped over him. The pig slid into the water and the otter towed it to the middle of the pond. In vain did the wolf and the fox run round the pond shouting at the otter.

'Give us our share, give us our share!'

The otter only laughed at them and ate up the whole pig himself.

How the Snakes Got Their Poison

While the world was still young and everything was different, there was no night. The sun always shone in the heavens and neither people nor animals could rest. Hardly had they begun to nod when the sun woke them up with its light and its heat.

Only the snakes could bear it and were always merry and lively. Secretly the snakes kept darkness and night hidden away.

This did not remain a secret long. When the Indians learned that the snakes possessed night and darkness they sent their great chief to the great chief of the snakes to beg from him a little night and darkness.

The great chief of the Indians went deep into the tropical forest where the chief of the snakes lived. He was not welcomed warmly.

'Who are you?' asked the snake chief. 'And why are you disturbing my peace?'

The Indian chief replied. 'I am chief of the Indians and I have come to ask you for a little night and darkness. I shall give you my best bow and arrow in return.'

But the snake was not interested in bows and arrows.

'What use would they be to me,' he said, 'when I have no hands and arms? You must bring me something else!'

The Indian chief returned to his people disappointed. He called a gathering of the Indian council and told the members what had happened. In the end they decided to offer the snake a rattle.

The chief of the Indians went back to the forest again. The great snake was waiting for him. When he saw the rattle, he shook his head and said.

'That is a fine rattle, but what use would it be to me, when I have no hands and arms?'

The chief of the Indians spoke. 'Listen!' he said. 'I shall tie this rattle to your tail.' And at once he did so. The great snake lashed his tail and listened to the sound it made. And the snake accepted the gift.

'It is not quite what I wanted,' he said, 'but I will be generous and give you a little night and darkness.'

And he ordered a small leather wallet to be brought to the Indian chief. The chief took the wallet and said.

'Thank you, great chief of the snakes, for this little portion of night and darkness. But tell me what must I give you in return for the whole of night and darkness?'

The big snake replied. 'The whole of night and darkness is almost priceless. This rattle is not nearly enough to pay for it. You would have to bring me a whole pitcher of poison in which we might dip our fangs.'

The great Indian chief did not know why the snakes should want so much poison, and he did not ask. He hurried with the leather wallet back to his people, and in the village he opened it. In

Indians once again decided to call a great council and it was decided that they would start at once to collect poison for the snake chief. Slowly they collected it, drop by drop, until at last the pitcher was full. Then the great chief of the Indians set out for the forest for the third time. The great snake was waiting for him.

'I knew you would come,' he said. 'Here in this large wallet you will find long night and darkness. There will be enough for you.'

The great Indian chief gave the snake the pitcher full of poison and took from him the large wallet full of night and darkness.

'Thank you, great snake,' he said. 'But now, tell me one thing. Why do snakes need our poison?'

The big snake replied. 'Most snakes are small and weak and are easily killed or injured. If they have poisoned fangs they will be able to defend themselves. Now go, but do not open the wallet

an instant night and darkness spread over the world and the Indians lay down and fell asleep. But they did not sleep long, for it was only a little portion of night and darkness.

Very soon it was day again and the sun woke them up once more.

And for a long time, on earth, the days were long and the nights were short. Hardly had people lain down to sleep when they were roused by the light of a new day. At last the

until you reach your village. If you open it sooner I would not have time to divide the poison fairly among all the snakes and that would bode ill for us and for you.'

The great Indian chief promised that he would not open the wallet until he reached his village, and happily he set out. But on the way a parrot saw him and at once let out a shriek.

'The great Indian chief is taking home a wallet of night and darkness from the snakes.'

At the parrot's shriek all the animals of the forest ran up to him demanding that he should open the wallet at once and let out the long night and darkness.

The great chief tried to pacify them. 'Wait

123

until I reach our village. I promised the great snake I would not open it until then.'

But the animals would not listen. They did not want to wait even for a moment and they snatched the wallet from the great chief's hands and opened it. At once light and darkness came down on the world.

In the depths of the forest the great snake had just begun to divide the poison. But in the darkness he could see nothing, and the snakes pressed round him one after another, and in the end the pitcher was overturned.

And that is how it came about that some of the snakes had much poison and others little and some none at all.

Today snakes are divided into those that are poisonous and those that are not. And among those that are poisonous is the family of the big chief of the snakes.

He always gives warning of his approach because he has a rattle on his tail.

The Tortoise and the Leopard

Once upon a time, the tortoise and the leopard were great friends. In those days the leopard did not eat meat, but like the tortoise he lived on grass, leaves or cabbage, especially cabbage.

But one day he said. 'I have had enough of cabbage. Let us go hunting for meat for a change!'

The tortoise too wanted to taste meat and so went willingly with the leopard. They set out for the woods, set several traps and by the evening had caught several antelopes.

One of them they killed at once and roasted it over the fire, the others they killed and put into several baskets they had woven out of leaves and branches.

The tortoise and the leopard were busy all evening, so they decided to spend the night in the woods and take the baskets of meat home in the morning.

After a good supper, the leopard slept well. But the tortoise could not sleep.

She kept thinking about the meat in the baskets. 'Why,' she said to herself, 'does the leopard need so much meat? Any time he is hungry he can go and hunt antelopes. But I cannot chase antelope. I shall keep all the meat for myself.'

And she got up very quietly and put all the meat in her own basket and filled the leopard's with stones. She covered the stones with leaves so that he would notice nothing.

Then, very pleased with herself, the tortoise went to sleep.

In the morning, the leopard and the tortoise rose, picked up their hampers, put them on their backs and hurried home. When he arrived at his shack, the leopard's wife was cooking cabbage.

'Throw that cabbage away, my dear,' said the leopard. 'I have had quite enough of it. I have something better here, some good meat.'

And he emptied the basket on the floor. But there was no meat in the basket. Only stones fell out.

The leopard roared menacingly. 'That is certainly the work of the tortoise. I shall settle with her.'

And he ran off immediately to look for the tortoise.

But the tortoise was expecting this and did not wait for the leopard.

With her basket she crept into her hole and there made a good meal of antelope meat.

The leopard never forgave her for her treachery. He declared war on all tortoises and whenever he comes across one, he turns it over on its back and eats it.

That is how the leopard learned to go hunting and to feed on meat, while the tortoise continues to eat grass, leaves and vegetables.

The Wolf, the Dog and the Dog Collar

One evening a dog and a wolf met in a field near a farm. The wolf had not eaten for so long that he was nothing but skin and bone and could hardly drag one leg after the other. The dog was strong and healthy and ran backwards and forwards like the wind. The wolf found this hard to understand.

'Tell me, Dog,' he said, 'who feeds you so well!'

The dog replied proudly. 'Who feeds me? Master, of course.'

The wolf was even more surprised. 'And why does he feed you so well?' he asked.

The dog replied. 'He feeds me because I serve him well. If you like you can come and work for him too.'

The wolf was interested and asked. 'What would I have to do?'

The dog explained. 'You would have to be always on guard, so that nobody robbed us.'

This seemed a good idea to the wolf. He had had enough of being cold and hungry. He decided to try out this service.

'Well, if that's all, I'll come with you,' he said. And he ran with the dog to the farm.

Just as they reached the gate, the wolf noticed that there were rough patches on his new friend's neck.

'Why are there patches on your neck, Dog?' he asked.

'Oh, that's nothing,' explained the dog. 'They are only from my collar.'

The wolf was taken aback. 'From your collar? Why do you wear a collar round your neck?'

The dog had to tell him the truth.

'Because that is what my master orders,' he replied. 'In day time he puts on my collar and fastens me to a chain so that I cannot go running about. In the evening the takes off my collar, and then I can run about wherever I like — and keep watch.'

The wolf shook his head. 'He ties you to a chain, does he? I did not know that. No, no, my friend, I do not envy you after all. Rather than wear a collar round my neck and be tied to a chain, I would go hungry. I much prefer to run around freely wherever and whenever I like.'

And with that he ran off to the fields and the woods.

The Frog Who Wanted to be Like a Bull

Once a frog wandered into a meadow where he saw a bull. He was grazing on the juicy grass and did not notice the frog. But the frog could not take his eyes off the bull.

'What a giant!' he gasped enviously. 'What would I not do to be like him. But what is not still can be. I shall just puff myself up until I too am as big as a bull.'

So the frog started to puff. It was hard work, but the frog did not give up. When he thought he had puffed himself up enough, he started to shout. 'Look, everybody. Don't you think I am like a bull?'

But people only laughed. 'You a bull? You silly frog!'

And the frog went on puffing and blowing even harder.

'Now, everybody, do I not look like a bull?'

They only laughed all the more. 'You a bull? You silly frog!'

The frog puffed and blew himself up even more. He puffed so hard that his skin would not stretch any more. He burst like an acorn, and all that was left of the frog who wanted to be like a bull was a little heap of skin and bones.

The Hyena and the Hare

The hyena and the hare once went fishing together. When they had caught enough the hyena said to the hare. 'Now we'll each smoke our own fish. You stay here, Hare, and I'll go to the other side of the river.'

Then he took his own catch, crossed to the other side of the river and they each smoked their own fish.

When the sun went down, the hyena called across the river to the hare. 'Hare! Don't go to sleep whatever you do. A robber might come and take all our fish.'

The hare did not answer. He just stuck an iron spit he had brought with him into the fire and lay down happily to rest.

In the middle of the night the hyena started to call to the hare very quietly, once, twice and a third time. The hare was not asleep, but he did not answer.

The hyena, sure that the hare was fast asleep, very quietly moved to the other side of the river.

In the darkness he stole up to the hare's fish. He seized one and ate it. The hare did not move. The hyena took a second fish, but hardly had he taken a bite when the hare jumped up, seized the spit from the fire and beat the thief with it several times across the back.

The hyena did not utter a sound, but went back to his own bank.

From there he called out to the hare. 'Hare! Did you have a visit from a robber?'

'Yes, he came all right,' the hare replied. 'But I gave him a good beating.'

'Yes, you certainly gave him something to remember,' said the hyena. 'I could feel the blows from here. Only tell me, please, what did you use to beat him with?'

'The red hot end of a spit,' replied the hare.

And ever since then the hyena has had stripes on his back.

128

The Fox
Who Took Beasts
to Pasture

One day a farmer's wife set out to find a herdsman who would take her beasts to pasture. She walked a long way until at last she met a bear.

'Where are you off to, Mistress?' asked the bear.

'Where am I going, Bear?' she answered. 'I am looking for someone to take my beasts to pasture.'

'You want a herdsman, do you?' said the bear. 'What about me?'

'Why not?' replied the farmer's wife. 'But you must be able to call them in a gentle voice.'

'Of course I can,' boasted the bear. And he growled: 'Grr . . . grrr . . . grr . . . !'

'That won't do,' said the farmer's wife. 'I do not like that voice at all.'

And she went on walking until she met a wolf.

'Where are you off to, Mistress?' asked the wolf.

'Where am I going, Wolf?' she answered. 'I am looking for someone to take my beasts to pasture.'

'You want a herdsman, do you?' said the wolf. 'What about me?'

'Why not?' said the farmer's wife. 'But you must be able to call them in a gentle voice.'

'Of course I can,' boasted the wolf. And he howled: 'Ow...ow...ow...'

'That won't do,' said the farmer's wife. 'I do not like that voice at all!'

And she went on walking until she met a fox.

'Where are you off to?' asked the fox.

'Where am I going, Fox?' she answered. 'I am looking for someone to take my beasts to pasture.'

'You want a herdsman, do you?' said the fox. 'What about me?'

'Why not?' said the farmer's wife. 'But you must be able to call the beasts in a gentle voice.'

'Listen and judge for yourself!' said the fox modestly. And he called: 'Halilee, haliloo!'

'Well, well,' said the farmer's wife, when she had listened a while. 'Yes, I like that.'

And she hired the fox to take her beasts to pasture.

The fox drove the herd to pasture. The first day he ate all the goats, the second day he ate the sheep and the third day he ate the cows.

When he came home alone in the evening the farmer's wife asked him where he had left the flock.

'The head is in the stream, the tail in the meadow replied the fox.

The farmer's wife was churning butter, but when she heard the fox's answer she wanted to go and look at this strange thing. She left the churn and ran outside.

That was just what the fox was waiting for. He stuck his head into the churn and lapped up all the cream.

When the farmer's wife came back and saw what the fox had done, she seized the last spoonful of cream and threw it after him. But she did not succeed in hitting the running fox — only the very tip of his tail.

And ever since then the fox has had a white tip to his tail.

130

The horse neighed. 'Why not? Do you see that stone? Can you strike it so hard that sparks will fly?'

The lion clenched his paw and hit out at the stone. But no sparks flew. The horse neighed.

'You see, you are not so strong. Now I shall try. And he kicked with his hoof at the stone till a shower of sparks flew from it.

When the lion saw this he was afraid. He put his tail between his legs and the King of the Beasts ran off in shame.

The Horse and the Lion

Once upon a time a horse wandered far into the steppes. There he met a lion. The horse had never before seen such an animal, nor had the lion ever seen a horse. They both stood still and each said to the other. 'Who are you, animal?'

The horse was not at all afraid. 'I am the King of Beasts,' he said boldly.

The lion did not like this. 'It is I who am the King of Beasts!' he roared.

But the horse stood his ground. 'I am the King of Beasts,' he neighed, 'because I am the stronger.'

'You will have to prove it,' the lion rumbled. 'At once!'

The Field Mouse
and
the Town Mouse

Once upon a time a rich mouse, who lived in the town, invited her poor relation, the field mouse, to visit her. She showed her all her riches — a loft full of grain, a pantry full of food, a wine cellar and a larder full of meat and bacon. The poor field mouse gasped in wonder.

'You are doing very well here,' she said. 'What a fine life you have here in the town.'

The town mouse only puffed herself up with pride. But suddenly she stopped feeling so pleased with herself. She crouched on a wooden beam and the field mouse crouched beside her. Beneath them on the floor slunk an animal with green eyes, great whiskers and a large tail. He was licking his lips in anticipation as he looked about him.

The field mouse asked softly. 'Who is it?'

It was of course a cat, but the town mouse wanted to make fun of the field mouse. 'Oh, that's nothing,' she said. 'It is only my grandmother, but you had better greet her politely.'

The field mouse was not very willing to do this. Nevertheless, she took courage and crept out to greet this grandmother mouse. The town mouse laughed and laughed so heartily that she rolled off the beam right in front of the cat. The cat, of course, wasted no time and gobbled her up.

The field mouse was frightened. She ran along the beam and fled through the first hole in the wall, and off into the fields.

When some time later she was talking about her visit she sighed. 'There is certainly plenty of food in the town, but I would not like to live there. Just imagine, grandmothers eat their own grandchildren.'

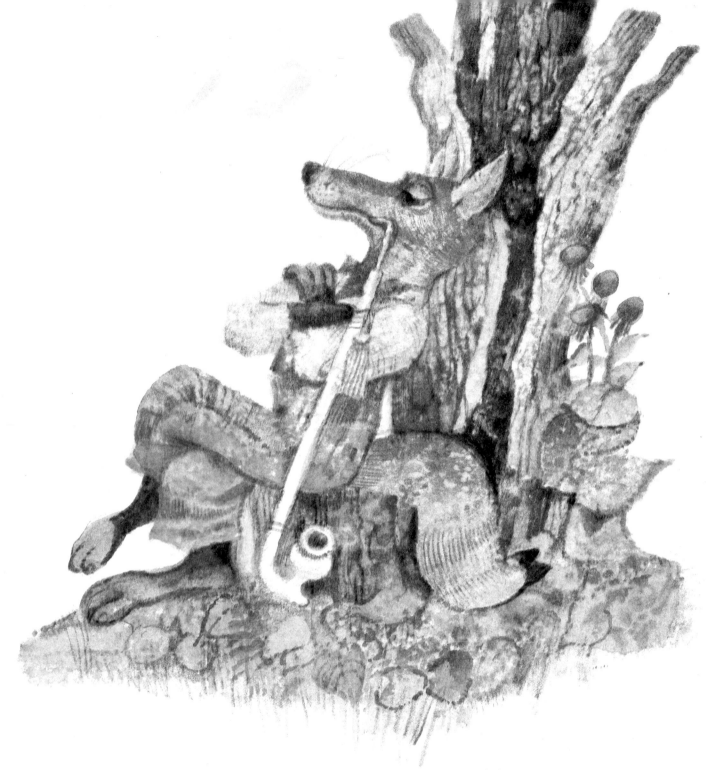

The Wolf and His Pipe

Once upon a time a fox sat in front of his hole smoking a beautiful pipe. When his neighbour the wolf saw this he was curious.

'What are you doing, Fox?' he asked.

The fox answered. 'As you can see I am smoking.'

'And is it pleasant?' asked the wolf.

'Of course it is,' replied the fox. 'Otherwise people would not smoke.'

'I must try smoking too,' said the wolf. 'If only I had all the things needed for it.'

'That's easily done,' the fox assured him. 'I can get everything for you. Over there, near the forest, a farmer is ploughing. He has left his coat by the path. I am sure he will have a pipe and tobacco in his pocket. Let us go and have a look!'

The wolf agreed and went with the fox to the field path. There in the grass lay the coat and under it a gun.

'That is a beautiful pipe,' cried the fox, pointing at the gun. 'It is a bit bigger than mine, but it will be all the better for you to smoke with. Just try it out!' And he pushed the barrel of the gun into the wolf's mouth. Then he said. 'And now I shall fill it and light it for you, Wolf. Just hold onto it well and breathe in.'

The wolf held on bravely and drew in his breath and the treacherous fox pressed the trigger. There was a crack like a clap of thunder and the poor wolf went rolling over. Three teeth had gone. Beside himself with anger, the wolf howled. 'I will never forgive you for this, Fox. Even if three of my teeth have gone, I still have enough in my head to tear you to pieces!' And he shot off into the woods.

Since that time the wolf has never yearned to smoke a pipe.

The fox does not smoke either: he is too busy taking care that the wolf does not catch him.

The Horse and the Stag

Once upon a time the horse roamed as free as the lion, the wolf or the stag. He could gallop over the steppes and through the forests, graze where he liked and drink freely at rivers and wells.

Once, however, at a certain well, he met a stag. The stag had come there to drink and this angered the horse. 'Go away at once, Stag!' he said. 'This is my well.'

The stag did not move. 'It is not yours,' he said. 'It belongs to me and to anyone else who comes here to drink. There is plenty of water for all. Just wait a little and you can drink when I have finished.'

The horse did not like this. 'I will not drink after you,' he said. 'You have polluted the water.'

The stag still did not give in. 'I have not polluted the water,' he replied. 'If anyone has, it is you.'

Words followed words and in the end a fierce argument developed between them. The angry horse forgot that he was thirsty and lashed out at the stag with his hoofs. But the stag did not wait and with a leap and a bound he was off. The horse chased him in vain; he could not catch up. He became even angrier. He decided to punish the stag. He went in search of man.

'Help me, man,' he said. 'The stag has insulted me and I want to pay him out.'

Man thought for a time. Then he said. 'All right, if you like, we will teach him a lesson together. You must take me to that well.'

'I shall take you, man,' the horse replied.

Man wasted no time. He put a bridle on the horse and taking a spear in his hand, climbed on his back. The horse quickly carried him to the well. In a little while the stag appeared. When he saw the horse and the man, he fled. But it was too late. The horse with the man on his back went racing after him.

At just the right moment, the man threw the spear and the stag fell to the ground.

The horse was satisfied now. He had his revenge.

'Thank you, man, for your help,' he said. 'But now jump down from my back. You are very heavy, and I want to graze and drink a little.'

But the man did not jump down.

'What do you mean, horse,' he said. 'One good turn deserves another. I helped you to settle with your enemy, and now you are going to serve me.'

And he tightened the rein, pressed the horse's flanks with his heels and rode home.

Since that time the horse has served man. His revenge cost him dear. While the stag runs freely through the forests to this day, the horse will always serve another.

Brother Rabbit and the Cow

Early one evening, Brother Rabbit went for a walk, and in a meadow he saw a cow. Her udder was full of milk and the rabbit thought how much he would enjoy some milk. But how could he get milk when he had nothing to buy it with. 'I shall try, even without money,' said Brother Rabbit to himself and greeted the cow very politely. 'How are you this fine evening, Cow?' he asked.

The cow answered. 'Quite well, thank you, Brother Rabbit. Only the grass is not very sweet today,' she said. 'It is very dry.'

Brother Rabbit immediately had good advice to give. 'Just try a few plums,' he said. 'They grow on that tree. You will see how they will improve your appetite.'

On the edge of the meadow there was a plum tree, weighed down with fruit. The cow looked at the rabbit and said. 'It is true, one or two plums would do no harm, but how can we get them down?'

As usual Brother Rabbit knew the answer. 'That's easy,' he said. 'Just hit the trunk of the tree with your horns and the plums will come tumbling down.'

The cow tried. She butted the tree with her horns. But the plums were still green and not one of them fell.

'You must butt harder,' said the rabbit. And the cow did butt the tree harder. But still no plums fell. 'You must run at it,' advised the rabbit, and the cow obeyed. She ran at the tree and butted it with all her strength. A few plums did fall down, but the cow did not get any of them. She had run at the tree trunk and butted it so hard that one of her horns was so deeply embedded in it that she could not pull it out.

This was just what Brother Rabbit had been waiting for. He ran home to fetch a bucket. He told his wife and children to come too with jugs and pots to fill with the cow's milk. Then Brother Rabbit sat down under the cow and milked and milked until she was dry.

'Thank you, Cow,' he said politely, 'for your excellent milk. Now we wish you goodnight!'

The cow was very angry, but what could she do? She still had one horn fixed firmly in the trunk of the plum tree, and no matter how she tried, she could not pull it out. It was not till morning that she succeeded in freeing her horn.

'I shall pay you back, Brother Rabbit,' she said to herself, as she went back to graze.

When evening came, she returned to the plum tree and pushed her horn into the hole as if she had been there all day long. She waited for the rabbit.

But Brother Rabbit came out for his walk a little earlier that evening and saw what the cow was doing. He waited till the cow reached the plum tree and then called out in greeting.

'I see you are still here, Cow!'

The cow groaned. 'It is bad, Brother Rabbit. I have been standing here all night and all day,

and I just cannot pull my horn out. Help me please. Hold me by the tail and pull!'

But the rabbit was not going to be caught like that. 'I am not strong enough to pull you out. I shall groan for you instead.' And he hurried over to the cow and began to groan. The cow thought the rabbit was near enough for her to take her revenge. She pulled her horn out of the tree trunk and turned on him. But Brother Rabbit was on his guard. As soon as she moved, he took to his heels and was off.

The cow, her tail in the air, went racing after him. But she could never run as fast as the rabbit, and in a few seconds he had vanished into the undergrowth. The rabbit hid among the leaves and only his big eyes were visible. As the cow raced past she saw the eyes, but did not recognize the rabbit, so fast was she running.

'Have you seen Brother Rabbit pass this way?' she called.

And Brother Rabbit answered in a thin little voice. 'Yes, I saw him just a moment ago. He was running along the road. If you hurry you might catch him!'

The cow ran faster than she had ever run before along the road and into the village. Only when she got there did she realize she would never catch the rabbit. She went back to her pasture tired and angry.

That was how Brother Rabbit tricked the cow twice.

But the cow never forgot, and Brother Rabbit knew this very well. After that, as soon as he saw her, he would race off as fast as he could in case he, like the plum tree, should feel the sharpness of her horns.

137

The Jackal, the Hyena and the Well

It was night and the moon was shining. But on the steppes it was still hot and the jackal was thirsty.

Suddenly he saw in front of him a well with a cross bar and two buckets. When one of the buckets went down into the well, the other came up full of water.

The jackal did not take long to make up his mind. He hopped into the empty bucket at the top and went down. Thankfully he drank his fill. But then he realized he was in difficulty. He had gone down quite easily, but how was he to get up again? The walls were too slippery for him to grip with his claws.

Happily for him, a hyena appeared at the well at that very moment. He, too, was thirsty. Looking down, he saw the jackal and at once forgot his thirst.

'What are you doing there, Jackal?' he said. 'And what is it that shines just beside you?'

Behind the jackal in the well was the reflection of the moon. The jackal had an idea.

'What am I doing?' he said. 'You can see for yourself, Hyena. I am eating cheese — a whole round yellow cheese.'

The hyena believed that it was a cheese and at once wanted some too. 'Leave me a bit!' he said. 'I am hungry.'

'Why not,' the jackal answered. 'I have already had enough. Hop into the other bucket and come down!'

The hyena did not need to be told twice. He jumped into the bucket and went sailing down into the well. He was heavier than the jackal, and his weight easily sent the jackal to the top.

Quickly he hopped out of the bucket, leaned over the well and said. 'Thank you, Hyena, I wish you a good appetite. You can have the whole cheese for yourself!'

How the hyena got out of the well no one really knows. Perhaps he was pulled up in the morning by the villagers.

The Vixen and the Eagle

Some fox cubs were playing outside their hole, and as they leapt and frolicked, an eagle spotted them. In a flash he swooped down, seized a fox cub in his talons and flew off with it to his nest to feed his young.

The mother vixen saw it happen and ran after the eagle. Under his nest she called up to him. 'Spare my child, Eagle, and I shall repay you!'

But the eagle, high up in his nest, only laughed.

The vixen changed her tone and began to threaten him. 'Spare my child, Eagle,' she said, 'or I shall have my revenge on you. Kill one of my children, and I shall destroy all of yours!'

The eagle was startled. He knew the vixen and was aware that she was not speaking wildly. He said. 'And how will you do it, when you are down there and my children and I are up here?'

'Just wait and see,' said the vixen.

And she ran off to the nearest meadow, where a fire lit by shepherds was still burning. Seizing a burning branch in her mouth, she ran back to the tree where the eagle had his nest and threw it on the dry grass round its roots. In a moment a flame shot up and the grass began to burn. Brushwood caught fire from the grass and a column of smoke rose to the eagle's nest.

The eagle realized that the vixen's threat had not been an empty one.

He cried out. 'Here is your child. But put out that fire or the nest will catch fire and so will my children!'

And he flew down with the fox cub. Then the vixen threw sand onto the burning brushwood and the fire was soon out.

In future, however, she kept a very watchful eye on her cubs. And the eagle since then has been careful to keep out of the way of foxes and fox cubs.

139

The Spider and the Magic Gourds

Once upon a time the spider and his family had nothing to eat. The spider had to go begging. He went from village to village.

'Good people, please give me some food,' he pleaded. 'I have a wife and six children at home, and they have nothing to eat.'

And the good people were always sorry for his wife and children. Once he brought home seven pancakes, another day seven nuts and a third time seven sweet potatoes known as batatas.

But most of this food was always eaten up by the spider himself.

'How shall we divide it?' his wife always asked, when she had counted what he had brought home. 'There are eight of us altogether, and there are only seven pancakes.'

'That is all right,' the spider always said. 'I do not need a whole one. I shall just break a piece off each of them.'

When they sat down to eat, the spider broke off a good half of each pancake or nut or sweet batata, and so he always had the most of all. Very soon he became as fat as a barrel. That was a mistake. When people see a fat beggar they do not believe that he is hungry and that his children have nothing to eat. So the spider had to go out into the world to seek a living.

He did not have to go far. Outside the nearest village he came upon a gourd growing close to the path. It was beautiful and it warmed his heart to see it.

'That is a beautiful gourd,' cried the spider.

'I am indeed,' said the gourd unexpectedly, 'and if you only knew what I can do!'

'Show me then!' said the inquisitive spider. He had scarcely spoken when there appeared before him a table laden with good things.

'That is a splendid trick,' said the spider, and ate his fill. Then taking the gourd with him, he returned home.

From that time on his wife and children never went hungry. Every day the spider brought home plenty of food. But he never said where it came from. In the morning he would go out with the gourd and in the nearby thicket he would order his dinner. What was left over he took home.

And so it went on, until one day, his youngest son discovered his secret. The young spider was even more wily than his father. He watched where his father went every day, hid in the thicket and saw and heard everything. In the evening, when the old spider went to visit his neighbours, the youngest son took the gourd, put it in front of him and said.

'That is a beautiful gourd!'

'I am indeed,' replied the gourd, 'and if you only knew what I can do!'

'Show me then!' said the youngest spider, and

before him there appeared a table laden with good food for the whole family. They sat down happily in front of it and started to feast.

After the meal they wanted to put the gourd back in its place, so that the old spider would notice nothing. But in their haste they dropped it on the ground and the gourd burst.

The spider noticed nothing until the next day when he put the gourd in front of him and said.

'That is a beautiful gourd!'

But the burst gourd did not answer.

'What is the matter with you?' asked the spider. Then he picked up the gourd and saw what had happened. He decided to punish his sons, but he did not yet know how he would do this.

As there was again nothing to eat in their cottage he set out once more into the world. But again he did not have to go far. Outside the next village he again saw a gourd growing close to the path.

'That is a beautiful gourd!' he said.

'I am indeed,' said the gourd, 'and if you only knew what I can do!'

'Show me then!' said the inquisitive spider. Next moment the spider was sorry he had spoken these words, for out of the gourd there jumped a whip made from an ox's tail. It started to beat the spider so hard he was lucky to escape with his life.

'That is a strange trick,' gasped the spider, when the whip at last stopped beating him. But he picked up the gourd and went home with it.

'At least I shall use it to punish my son', he said to himself.

And punish him he did. Hardly had he left the house in the evening when his youngest son seized the new gourd, set it in front of him and said.

'That is a beautiful gourd!'

'I am indeed,' replied the gourd, 'and if you only knew what I can do!'

'Show me then!' said the youngest spider, and the gourd did not need to be asked twice. Out jumped a whip made from an ox's tail and started to beat him so hard he was lucky to escape with his life.

When the little spiders saw what was happening, they and their mother ran off to hide away in every corner and crevice they could find in the cottage.

And there they stayed, even when the whip went back into the gourd and vanished with it for ever. You can find them and their father even today hiding in dark corners and crevices.

The Wolf
and
the Stork

A wolf one day caught and killed a quail. He was eating it so fast and so greedily that a piece stuck in his throat and he nearly choked.

By a happy chance a stork came by. The wolf begged him in a strangled voice. 'Help me, Stork. A piece of bone has stuck in my throat. If you do not pull it out, it will kill me. Help me and I shall reward you.'

The stork was not very willing to help the wolf. He did not like the idea of putting his beak down a wolf's throat.

But tearfully the wolf pleaded with him, and at last the stork took pity on his plight. 'Open your mouth wide,' he said. 'I shall try to help you.'

The wolf obediently opened his mouth, the stork put his long beak down the wolf's throat and pulled out the piece of bone.

'There it is, Wolf. And now what is my reward to be?' he asked.

The wolf simply shook himself, and said. 'Reward did you say? I have already rewarded you. I have not eaten you up as I did the quail. Is that not enough? If I had shut my mouth, it would have been the end of you.'

'That is what they call a wolf's gratitude,' said the stork.

And flapping his wings he flew off before the wolf could change his mind.

The Pig and His Short Snout

Once upon a time a crab stole the lion's wife and hid her in his lair by the river. The lion was angry. He called together all the animals from the woods and thickets and told them. 'The crab has stolen my wife. Which of you will help me to get her back?'

'I,' said the elephant. 'I have strong tusks and with these tusks I will dig up the crab's lair.'

But the lion did not like the idea. He was afraid the elephant might hurt his wife.

'All right,' said the buffalo. 'I will get her back for you. I have strong hoofs and with them I will trample the crab's lair.'

But the lion did not like this idea either.

'All right, I will get your wife back for you,' declared the pig.

In those days the pig had a long snout, even longer than the elephant's trunk.

'I will pull her out of the crab's lair with my snout,' said the pig.

The lion thought that this was the best idea. So he sent the pig to the crab's lair and the elephant and the buffalo went with him to help.

When they came to the crab's lair, the pig said. 'I will push my snout inside. You must give me a push from behind so that I can get as far in as possible.'

The pig stuck his long snout into the crab's lair and the elephant and the buffalo pushed him from behind with all their strength.

In the lair the crab was discussing with the lioness what they would have for supper. The lioness said she would like a piece of meat.

'Well, here it is!' cried the crab, when he saw the pig's snout coming into the lair. And with his pincers he nipped off a piece, just big enough to make a supper for the lioness.

Outside the lair, the pig let out a cry of pain. But the elephant and the buffalo thought he was shouting in triumph and again pushed him with all their strength. The pig's snout went still deeper into the lair and the crab nipped off another piece for his own supper.

At that the pig started to shriek terribly. The elephant and the buffalo stopped pushing him and the pig eventually pulled his snout out of the crab's pincers. It was red and short — just as short as it is today.

When the elephant and the buffalo saw what had happened they were frightened and fled. They never went to help the pig again.

As for the pig, he stopped being friends with the wild animals. With his short red snout he prefers living with people.

The Lion Who Wanted to Outwit the Horse

A horse was one day grazing in a meadow. In the thicket nearby a lion was lying in wait for him. The lion was hungry, but he did not want to have to chase such a fast runner as the horse.

'It would be better to try a little guile,' he thought. And he came out of the undergrowth and greeted the horse politely. 'Do not be afraid,' he said. 'I shall do you no harm. Just the opposite in fact, for I am a doctor.'

The horse was no fool and pretended to believe the lion. 'That is fortunate,' he said. 'For I have just stepped on something and my hoof hurts so badly I can scarcely walk. Would you have a look at it for me?'

The lion was only too willing. 'Of course, my friend, I shall certainly have a look,' he said. 'Show it to me!'

The horse obediently raised his hind leg and the lion bent over it as if he really wanted to examine the horse's hoof. But he had quite a different idea in mind as to how he would cure him. However, the horse did not wait. As the lion came close, he let fly with his hind legs, kicking him on the head so hard that he rolled over.

So the King of Beasts remained hungry. When he recovered his senses the horse was already far away, and the lion was left with a large lump on his head.

How the Sparrow Got the Better of King Eagle

King Eagle one day summoned the parliament of the birds.

'Which one of you birds who fly by day and by night over the mountains and plains has ever heard a stronger voice than mine?' he asked.

The birds said nothing, for they knew the eagle had the strongest voice of them all.

'Which one of you birds who fly by day and by night over the mountains and plains can fly as high as I?' the eagle then asked.

The little sparrow became impatient with the boastful eagle, and chirped. 'I, Eagle, I can fly higher than you!'

'You?' sneered the eagle in disbelief.

'I, Eagle.' And the sparrow fluffed up his feathers.

Next day the little sparrow and the huge eagle stood side by side. The eagle spread his wings, the birds gasped in admiration and no one noticed that the little sparrow had hopped onto the eagle's back.

The eagle flew up and up, higher than the highest mountain, and he called out in his eagle's voice. 'Where are you, Sparrow?'

'Here I am, Eagle,' a little voice chirped above him. The eagle was bewildered, but he flew even higher above the clouds, and called out again. 'Where are you, Sparrow?'

The sparrow clutched the eagle's feathers as firmly as he could and answered bravely. 'Here I am, Eagle.'

The eagle became angry. He circled round, then flew even higher. But his strength had gone and the proud eagle dropped from that dizzy height like a stone and was shattered on the rocks below.

And the fluffy, little sparrow flew away.

The Shining Fish, the Golden Sparrow and the Stone Lion

Once upon a time there was a poor boy whose name was Little Wang Siao. His father died when he was still very young and since that

once, but he was obedient and did what his mother told him. He went to the landlord's house with a basket of the choicest melons,

day he and his mother had lived alone. His mother worked hard to provide for her son and when Wang Siao grew older, he in turn worked hard to help his mother. He was a good son, kind and loving, as well as hard-working.

From morning till night, he tended their little piece of land, and that was why he had the best crops in the village. His melons, in particular, were bigger and juicier than anyone else's and people fought in the market to buy them.

One year, Wang had an especially fine crop of melons. When he had gathered them his mother picked out the very best and ripest and put them in a basket.

'Take these to our landlord, my son,' she said. 'You know that the first melons belong to him. Then we ourselves shall taste them before we take the rest to the market.'

Siao would have liked to taste his melons at

knocked on the gate and entered the courtyard.

The landlord was not at home, but his beautiful daughter was there. When she saw the fine melons, she wanted to taste one at once and she sent her servant to bring Siao to her.

Siao followed the servant into the beautiful garden behind the courtyard where no villager had stepped before. And Siao looked about him in wonder. Everywhere flowers bloomed, bushes blossomed and birds sang in the tree tops. Then along a path towards him came the most beautiful girl he had ever seen. At that moment Siao thought she must be a nymph such as he had heard of in fairy-tales. She was no nymph he quickly realized, but the landlord's daughter Ying Ying.

'Bring me one of those melons so that I may taste it,' she commanded her servant.

When Siao heard this he put his basket on the

146

ground and without hesitation picked up the most beautiful melon, broke it into four pieces and he himself offered one to the beautiful Ying Ying.

'How dare you, peasant,' the servant scolded. 'You will frighten our young lady!'

But Ying Ying only smiled. 'Leave him alone. Why should I be frightened? You had better ask him how much we owe him.'

Wang Siao protested that she owed him nothing. But Ying Ying insisted and the servant was ordered to bring him a silver coin. Siao had never before seen such a coin, but what pleased him more than the silver was Ying's lovely smile

From that day on Wang Siao thought of nothing but the landlord's beautiful daughter. He saw her before his eyes day and night, heard her voice and smelt her fragrance as if she were standing beside him. He walked as if in a dream, and neither ate nor drank nor slept. His mother became more and more worried about him. She urged him to tell her what was wrong. Finally he told her.

'Mother, I took the melons to our landlord,' he said. 'I saw his daughter, the beautiful Ying Ying. Since then I can think only of her. If she does not become my wife I shall die of love.'

His mother was startled. 'What has given you such an idea, my son?' she said. 'Who has ever heard of the daughter of a rich landlord marrying a poor man? Forget her and let me find you another bride.'

But Wang Siao would not hear of another bride. He continued to walk about like a shadow. He neither ate, drank or slept, until at last he became so ill he was forced to remain in bed. His mother convinced now that her son was indeed dying of love went to the landlord to ask on his behalf for the hand of his daughter.

The landlord could scarcely believe his ears. At first he was angry, then he started to laugh.

'All right,' he said. 'If that son of yours is so bold, tell him that I shall give him my daughter. But first he must bring her a shining fish and a golden sparrow as wedding gifts. Keep him out of my sight till then, or I will have his head.'

The mother ran home weeping and gave Siao the landlord's message. She thought that it would be the end of her son. But Siao jumped out of bed immediately and started to get ready for his journey.

'Do not worry, Mother,' he cried. 'If a shining fish and a golden sparrow exist anywhere in the world, I shall find them and bring them back to my beloved.'

Next morning Wang Siao said goodbye to his mother and set out into the world. He wandered from village to village, from town to town, until at last he learned from a blind beggar that the King of the Sea Dragons possessed a shining fish in his palace.

So Siao set out towards this palace in the sea. It was a long journey and when he arrived at the sea and saw the wide expanse of water, he sighed sadly.

'I have reached the sea, but how can I get to the palace of the King of the Sea Dragons? I shall just have to dry up the sea.'

Thereupon he took out his bowl and began to ladle the water into the sand. He worked for a whole day, then for a whole week, then for a whole month, until one day the guard of the Dragon King, the Great Crab, saw him.

He swam to the shore. 'Tell me, good man,' he said. 'Why are you taking the water out of our sea?'

Wang Siao answered. 'Because I want to dry it up, dear sir.'

The Great Crab started to laugh. 'Do you really think that you will dry up the sea with that little bowl of yours?'

But Wang Siao would not be put off. 'Why shouldn't I? If I work for a whole year or for ten years, I shall dry up your sea in the end.'

This answer frightened the Great Crab. What if this obstinate young man succeeded in the end, as he promised? Without delay he hurried to his master and told him what he had seen and heard. The King of the Sea Dragons was also alarmed.

'Let us offer him a present,' he said. 'Tell him he may have the shining fish if he will stop drying up our sea.'

'That would be best, mighty ruler,' said the Great Crab, bowing low. 'I shall go at once and make this offer.'

Wang Siao was overjoyed to have the shining fish he sought, and at once he stopped drying up the sea. He had the first wedding gift for Ying Ying. Now he must go in search of the other.

So once again he journeyed from village to village and from town to town, until at last he learned from a blind beggar that there was only one golden sparrow in the whole world. It nested at the top of a pine tree which grew on the highest peak of the highest mountain of the West.

Wang Siao set out westward, and after many months arrived at the western mountains.

Standing on the first ridge, he sighed sadly. 'I have reached the western mountains, but how I shall reach the golden sparrow I do not know. I shall have to climb these mountains one after another until I reach the highest peak.' And Siao began to climb.

He climbed for one day, he climbed for a week, he climbed for a month, until he reached the highest mountain. A pine tree grew there and at the top was a nest. But the nest was empty. Wang Siao, exhausted, sat down under the pine tree and fell asleep. Suddenly he was awakened by beautiful singing. A little golden bird, perched on a branch right above his head, was singing merrily. But as soon as Siao stretched out his hand, the golden sparrow spread its wings and flew off to another pine tree. Siao ran after it from tree to tree, from one mountain to another. He ran after it for a day, he ran after it for a week, he ran after it for a month. At last, the golden sparrow was too tired to go on.

It flew away from the mountains down to the valley and from the valley to a large town. At the gate of the town the sparrow's wings could take him no further and it hopped into the mouth of a large stone lion and tried to hide. Wang Siao, who had followed the sparrow all the way, put his hand into the lion's mouth. But alas for him, the golden sparrow was a magical bird and whatever it touched came to life.

The stone lion at once came to life, and as Siao put his hand into its mouth, the lion closed its jaws and Siao and the golden sparrow were trapped together. Wang Siao could not pull his hand out of the lion's mouth again.

Siao had found both wedding gifts for his beloved Ying Ying, but he could not give them to her. He had to stand there by the city gate, while good people took pity on him, give him food and sent messages to his mother and his bride.

His mother went straight away to see and weep over her son. But for a long time Ying Ying's father forbade her to visit Wang Siao. At last he relented when he learned that Siao had the shining fish and the golden sparrow. He did not want to lose such treasures.

And so it came about that Siao saw his bride at last. Beautiful Ying Ying wept over Wang.

'Poor Siao, you have had to suffer so much

for me,' she whispered. 'And now you may even die here because of me. I would give my life for you, if it could save you.'

The stone lion's heart was made of stone too, but when it saw such faithful love, it took pity on Siao and Ying Ying. The lion opened its mouth and Wang and the golden sparrow were free. Now there was nothing to stop him from going back to his village and making the beautiful Ying Ying his wife.

The landlord, her father, was not pleased, but in the end he had to accept the poor bridegroom. After all, his son-in-law was now richer than himself. Even the Emperor did not possess a shining fish and a golden sparrow.

And so everything ended happily, and Wang Siao, who grew the best melons in the district, married his beloved and faithful Ying Ying.

And they lived contentedly together for the rest of their lives.

How the Cat
and the Mouse
Danced Together

In the days when all the animals still lived together in one village, the spider once held a ball, and to this ball he invited, among others, his neighbours the cat and the mouse.

Everyone was delighted to accept the invitation because the spider was known to be an excellent musician. He could play beautifully on the fiddle and sing well too. When he began to play and sing everyone wanted to dance.

And so it was at the ball.

The spider played and sang, the guests made merry and danced as long as they had breath.

'Hey, hey, let us go on dancing for ever,' cried some of his guests.

'Enough, enough, let us stop now,' cried others.

But the spider did not listen to any of them and went on playing. The longer he played the livelier was his music. The longer he played the quicker was his music. At last no one could dance another step, no one except Neighbour Mouse and Neighbour Cat. They danced on and perhaps they would still be dancing today if the mouse's trousers had not fallen down. They slipped to the ground and the poor dancing mouse tripped and fell over.

When the animals saw this they laughed heartily.

Only the cat did not laugh. She was so angry that sparks flew from her whiskers.

'What a shameful thing to do to me!' she cried.

And she spread her claws and struck out at the mouse.

The poor mouse was frightened now as well as ashamed. When he saw the cat getting ready to attack him again, he took to his heels and fled down the nearest mousehole.

Ever since then cats have not danced and mice have lived in holes.

The Wolf
Who Wanted Boots

A farmer was one day ploughing his field. Suddenly an angry wolf appeared before him.

'I am going to eat you up,' he growled.

'Don't eat me, Wolf,' the farmer said, 'and I'll make it worth your while.'

'All right,' said the wolf. 'Tomorrow bring me two pairs of boots — one for Sundays and holidays, the other for weekdays, so that I won't always have to go barefoot.' He had long wanted to possess boots.

'As good as done,' the farmer promised him. 'You shall have them tomorrow morning.'

The next morning the farmer came to the field with a cart covered with a tarpaulin. The wolf was waiting for him.

'Where are my boots?' he burst out angrily. 'You promised to bring them and I can see no sign of them.'

The farmer replied. 'It's true, I have not brought them. But I've brought two cobblers with me to measure you for your boots. Just look in the cart!'

The wolf went up to the cart and lifted the tarpaulin. Out sprang two enormous dogs.

The wolf took to his heels, and in a few seconds had vanished into his lair. At least everything vanished except his feet. He had not been quick enough and now the dogs were hanging onto his feet as if they would never let go. The wolf set up a great wailing.

'Oh, my poor feet, my poor feet!' he cried. 'Take my tail, eat my tail but don't take my feet!' he begged.

The dogs would not let go, but dragged him right out of his lair.

And the farmer laughed. 'Cobblers don't measure tails!' he said.

It was a long time before the 'cobblers' stopped measuring the wolf's feet, and since that day the wolf has preferred to go barefoot.

Why the Spider Sits in the Corner Catching Flies

Once upon a time a spider had no money to pay his taxes. 'It will be quite easy for me to borrow some money,' he thought. And he set out for the village.

On the way, he met a mouse. 'Mouse, lend me a dollar,' he said. 'Tomorrow I shall pay it back.'

The mouse gave him the money. 'Here is a dollar,' he said. 'I shall come for it tomorrow.'

'Come, by all means,' said the spider, and hurried on until he met a cat.

'Cat, lend me a dollar,' he begged. 'Tomorrow I shall pay it back.'

And the cat, too, lent him a dollar. 'I shall come for it tomorrow,' he said.

'Come, by all means,' said the spider, and hurried on until he met a dog.

'Dog, lend me a dollar,' he begged. 'Tomorrow I shall pay it back.'

The dog, too, lent him a dollar. 'I shall come for it tomorrow,' he said.

'Come, by all means,' said the spider and hurried on until he met a tiger.

'Tiger, lend me a dollar,' he begged. 'Tomorrow I shall pay it back.'

The tiger, too, lent him a dollar. 'I shall come for it tomorrow,' he said.

'Come, by all means,' said the spider, and hurried on until he met a lion.

'Brother Lion,' he begged, 'lend me a dollar. I shall pay it back at midday tomorrow.'

And so the lion, too, lent him a dollar. 'I shall come for it tomorrow. I shall need it,' the lion added.

'Come, by all means,' said the spider, and hurried home with the five dollars. He was happy, for he had the money he needed. Then he began to plan how he would pay back the money. The whole afternoon he spent digging a deep pit behind his cottage.

At noon next day, the mouse knocked at the spider's door. The spider hurried to open it.

'Come in, Mouse, I shall give you your dollar at once!' cried the spider to the mouse.

He let the mouse in and started to chat. He chatted and chatted until there was a knock at the door. It was the cat.

'I'm coming,' said the spider. But before opening the door to the cat, he told the mouse to go into the back room. 'Hide there for a while,' the spider said. 'It would be a pity if the cat saw you!'

The mouse scuttled off to hide and the spider opened the door. 'Come in, Cat,' he said. 'I shall give you your dollar at once.'

He let the cat in and started to chat to her. He chatted and chatted until there was a knock at the door. It was the dog.

'I'm coming,' said the spider. But before he

opened the door to the dog, he let the cat into the back room. 'Hide there for a while,' the spider said. 'It would be a pity if the dog saw you.'

The cat, very frightened, ran into the back room to hide. But when she saw the mouse she forgot her fear of the dog. She pounced on the mouse and gobbled him up.

Meanwhile the spider opened the door to the dog. 'Come in, Dog!' he said. 'I shall give you your dollar at once.'

He let the dog in and started to chat with him. He chatted and chatted until there was a knock at the door. It was the tiger.

'I'm coming,' said the spider, but before he opened the door to the tiger, he let the dog into the back room. 'Hide there for a while,' the spider said. 'It would be a pity of the tiger saw you.'

The dog, very frightened, ran into the back room to hide. But when he saw the cat, he forgot his fear of the tiger. He sprang at the cat and killed her.

Meanwhile the spider opened the door to the tiger. 'Come in, Tiger!' he said. 'I shall give you your dollar at once.'

He let the tiger in and started to chat to him. He chatted and chatted until there was a knock at the door. It was the lion.

'I am coming,' said the spider. But before he opened the door to the lion, he let the tiger into the back room. 'Hide there for a little while,' the spider said. 'It would be a pity if the lion saw you here.'

The tiger, very frightened, ran into the back room to hide, but when he saw the dog, he forgot his fear of the lion. He sprang at the dog and killed him.

Meanwhile the spider opened the door to the lion. 'Come in, Lion!' he said. 'I shall give you your dollar at once. But first may I offer you a meal? In the back room dinner is waiting for you!'

The lion did not need to be asked twice. He went into the back room. When he saw the tiger there, he leapt at him and killed him. And a very good dinner he made.

Then the spider took the lion to the door. 'I shall give you your dollar in the yard,' he said.

The lion ran out at once. But he had scarcely taken a step when the ground gave way beneath him and he fell straight into the pit the spider had dug the day before.

And that was how the spider paid his debts. Since that time no one will lend him money — not even a penny. And there is nothing else for the spider to do but sit in the corner, weaving a web to catch flies.

The Jaguar and the Fire

Long, long ago the jaguar made friends with fire. Fire was then yellow and red, while jaguar had a coat as white as milk.

The jaguar would go, in his white coat, day after day to visit his friend the fire. He would sit down beside it, talk to it and then go home again. But the fire never went to visit the jaguar.

Once the jaguar asked. 'Why do you never come to see me? I come to you every day, but you have never yet visited me.'

The fire replied. 'You are right, but it is better that way.'

The jaguar was surprised. 'Why?' he asked.

So in the evening the fire set out to visit the jaguar. It went through the grass, it went through the undergrowth, it went through the woods, always moving forward. And wherever it

set foot everything was burned, wherever it passed nothing remained but ashes. It went on and on to the hut where the jaguar lived. When the jaguar saw it coming, he was afraid.

'Stop, friend fire,' he shouted. 'Go home again!'

But the fire kept coming on. 'Did I not tell you,' it said, 'that you would be afraid of me? Did I not tell you that if I came I would never go back?'

And it came right up to the door of the jaguar's hut.

In a few minutes the hut was in flames. The jaguar leapt out at the very last moment and escaped with his life, but a reminder of the visit of his friend, the fire, remained with him. The falling sparks left dark spots on his white coat which he has to this day.

And to this day he is so terrified of fire that he no longer looks on it as a friend, and no longer does he live in a hut.

And the fire asked. 'Will you not be afraid if I come?'

'Certainly not,' answered the jaguar.

'You had better think it over,' said the fire. 'If I do one day leave this place, I shall never return.' But the jaguar still insisted. 'Come!'

The Lion and the Three Bulls

Once upon a time there were three bulls who were friends. They went out together to graze, they went together to the river to drink and for many years they lived quietly and happily. Because of their great strength they were feared by all and left in peace.

Even the lion was afraid of them, much as he would have liked a taste of bull. One bull he could take on, but not all three together. For a long time he wondered how he could separate the three friends. At last he had an idea.

The next time the lion met the three bulls he greeted them respectfully, conversed with them politely and it was not long before all four of them had become firm friends. This was just what the lion had planned.

Early one morning, the lion stole up quietly to the oldest bull.

'Watch out for your younger friends,' he rumbled. 'Look how they're avoiding you. They must be plotting something against you. But don't be afraid, I'll be on your side.'

And the oldest of the bulls believed him.

Next day, the lion went to the youngest of the bulls with the same story.

'Watch out for your older friends! Look how they're avoiding you. They must be plotting something against you. But don't be afraid, I'll be on your side.'

And the youngest of the bulls believed him. So it was that the old friends were separated for good.

Each of them sought a different meadow and went to graze by himself.

After that the way was clear for the wily lion. He could easily settle with one bull at a time. And it was not long before all three bulls fell victim to his claws.

The Snake
and the Raven

A raven and his wife once built a nest in the branches of an old tree in the forest. But alas, when their baby ravens hatched out they were gobbled up by a snake who had made its lair at the foot of the tree. The first time this happened the ravens were full of grief, but the second time the raven's wife was ready to peck out the snake's eyes.

But the raven warned her. 'Do not forget that as well as eyes the snake has poisonous fangs. The only thing for us to do is to trick him. Just leave it to me and you will see!'

The raven's wife obeyed and left him to plan their revenge. The raven did not waste time.

He knew that the prince of the land came often to bathe in a nearby lake. Next day the prince arrived with his servants. The raven watched and waited as the prince undressed and took the gold chain from around his neck. Then the raven swooped down, and seizing the chain in his beak flew off.

The prince and his servants were at first struck dumb with surprise. Next moment the royal servants had set off in pursuit. They did not have to go far. At the foot of the raven's tree the bird opened his beak and dropped the chain into the snake's lair.

The servants were about to fling themselves upon it when they heard a violent hissing coming from the lair. Such hissing terrified the raven, but it did not worry the prince's servants. They found some sticks in the wood and returned to the lair where they beat the snake until it was dead. Then taking up the gold chain they went back to their master.

And from that day on the clever raven and his wife were left in peace to rear a whole flock of baby ravens in their nest in the old tree in the forest.

The Donkey,
the Dog,
the Mouse
and
the Naughty
Goat

Once upon a time an old woman was sweeping the path in front of her cottage when she found a penny.

'What shall I buy with this penny?' she

wondered. 'If I buy plums I shall have to throw away the stones. If I buy a carrot I shall have to throw away the leaves. If I buy some nuts I shall have to throw away the shells. I'll buy some flour and make a cake with it.'

And so the old woman bought some flour and baked herself a cake. She put the hot cake by the window to cool and went out again to the path in front of the cottage.

Hardly had the old woman gone out when a goat came running up from the meadow. When she smelt the cake she jumped through the open window into the room and gobbled up the cake.

A little later the old woman decided to cut herself a slice of the cake. But she could not get into the house. The goat was on the other side of the door and would not let her in. What could the poor old woman do? She sat down in the doorway and moaned and cried her heart out. While she was moaning and crying a donkey came by.

'Why are you crying your heart out, Granny?' he asked.

The old woman answered. 'Because the goat won't let me into my house.'

The donkey tried to soothe her. 'Don't cry, Granny,' he said. 'I'll chase the goat out.' And he went and knocked at the door.

'Who's there?' asked the goat from the other side of the door.

'The donkey,' came the reply. But the goat was not afraid of the donkey.

'And this is the goat!' she bleated fiercely. 'And I tell you I have two horns on my head. If you don't go away at once, I'll pierce you to the bone.'

The donkey took fright and fled. The poor

In a few moments a little mouse ran up. When he saw the old woman crying, he asked. 'Granny, why are you crying your heart out?'

The old woman answered. 'Because the goat won't let me into my house!'

'Don't cry, Granny, don't cry!' said the little mouse. 'I'll chase the goat out!'

'But how will you do it?' said the old woman. 'The donkey said he'd chase her out and he couldn't. The dog said he'd chase her out and he didn't. So how do you think you'll be able to?' But the mouse just went to the door and knocked.

'Who's there?' called the goat from the other side of the door.

'The mouse,' the little mouse said. But the goat wasn't afraid of the mouse.

'And this is the goat,' she bleated fiercely. 'And I must tell you, I have two horns on my head and if you don't go away at once, I'll pierce you to the bone.'

But the little mouse knew how to frighten people. 'And this is the mouse,' he shouted threateningly. 'If you don't go away at once, I'll lose my temper and scratch your eyes out!'

When the goat heard this she was really frightened. Next moment she had jumped out of the window and was off. The mouse and the old woman went into the house together and from that day on they lived together very happily.

old woman sat down again in the doorway and moaned and cried her heart out. In a few moments a dog ran up.

When he saw the old woman crying, he asked. 'Granny, why are you crying your heart out?'

The old woman answered. 'Because the goat won't let me into my house.'

The dog tried to soothe her. 'Don't cry, Granny,' he said. 'I'll chase the goat out!' And he went and knocked at the door.

'Who's there?' asked the goat from the other side of the door.

'The dog,' came the reply. But the goat wasn't afraid of the dog.

'And this is the goat,' she bleated fiercely. 'And I tell you I have two horns on my head and if you don't go away at once, I'll pierce you to the bone.'

The dog took fright and fled. The poor old woman sat down again in the doorway and moaned and cried her heart out.

159

The Cock
Sparrow
and
the Worm

Once upon a time there lived a tiny cock sparrow. He had a nest under the eaves of the barn and there he lived with his wife and his seven sons.

The poor little cock sparrow had more than enough to do to feed his big family. He flew backwards and forwards all day long, and it was a wonder his wings did not fly off. But he could never get enough food for them all and his wife complained every day that he brought home so little. All the same she and the children were as round as little balloons while the poor cock sparrow was as tiny as a wren.

One day he had had enough of her constant complaints. He said. 'If you think, my dear wife, that I bring home too little, go yourself for a change. Tomorrow I'll stay at home and you can go and look for food.'

The hen sparrow preened her feathers. 'Yes, I'll go,' she said, 'and then we'll see who brings home the most.'

The next morning, the hen sparrow flew out of the nest as soon as dawn broke. She wanted something for breakfast, and she was in luck. In the garden, by the house, she saw a large worm. Half of it was out of the ground, the other half was still buried. If the hen sparrow could pull it out they would have enough food for the whole day.

'Won't the cock sparrow be surprised when I bring it home?' she thought.

She at once fell upon the worm and started to pull. She pulled and she pulled with all her strength, but she could not pull the worm out of the ground. There was nothing for it but to go for help. Breathlessly she flew to the nest and quietly woke up her eldest son.

'Get up, quickly,' she chirped. 'You must help me. There is a very big worm in the garden, and

I can't pull it out by myself. But don't wake your father whatever you do.'

The oldest of the little cock sparrows got up and flew after his mother to the garden. His mother caught hold of the worm and the oldest little cock sparrow caught hold of his mother and they started to pull. They pulled and they pulled with all their strength, but they could not pull the worm out of the ground.

There was nothing for it but to go for help. Quite breathless, the oldest little cock sparrow flew to the nest and quietly woke up his younger brother.

'Get up quickly. You must help us,' he chirped. 'There's a very big worm in the garden, and we can't pull it out of the ground by ourselves. But don't wake father whatever you do.'

The second little cock sparrow got up and flew with his older brother to the garden. Now there were three of them. The mother bird caught hold of the worm, the first little cock sparrow caught hold of his mother and the second little cock sparrow caught hold of the first, and they started to pull. They pulled and they pulled with all their strength, but they could not pull the worm out of the ground.

There was nothing for it but to go for help. Quite breathless, the second little cock sparrow flew to the nest and quietly woke up his younger brother.

'Get up quickly. You must help us,' he chirped. 'There's a very big worm in the garden, and we can't pull it out of the ground by ourselves. But don't wake father whatever you do!'

The third little cock sparrow got up and flew with the second one to the garden. Now there were four of them. The mother bird caught hold of the worm, the first little cock sparrow caught hold of his mother, the second of the first, and the third of the second and they started to pull. They pulled and they pulled with all their strength, but they could not pull the worm out of the ground.

There was nothing for it but to go for help. Quite breathless, the third little cock sparrow flew to the nest and quietly woke up his younger brother.

'Get up quickly,' he chirped. 'You must help us. There's a very big worm in the garden, and we can't pull it out of the ground by ourselves. But don't wake father whatever you do!'

The fourth little cock sparrow got up and flew with the third to the garden. Now there were five of them. The mother bird caught hold of the worm, the first little cock sparrow caught hold of his mother, the second of the first, the third of the second, the fourth of the third and they started to pull. They pulled and they pulled with all their strength, but they could not pull the worm out of the ground.

There was nothing for it but to go for help. Quite breathless, the fourth little cock sparrow

flew to the nest and quietly woke up his younger brother.

'Get up, quickly,' he chirped. 'You must help us. There's a very big worm in the garden, and we can't pull it out of the ground by ourselves. But don't wake father whatever you do!'

flew to the nest and quietly woke up the last little brother.

'Get up, quickly,' he chirped. 'You must help us. There's a very big worm in the garden, and we can't pull it out by ourselves. But don't wake father up whatever you do!'

The seventh little cock sparrow got up and flew with the sixth to the garden. Now there were eight of them. The mother bird caught hold of the worm, the first little cock sparrow caught hold of his mother, the second of the first, the third of the second, the fourth of the third, the fifth of the fourth, the sixth of the fifth and the seventh of the sixth, and they started to pull. They pulled and they pulled with all their might, but they could not pull the worm out of the ground.

Whatever were they to do now? At home in the nest there was now only father cock sparrow himself. But before they had time to think whether they should go for him or not, the cock sparrow was with them.

He looked at the worm and said. 'Let me have a look. I'll try by myself!'

He caught hold of the worm firmly, close to the ground, and with one jerk he pulled the whole worm out. It was such a big worm that there was enough to feed them for the whole day. But this time the biggest portion went to father cock sparrow himself.

All the family had to admit that he was by far the strongest, even if he did look like a wren, while all the rest were as round as little balloons.

The fifth little cock sparrow got up and flew with the fourth to the garden. Now there were six of them. The mother bird caught hold of the worm, the first little cock sparrow caught hold of his mother, the second of the first, the third of the second, the fourth of the third, the fifth of the fourth, and they started to pull. They pulled and they pulled with all their strength, but they could not pull the worm out of the ground.

There was nothing for it but to go for help. Quite breathless, the fifth little cock sparrow flew to the nest and quietly woke up his younger brother.

'Get up, quickly,' he chirped. 'You must help us! There's a very big worm in the garden, and we can't pull it out of the ground. But don't wake father whatever you do!'

The sixth little cock sparrow got up and flew with the fifth to the garden. Now there were seven of them. The mother bird caught hold of the worm, the first little cock sparrow caught hold of his mother, the second of the first, the third of the second, the fourth of the third, the fifth of the fourth, the sixth of the fifth and they started to pull. They pulled and they pulled with all their might, but they could not pull the worm out of the ground.

There was nothing for it but to go for help. Quite breathless, the sixth little cock sparrow

Brother Rabbit and the Wild Cat

Once upon a time a rabbit went for a walk in the woods. Suddenly something jumped on him from behind. The attack was so unexpected that Brother Rabbit nearly died of fright. Perched on his back was a wild cat. He had been lying in wait for wild turkeys, but when none had come his way he thought he would make do with a rabbit.

Brother Rabbit knew he was in great danger. 'What are you doing, Brother Cat?' he asked. 'Surely you do not want to eat me!'

The cat replied. 'Of course I do. I have been waiting in vain all day for wild turkeys and now I am hungry.'

Brother Rabbit shook his head. 'I would not make a very good meal for you, Cat,' he said. 'But if you like I will help you to catch those turkeys. But you must let me go free and do just what I tell you.'

The cat preferred to eat turkeys, so he let himself be persuaded, and he set the rabbit free.

'Lie down on the path and pretend to be dead,' said the rabbit. 'Do not move until the turkeys are within reach of your claws. Otherwise the plan will fail.'

The cat did what the rabbit told him and lay down across the path and pretended to be dead.

In the meantime, Brother Rabbit hid in the undergrowth and began to cheep like a turkey chick. He did it so well that very soon he had attracted a whole flock of inquisitive turkeys. From every corner of the forest they came running.

But when they saw the cat lying across the path, they were puzzled.

'There's a cat lying there, and he's dead,' gobbled one turkey.

'It is a cat, but he is not dead. He is only pretending to be dead,' gobbled another.

'He is dead!' gobbled a third.

'He's not, he's not!' declared a fourth.

And soon the noise of squabbling turkeys could be heard for miles.

The cat listened for a time without moving, but at last he could keep still no longer. The hubbub was deafening, and he was getting hungrier and hungrier. When one of the turkeys came a little closer, he pounced. But the turkey was not close enough. It flapped its wings and flew to the top of the nearest tree far out of the cat's reach.

The other turkeys flew off too. And Brother Rabbit, watching from the undergrowth, laughed. Then he too took to his heels and vanished like the turkeys.

So the cat remained hungry. He had freed the rabbit and had not caught a turkey.

'But it was his own fault,' Brother Rabbit always said. 'If he had waited and gone on pretending to be dead a little longer, he might have caught all the turkeys.'

And he would laugh when he remembered how he had tricked the wild cat.

163

How the Cock Became a Domestic Bird

When the world was still young and everything was different, all the birds lived together in one village on the slopes of a high mountain. They went hunting together, they worked together in the fields and in the evening they sang and danced together round a great fire.

It happened, one night, that they danced so long and so late that they forgot about the fire. When they woke up in the morning the fire was out; not even a glowing ember remained.

The birds started to lament. 'Who is going to light our fire?' they wailed.

The brave cock, Cockadoodle, chieftain of the birds, promised the others that he would help them; he would bring them a new fire. Without delay, he spread his strong wings and flew off in search of fire. He flew on and on without resting. For two days he flew until he reached the seashore.

On the shore stood a house, and inside, by the fire, sat a beautiful girl with black hair and eyes like stars. The cock, Cockadoodle, flew up to her.

When the girl with eyes like stars saw her guest, she thought she had never seen anyone so handsome. She gave him a warm welcome and asked him to stay with her. She told him she lived quite alone and would like him for her husband.

But the cock, Cockadoodle, had no wish to be married. He thought only of his promise to take a new fire to his friends. He seized a burning branch from the fire and without a word flew off with it into the air.

When the girl with eyes like stars saw this, she cried after him. 'At least tell me where I shall find you!'

'You will find me far away in a village on a mountainside, where all the birds live and work and sing and dance,' cried the cock, as he disappeared into the distance. The girl with eyes like stars was again all alone.

When her parents came home in the evening, she cried so bitterly and begged so earnestly that they find the handsome cock, that at last they agreed.

As soon as it was light, all three set out to look for the cock, Cockadoodle. They went by boat, taking with them some coconuts on the voyage. All day they rowed and all night, until suddenly the girl heard a far-off sound.

'Stop, I can hear the birds,' she cried.

'That is not the sound of birds. It is only children playing,' replied her parents, and rowed on.

They rowed all day and all night, until the girl again cried out. 'Stop, I can hear the birds!'

And this time she was right. On the slopes of a high mountain was a village, and in the middle of the village a big fire was burning and round

that fire the birds were dancing and singing. Every bird was beautiful, but which of them was the cock, Cockadoodle, the girl could not tell in the light of the fire. She would have to wait till morning.

When morning broke, a cold wind blew down from the mountain, the stars went out and the birds began to wake up and come out of their shelters. The first to appear was a hornbill.

'Is that your sweetheart?' the father asked the girl with eyes like stars.

'No, it is not. My sweetheart is even more beautiful,' said the girl.

The next to come out was a parrot. 'So that is the one,' said the father.

'No, it is not. My sweetheart is even more beautiful,' said the girl.

The third to appear was a bird of paradise. 'So this must be the one,' said the father.

'No, it is not,' answered the girl. 'My sweetheart is even more beautiful.'

At last the cock, Cockadoodle, chieftain of the birds, came out of his shelter.

'That is the one,' cried the girl, taking the coconuts out of the boat. And she called. 'Come and look, my Lord and Master, what I have brought for you!'

'I shall not come,' replied the cock, Cockadoodle, proudly, because he was a chieftain and did not obey anyone. 'You may bring it here to me.'

'I should like to,' said the girl with eyes like stars, 'but I cannot. It is too heavy and there is too much of it. You are so strong that you could easily carry it from the boat by yourself.'

The cock, Cockadoodle, was curious to see what the girl had brought him. And he was also proud and pleased that the girl thought him so strong. He went to the river, stepped into the boat and looked around him. The boat was full of coconuts.

But alas, before he could carry one of them to the bank, a net was thrown over his head and he was caught.

The father and mother sat down at the oars and the boat shot away like an arrow. In three days and three nights they were home in their cottage by the sea. And since that time the cock has lived among people.

Without their chieftain, the birds of the village dispersed. The hornbill flew off to a hollow tree, the quail found a new home in the grass, the lapwing settled on the water.

Each bird found its own place and soon not a trace remained of the birds' village on the mountainside.

The Lion, the Mosquito and the Spider

'Why should the lion be proud of his strength,' the mosquito said to himself one day. 'I am stronger and I am bolder,' he buzzed. And he flew to the lion to challenge him to a duel.

At first the lion took no notice, but the mosquito was persistent.

'Do not be a coward, Lion. Come and measure your strength against mine,' he said.

'All right, Mosquito,' the lion roared, 'but it will be the end of you.' And he lashed out so hard with his paw that it would have killed a bull. But it did not kill the mosquito who dodged quickly and stung the lion on his nose. The lion lashed out again, but again it was in vain. The mosquito dodged and stung the lion on the eyelid.

The duel went on for a long time, with the lion roaring and lashing out with his paws and the mosquito buzzing and stinging, first in one place, then in another. In the end the lion could go on no longer. His nose and eyes were swollen, he could hardly see and scarcely breathe.

'Stop, Mosquito!' he begged. 'I cannot bear any more pain.'

The mosquito was satisfied. 'You see, Lion, I *am* stronger. You ask for peace and you shall have it.' And, very pleased with himself, he flew off to tell all the animals how he had defeated the lion.

But the mosquito was not looking where he was going. He did not see the fine web the spider had spun among the trees.

Next moment he was caught. He had defeated the lion, but was unable to free himself from the spider's web. The more he struggled the more he became entangled in it. And so it came about that the victorious mosquito was defeated by a little spider.

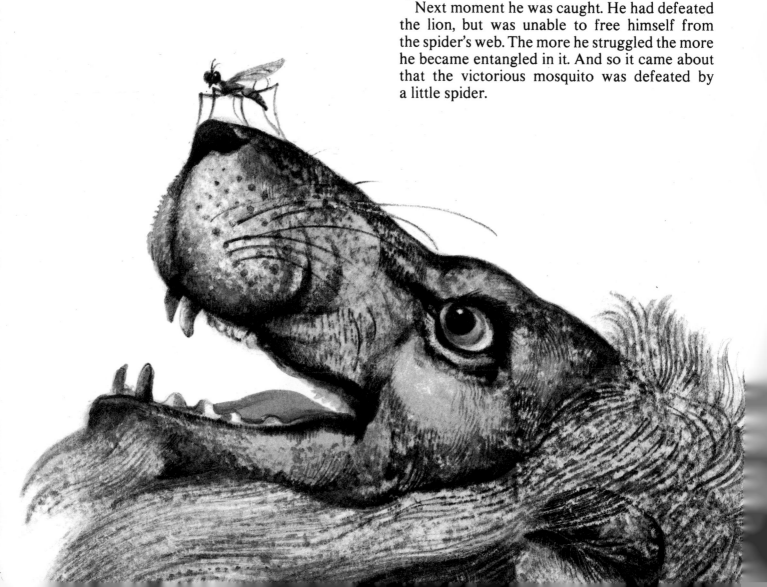

The Hoopoe Bird and the Cuckoo

Long ago the cuckoo wore a crest on her head. It was so beautiful that she looked like a princess wearing a crown. Now and then someone would borrow the cuckoo's crest to go to a wedding, a banquet or a ball, and the cuckoo would lend it to all of them with pleasure.

One day the hoopoe was going to a wedding. He was to be best man to his friend, the lark. The hoopoe was looking forward to the wedding, as he put on his best feathers and polished his long beak. But he could not decide what to wear on his head. Then he remembered the cuckoo, and went to her to ask if she would lend him her crest.

'With pleasure,' said the cuckoo, 'but you must bring it back tomorrow.'

'Of course I will,' promised the hoopoe. He put the crest on his head and went off to the wedding.

At the wedding, everyone admired him. 'What a beautiful crest you have,' they said. 'Where did you get it?'

And the hoopoe bird replied boastfully. 'It was given to me by King Solomon because I advise him well!'

'You are the adviser of King Solomon?' they all cried. And the birds admired the hoopoe still more.

The next day the wedding was over and also the hoopoe's day of glory. The time had come to give the crest back to the cuckoo. But the hoopoe was not willing to return it.

'It suits me better than it suits the cuckoo,' he said. 'And what would the birds say now if they saw me without it? What would King Solomon say?'

And so he did not give back the crest. The cuckoo waited one day and then two days, but on the third day she went to the hoopoe.

'Hoopoe, give me my crest!' she said.

'What crest?' snapped the hoopoe bird.

'The one you have on your head!' said the cuckoo.

'You want my crest, do you? I was given it by King Solomon!' cried the hoopoe. 'Just ask any of my neighbours!'

And the neighbours repeated what the hoopoe had told them. They even swore in court that the hoopoe had been given it by King Solomon in return for his good advice.

Mournfully, the poor cuckoo left the court and went into the forest to search for the treacherous hoopoe.

'Hoopoe, hoopoe,' she called. And the sound echoed from tree to tree.

She is still calling to this day. And although people say she calls 'Cuckooo', listen again when you go into the woods. You will hear that she is not calling 'cuckoo, cuckoo,' but 'hoopoe, hoopoe!'

And why else would the hoopoe bird always hide in a hollow tree?

How the Fox and the Rabbit Went Fishing

The fox and the rabbit were once friends. But that was long, long ago when the rabbit still had little ears and a long, shaggy tail.

One day, Brother Rabbit said to the fox. 'You know, Fox, I should like to go fishing.'

'Fishing? That's a good idea,' said the fox. 'I should enjoy nice baked trout for supper.'

'But we do not have a rod and line,' said the rabbit.

'That is no problem,' said the fox. 'Just try catching fish with your tail. You have a nice, long shaggy tail, the fish will bite it and you will just have to give it a twitch and the fish will be on the bank.'

'That is a good idea,' the rabbit nodded his head. 'But why will you not fish with your tail, Fox?'

'I could try, Rabbit,' said the fox, 'but mine is not as long, and shaggy as yours. You will be a much better fisherman.'

The rabbit was pleased that the fox had praised his tail, and he went with the fox to the river. He dropped his fine tail into the water and waited for a fish to bite. And the fox gazed into the water and waited to see what would happen next.

Suddenly the rabbit felt something catch hold of his tail. He said to the fox. 'Fox, look and see what is holding onto my tail. It is probably a large carp, for it nearly pulled me down into the water.'

The fox looked. 'Goodness me, brother, that is not so good,' he said. 'It is an old turtle. She will pull you down into the water and you will drown!'

It was true. The old turtle held the rabbit firmly by the tail and was pulling him down with all her strength into the river.

'Help!' cried the rabbit. 'Hold on to me, Fox, and pull. Otherwise the turtle will drown me!'

The fox grabbed the rabbit by the ears and pulled and pulled, until he nearly pulled his ears off. Ever since then the rabbit has had long ears.

In the end the fox pulled the rabbit away from the turtle, but almost the whole of the rabbit's tail stayed in the turtle's mouth. And that is why today the rabbit has a tiny little tail.

The Mosquito
and
the Earwig

The earwig and the mosquito were friends, but they were both very poor.

One day the earwig came to the mosquito and said. 'Come, Mosquito, let's go to the forest and gather coconuts. We'll make some fine oil from them, sell it at the market and earn money. Then we shan't be quite so poor.'

'That's a good idea, Earwig,' the mosquito agreed readily. And so the mosquito and the earwig set out together for the forest. When they came to the first palm tree, the mosquito said to the earwig. 'Come on, Earwig, climb this palm and throw the nuts down to me!'

But the earwig did not want to. 'You climb. I'll stay down here and pick up the nuts.'

The poor mosquito did not yet know what his friend, the earwig, had planned for him.

'All right,' agreed the mosquito. And he climbed the palm tree and started to throw down the coconuts.

But the earwig just sat at the foot of the tree and did not pick up the nuts.

When the mosquito came down from the palm tree, all the coconuts still lay on the ground.

'Pick them up yourself,' said the earwig to the mosquito. 'I'll carry them home.'

'Good,' agreed the mosquito, and gathered all the coconuts into a basket. But when the basket was filled, the earwig still did not want to work.

'You carry them home yourself,' he told the mosquito. 'I'll make them into oil!'

'Very well,' agreed the mosquito. He put the basket of coconuts on his head and carried it home. But when he got home and put them on the ground, the earwig again did not want to work.

'You make the oil yourself,' he told the mosquito. 'Then I'll take it to market and sell it.'

'Very well,' agreed the mosquito. And he cooked the nuts, pressed out the oil and poured it into an earthenware pot.

Afterwards he felt tired and lay down to rest.

He thought that the earwig would again refuse to work, and that he himself would have to take the oil to market in the morning.

But this time the earwig was not lazy. Before the mosquito awoke, the earwig rose, took the earthenware pot full of oil and hurried to the market in the town. There he sold the oil for a good price and set off home again with the money.

But he did not want to share the money with the mosquito.

He was almost home when he saw the mosquito coming to meet him.

'Where's my money, Earwig?' the mosquito called. 'How much did you get at the market?'

The earwig pretended not to hear and walked past the mosquito. His friend ran after him shouting. 'Earwig! Surely you don't want to rob me of what I've earned by all my work?'

But the earwig hurried on, looking for somewhere to hide. And because he could not find any other shelter, he crept quietly into the ear of a little boy who was lying asleep by the path.

The mosquito did not give up. He flew to the sleeping boy and began to buzz round his ear, shouting angrily. 'I'll find you, you robber. I'll find you, you good for nothing!' And he squeezed his way into the boy's ear where the earwig was sitting quietly with his money.

If the mosquito had not shouted and buzzed so much, perhaps he would have been able to pull the robber earwig out of the boy's ear and get the money he had earned.

But he buzzed and shouted so loudly that the boy woke up and began to flap his hand wildly about his head. The poor mosquito was forced to flee, still buzzing angrily. And so it was that he never got his share of the money.

He never forgot or forgave the earwig for tricking him.

To this day he flies round people's ears. To this day he buzzes angrily as he searches for the earwig who stole from him. And to this day the earwig hides in people's ears.

The Spider and the Bananas

Once upon a time a spider set out on a journey into the world. He wanted to be wiser than all other living creatures. He took with him a big jug with a lid. Into this jug he threw everything wise he heard in the world.

'When I get home with this treasure,' he said to himself, 'no one will be my equal in wisdom.'

But as he travelled through the world, the jug on his back became heavier and heavier each day. In the end it was so heavy that the spider could not even raise his head.

One day, tired and thirsty, he came to a pool. 'I shall rest here and drink from the pool,' said the spider, and bent down to the water. And in the water he saw, to his surprise, beautiful yellow bananas.

'Now, I shall eat as well as drink,' he said. And wasting no time, he slipped with the precious jug on his back, into the water.

But search as he might he could not find the bananas. He crawled sadly out of the pool, saying. 'Well, at least I shall drink.'

But as he bent down to the water for a second time, he saw the bananas again. He grew cheerful again. 'I will eat after all,' he said, and went into the water for a second time. But again he could find no bananas in the pool. He crawled out, and consoled himself by saying. 'Well, at least I shall have a drink.'

But as he bent down to the water and started to drink, he saw the bananas for a third time. 'Now they really are mine,' he said happily, and

jumped into the water once more. But again it was in vain. When he crawled out of the water for a third time — still hungry — he heard someone laugh. On the opposite side of the pool some monkeys were watching him. They called.

'Whatever are you doing, Spider?'

The spider said. 'I am searching for the beautiful yellow bananas I see in the water, but I cannot find them.'

The monkeys laughed all the more and cried. 'Try raising your head and looking above you!'

The spider wanted to raise his head but he could not, thanks to the heavy jug full of all the wisdom in the world. There was nothing for it but to throw it from his shoulders. And when at last he raised his head and looked up, he saw a palm tree covered in bananas. It was their reflection he had seen in the water.

The spider was angry. 'I have collected wisdom from all over the world; I have a jug full of it, but of what use is it to me? I am less wise than the monkeys.'

And he picked up the jug, struck it on a stone and the wisdom of the world spilled out in all directions.

And so the spider who had searched the world for wisdom learned that it cannot be bought or found, and that everyone must have it in his own head. And above all, he learned that everyone should first look up before diving into the water for bananas.

The Blackbird and His Yellow Beak

Once long ago when the blackbird was still as white as snow, he watched a jackdaw hiding a gold ring in a hollow tree.

The blackbird was amazed. 'Where did you get it?' he asked. 'I should like to have a ring like that.'

The jackdaw replied. 'You would have to go into the depths of the earth to the king of hidden treasure. If you like I will show you the way to him.'

And he took the blackbird to a cave hidden in the mountains. 'Here it is,' he said. 'When you go inside, you will come first to a chamber full of objects made of pure copper, then to a chamber full of pure silver and finally to a chamber full of pure gold. But you must not touch anything. Go on to the fourth chamber where, sitting on a diamond throne, is the king of hidden treasure. When you ask him he will give you what you want. But if you touch anything without his permission, it will be the worse for you.'

The blackbird thanked him and boldly flew into the cave. Everything was as the jackdaw had said. The first chamber was full of beautiful things made of red copper, the second full of treasures of white silver and in the third, everything was of glittering yellow gold.

In the first chamber, the blackbird only looked about him, in the second he stopped for a little while, but in the third he could not hold back, and he dipped his beak into the gold sand with which the floor was scattered. He wanted to take just a little of it back to his nest.

But scarcely had the blackbird touched the gold sand when one of the guardians of the hidden treasure leapt up with a rattling sound. Flames shot from his eyes and smoke from his mouth.

The blackbird narrowly escaped from his claws. But a reminder stayed with him for the rest of his life. His white feathers were blackened by the flames and smoke and have remained black to this day.

And to this day his beak has remained yellow where he dipped it into the gold sand in that chamber of the king of hidden treasure.

Why
the Toad's Skin
is Full of Cracks

Once upon a time when all the animals still lived together in one place, the Good Spirit arranged a celebration in heaven and invited all the animals who were good musicians.

Among others, he invited the rook who played beautifullly on his lute. But he forgot to ask the toad, although he was a fine drummer. The disappointed toad hurried to the rook and said.

'Rook, take me with you up to heaven to the celebration. I want to play my drum.'

But the rook would not listen. 'You are much too heavy, Toad,' he said. 'I could not carry you. Besides you have not been invited.' But these were only excuses. The rook did not want the

toad to drown the sound of his lute with his drumming.

When the toad realized that the rook could not be persuaded to take him to heaven, he said no more. He waited for the rook to leave his nest, then he crept into his lute.

The rook came back and flew off to heaven. On his back he carried his lute which, to his surprise, seemed to become heavier and heavier, the higher he flew. It was not till he reached heaven that the rook found out the reason.

'Thank you, Rook, for bringing me here,' laughed the toad, as he scrambled out of the lute and started to beat gaily on his drum.

The rook was angry, but he kept his anger to

himself. All he said was. 'Just wait, Toad, until you want to get home.'

When the celebrations were over, the toad did begin to worry about how he was going to get back to earth. But there came a moment when the rook was not looking. Again the toad squeezed himself into the lute and waited.

At last the rook put the lute on his back, spread his wings and slowly floated down to earth. But he did not go all the way down. In the clouds he took the lute from his back, turned it over and shook out the toad.

'Who has the last laugh now,' he cried.

Indeed the toad did not feel like laughing. He fell, and as he fell, he dried loudly. 'Stones, stones! Get out of my way, or else I shall be killed.'

But stones are deaf, they could not hear his plea and did not get out of the way. And the toad landed on the stones with such force that the skin split and cracked all over his body.

And to this day the toad has had a wrinkled skin, and no longer is he the best drummer among all animals.

But neither does the rook play his lute. For when he took it off his back in the clouds to shake out the toad, it slipped through his claws and fell to the earth. It broke into a thousand pieces and today the rook still searches for these pieces. He hops across the fields and meadows, pecking at the ground, calling, 'Caw . . . caw . . . caw . . .'

The Pig and the Elephant

A pig wanted to grow bigger so he went to the elephant for advice.

'Tell me, Elephant,' he said, 'what do you eat that makes you so big? I too want to be big.'

'I will not tell you what I eat,' replied the elephant. 'But as a favour, I shall bring you a few fresh leaves every day, and you will see how big you will grow.'

That same evening, the elephant brought the pig a bundle of fresh leaves. And every day, as he had promised, he continued to bring him the leaves. The pig always ate them with relish and in a short time he did begin to grow bigger.

'Soon I shall be as big as the elephant,' said the delighted pig. 'Very soon I shall be bigger than all these lesser creatures running about in the world,' he said proudly. And he stopped talking to the other animals. He went through the woods and the undergrowth, stamping, snorting and snuffling, as if he really was an elephant, and he was pleased when all the other animals took fright and ran away.

One evening, the elephant himself heard the stamping and snorting. He was very surprised. 'Who is there,' he cried, 'stamping and snorting in the undergrowth?'

The pig did not recognize the elephant. 'It is I,' he grunted. 'An animal bigger than an elephant!'

The elephant was even more surprised, 'Oho!' he said. 'Such an animal I have never seen in my life! You must be worth looking at!'

And he trotted into the undergrowth. But

what did he see there but the pig wallowing in a puddle of water.

'Oh, it is you, is it?' said the elephant, still more surprised. 'I bring you leaves so that you will grow a bit bigger, and you are already boasting that you are bigger than I am and threatening all the other animals. As a punishment I shall bring you no more leaves and you will stay as you are.'

And so the pig did not grow any bigger. It is true he has eyes, ears, a snout and teeth rather like those of an elephant, but otherwise he is small. And he will always remain small, however much he eats and however much he snorts and stamps.

The Three Fishes

In a fishpond there once were three fishes. They had lived there happily for a long, long time. Then one day three fishermen came to the pond.

'Tomorrow we shall fish in this pond,' they said to each other.

The fish were frightened. One fish said wisely. 'What we can do today we must not put off till tomorrow.' And straightaway it made for an outlet in the fishpond and swam into the stream, and safety.

The second fish was more easy going. 'There's plenty of time before morning,' it said, and went on swimming in the pond. When morning came, it swam to the outlet. But the hole had been blocked with a net.

There was nothing for it but to think of another plan. It floated to the surface, tummy uppermost, pretending to be dead. One of the fishermen picked it up and threw it onto the bank.

The fish gave a wriggle, jumped into the stream and swam off.

The third fish was still more easy going. 'What will be, will be,' it thought, and it did not worry, even when the fishermen put a net in the water. But when he felt the net being drawn in, the fish was frightened. It swam like lightning from one end of the net to the other, trying to break through. But the net was strong and there were no holes in it.

Then, too late, the fish was sorry it had not tried to save itself.

It was not long before the fishermen had caught and killed it. And next day it was sold at the market.

The Frog
from Osaka
and
the Frog
from Kyoto

Once upon a time there were two frogs who lived in Japan. One had his home in a ditch in the port of Osaka, the other in a stream in the imperial capital, Kyoto. The Osaka frog decided he wanted to see Kyoto, and the Kyoto frog wanted to see Osaka. So one day, early in the morning, they set out at exactly the same time.

Half way between the two towns, in the middle of a desert, there was a high hill. The frogs struggled hard to climb its steep slopes and it took a long time for them to reach the top.

On the summit at last, the two frogs met. At first they stared at each other in amazement. Then they greeted each other and began to talk.

They told each other where they were going and were amazed that they both had had the same wish.

When they had rested and it was time for them to continue their journeys, one of the frogs sighed.

'What a pity we are not like other animals,' he said. 'If we were bigger, we would be able to see from the top of this hill just where we were going. At least we would know if it was worth the effort.'

'But that can easily be solved,' said the other frog wisely. 'If we stand face to face propping ourselves up against each other with our front legs we shall be able to see just where we are going.'

And the frogs tried.

They stood on their broad hind feet, holding on to each other with their front paws so that they would not fall, and they stretched up their heads as high as they could.

They each looked at the towns that lay in the distance. But the frogs had forgotten that like all frogs, their eyes were on top of their heads. So when they stretched up their heads, both of them were looking backwards at the town they had come from.

'What do I see?' cried the frog from Osaka in amazement. 'Kyoto looks exactly like Osaka. I might as well save myself the journey.'

'And indeed Osaka looks just like Kyoto,' cried the frog from Kyoto.

For a long time they stood face to face, holding on to each other, amazed at how similar were Kyoto and Osaka.

And when they had gazed enough, they let go of each other, bowed respectfully, wished each other a pleasant journey and set off for home.

To the very end of their lives they were both firmly convinced that Osaka and Kyoto were as alike as two peas in a pod, although in fact the very opposite is true.

The Hyena and the Lion

A hyena was once hungry, so hungry that he could scarcely walk for weakness. But he did not dare go hunting by himself.

He went to the den where the lion was resting and said. 'They say you are the strongest of all the animals, but I am even stronger.'

'We shall see,' growled the lion. 'Come, show me your strength as a hunter. We will go and hunt gazelles.'

And so they went off hunting, the lion in front, the hyena following. When they caught up with a herd of gazelles, the lion jumped on the biggest and killed it.

The hyena only dared to go for the smallest, but he could not even catch that. When he sprang after it, the gazelle shook itself and ran off.

After the hunt, the lion asked. 'Where is your gazelle, Hyena?'

The hyena made excuses for himself saying, 'They were afraid of me and fled before I could spring on any of them.'

'All right,' growled the lion, 'come and share mine with me.'

They ate the gazelle the lion had killed. Then the lion said. 'Now we shall hunt zebras.'

They went into the undergrowth — first the lion, the hyena following. When they came upon a herd of zebras, the lion jumped on the biggest and killed it.

The hyena could not even catch the smallest. When he sprang at it, the zebra took fright and was off.

The lion was surprised. 'Where is your zebra, Hyena?' he asked later.

The hyena again made excuses for himself. 'They were afraid of me,' he said, 'and they fled before I could spring on them.'

'All right,' growled the lion, 'come and share mine with me.'

They ate the zebra the lion had killed. Then the lion decided that they would hunt buffalo.

They went into the undergrowth — first the lion, the hyena following as before. When they came on a herd of buffalo, the lion leapt on the biggest and killed it.

The hyena, however, could not even kill a buffalo calf. When he leapt on it, the calf took fright and was off.

When they met after the hunt, the lion asked. 'Where is your buffalo, you powerful beast?'

The hyena made the same excuse for the third time. 'They were afraid of me and fled before I had time to spring on one of them,' he said.

'All right,' growled the lion, 'we can share mine.'

But when they had eaten the buffalo the lion had killed, the King of Beasts turned to the hyena and said.

'So far, only I have proved my strength. Now it is your turn. We shall have a wrestling match. But if you lose, woe betide you! I shall kill you without mercy!'

The hyena had no wish to have a wrestling match, especially with the lion. So he said. 'Lion,

I thought I was stronger because I was hungry. But now that I have eaten well, I admit that you are the stronger.'

With that, the hyena took to his heels and vanished into the thicket.

The Fox Cub and the Three Bears

Once upon a time there was a fox cub who was very inquisitive and very adventurous. In vain did Mother Vixen scold her, in vain did Daddy Fox shake her; it was no use, she kept on going her own way. She ran away from home, wandered through the woods and several times did not even come home for dinner.

One day her mother said to her. 'If you are not careful, you will get lost completely or a bear will catch you in the woods and you will never see us again.'

Her mother was right. One day she really did get lost. She had gone further from home than usual when suddenly she found herself in a deep wood where there was not a living thing to be seen. Quite unafraid, the little fox cub went on and on, following her nose, until she came to a clearing. In the middle of the clearing stood a little house.

Any other fox would have first called out or knocked at the door, but not she. Quietly she crept up to the door, tried the lock and the door opened a little. The cub waited a moment and then pushed the door again. Then she pushed her muzzle into the opening, but still she heard and saw nothing. She gave the door a bigger push and her whole head was inside.

The cottage was empty and bare. In the middle of the room was a table and round the table were three chairs: one big, one middle-sized and a third that was tiny. On the table were three plates of porridge: one big, one middle-sized and one tiny little plate. In one corner of the room were three beds: one big, one middle-sized and a tiny one.

The fox cub was as hungry as a wolf after her long journey and her legs were so tired they could hardly carry her. When she saw the three plates of porridge on the table, she did not wait to be asked. She jumped up onto the biggest chair, seized the spoon and began to sup the porridge. But the chair was too tall and too hard, the spoon was too big and heavy and the porridge was too hot and salty.

'I do not like this,' she said to herself, and she spat out the porridge, threw down the spoon, pushed the chair away from the table and climbed onto the second chair.

But this was not much better. The second chair was too high and too hard, the second spoon was still too big and too heavy and the porridge in the second plate was only a little sweeter.

'I do not like this either,' she said to herself, and she spat out the porridge, threw down the spoon, pushed the chair away from the table and climbed onto the third chair.

This one was just right — not too tall and not too hard. The fox cub began to enjoy herself. She seized the spoon and began to sup the porridge. It was as sweet as honey and just hot enough to eat. And in a very few minutes the fox cub had supped it all up.

'That was just what I needed,' said she happily. 'Now I shall have a little nap.' She wiped her whiskers, threw down the spoon so carelessly that it fell on the floor and pushed back the chair so hard that it fell over.

Then she inspected the beds. First she tried the biggest bed. But the sheets and blankets came right over her head and the fox cub could not get to sleep.

'This is not for me,' said the fox cub. And she threw off the quilt, jumped down to the floor and climbed into the second bed.

But that was no better. The second bed had too many blankets and the fox cub could not get to sleep.

'This is not the bed for me either,' said she, and she threw off the quilt, jumped to the floor and climbed into the third bed.

This one was just right. The sheets and blankets did not come over her head, there were not too many blankets and it was soft and comfortable.

The fox cub fell asleep and slept and slept.

The fox cub was still sleeping peacefully when the owners of the little house — a big bear, a middle-sized bear and a little bear — arrived home. They had been for a walk in the forest and now were looking forward to their supper. In the doorway they stopped.

'Someone has been here!' growled the big bear in his deep voice.

'Someone has been here,' said the middle-sized bear in her middle-sized voice.

'Someone has been here,' squeaked the little bear in his thin little voice.

They went into the room and looked round.

'Someone has been sitting in my chair!' growled the big bear in his deep voice.

'And in mine too!' said the middle-sized bear in her middle-sized voice.

'And in mine too!' squeaked the little bear in his thin little voice. 'And has knocked it over!'

They went up to the table and looked down.

'Someone has been eating from my plate!' growled the big bear in his deep voice.

'And from mine too!' said the middle-sized bear in her middle-sized voice.

'And from mine too!' squeaked the little bear. 'And has eaten up all my porridge!'

They walked up to their beds and looked down.

'Someone has been sleeping in my bed!' growled the big bear in his deep voice.

'And in mine too!' said the middle-sized bear in her middle-sized voice.

'And in mine too!' squeaked the little bear in his thin little voice. 'And is still asleep there!'

The big bear, the middle-sized bear and the little bear all leaned over the bed and looked down at the sleeping fox cub.

Suddenly she opened her eyes. When she saw three angry bears gazing down at her, she leapt up in terror. But she was not quick enough to

escape. The big bear held her by her forelegs, the middle-sized bear by her hind legs and the little bear by her tail.

'What shall we do with her?' growled the big bear in his deep voice.

'What shall we do with her?' echoed the middle-sized bear in her middle-sized voice.

'What indeed?' squeaked the little bear in his thin little voice.

'We'd better kill her!' growled the big bear in his deep voice.

'We'd better drown her!' said the middle-sized bear in her middle-sized voice.

'We'll throw her out of the window!' squeaked the little bear in his thin little voice.

'One, two, three . . .'

And they swung the fox cub once, they swung her twice, then they threw her straight out of the open window.

She landed on all four feet. Like lightning she was off. She ran and she ran and did not stop running until she reached home.

No one knows how she found her way there, but she did. And since that day she has never run away again, nor has she strayed into the house of the three bears.

Brother Rabbit
and
the Melons

Brother Rabbit was extremely cunning, and this story tells how his cunning once saved his life. At that time the rabbit's neighbour, the bear, was growing melons in a field. He worked very hard and his efforts were rewarded. When the melons began to ripen, they were as sweet as honey. Then one day he noticed that some of his best melons were disappearing.

'Who is taking them?' said the puzzled bear to himself. 'Could it be Brother Rabbit?'

Brother Rabbit was indeed the thief. He had watched the melons ripen, and to annoy the bear and enjoy their sweetness himself, he began to steal them.

Brother Bear was angry. 'I'll steal a march on that rabbit!' he thought, and early one morning, before daybreak, he went to his melon field, taking his son, Bruin, with him.

They arrived in the field just as the rabbit was choosing the ripest melons. He was so busy he did not even hear the bears approach. And when he saw them it was too late.

Father Bear grabbed him by the ear. 'I've got you this time, Brother,' he growled. 'This time you will not escape the oven.'

Then he said to his son. 'Take Brother Rabbit home, and before the cock crows in the evening, put him in the oven and we'll have him for supper. In the meantime, I'll call on Brother Fox and invite him to the feast.'

Young Bruin seized hold of Brother Rabbit, threw him over his shoulder and set off for home. There was still plenty of time before the cock would crow in the evening. Brother Rabbit knew he had some hours to think of a way out of this awkward situation. In a little while an idea struck him. 'Can you remember exactly what your father told you to do?' he asked young Bruin.

Bruin stopped, scratched his head and growled. 'Of course I can! I am to take you home, Brother, and before the cock crows in the

evening, put you in the oven so that Father, Brother Fox and I will have you for supper.'

Brother Rabbit laughed heartily. 'You would be in trouble if you did that, Bruin. That's just the opposite of what he said. What your father said was: take Brother Rabbit home, and before the cock crows, put the cock in the oven so that there will be something for his supper.'

Bruin stood stock still with his mouth open. 'You are right, Brother. And to think I was nearly going to roast you. Thank you for putting me right.'

And he hurried home before he made any more mistakes. As soon as he arrived he set to work. He killed the cock before it had time to crow in the evening and put it in the oven. When it was nicely roasted he brought it to the rabbit. Brother Rabbit ate it up with relish.

'It was very good, Bruin,' he said. 'Now I'd like to take a little nap before Brother Bear comes home. Just bring me a blanket and I'll lie down in the garden.'

Bruin obediently brought a blanket and Brother Rabbit carried it off to the garden. But he did not lie down himself. He rolled up a small log of wood in the blanket, then hid behind the fence to watch and wait.

Towards evening Brother Bear appeared. He was in a jovial mood and looking forward to his supper of roast rabbit. As he came to the door he called to his son.

'So young Bruin, where have you got this rabbit?' Bruin pointed to the garden.

'He's lying down out there. He wanted to have a nap after his supper,' said Bruin.

Brother Bear was furious. 'What are you saying, you fool? Didn't I tell you to put him in the oven?'

'Yes, you did,' said Bruin, 'and I did put him in the oven.'

The bear was angry. 'What do you mean? You told me he was in the garden, didn't you?'

'Brother Rabbit is in the garden. I put the cock into the oven as you told me,' Bruin replied.

Brother Bear was beside himself with anger. 'But I told you to put the rabbit, not the cock, in the oven. I should have guessed that Brother Rabbit would make a fool of you. But don't try to make a fool of me!'

And he took up a big stick and went into the garden. There in the grass lay the blanket, and something was wrapped up in it. Brother Bear without stopping to think beat it with his stick. The stick broke. One end remained in his hand, the other flew up and hit him on the head so hard it nearly knocked him senseless.

A huge lump appeared on his head; and at the same time he heard someone laughing on the other side of the fence. It was Brother Rabbit.

He called out. 'Well, Brother, I caught you out nicely, didn't I?'

And Brother Rabbit ran off home very pleased with himself.

But he never came again to steal Brother Bear's melons. He was afraid he would not catch out Brother Bear a second time.

The Frogs and Death

When death came to the world, all creatures began to die when their time came. Only the frogs did not die. Death had forgotten them. They lived far away from people and animals in the middle of a marsh. They increased and multiplied, they grew larger and grew old peacefully, but they did not die.

In time there were more of them than all the other animals put together.

But while the frogs flourished, the storks fared badly. At that time they lived in the steppes and had many enemies. Their worst enemy was one hunter who killed so many of them with his arrows that in the end only three storks remained. They were brothers, and when they realized they were the last of their family, they decided it was time to look for a new home.

'Before leaving the steppes, we must be sure we are going to a better place,' said the oldest stork. 'I shall go out and search for our new home.'

He flew off and arrived at last at the marsh where the frogs lived. He greeted them politely and the frogs welcomed him warmly.

'Where do you come from, and what are you looking for?' they asked.

'I am looking for a new home for myself and my brothers,' said the stork. And he told the frogs what had happened to his family.

'If we do not move,' he said, 'death is waiting for us. The hunter will kill us all.'

The frogs were amazed. 'What is death?' they asked. 'We do not know anything about death here. In the marshes no one dies. Perhaps that hunter kills you because you live freely in the steppes. But here there are no hunters and no death!'

'Then we will come and live here with you,' decided the stork. And he flew off to tell his brothers about their new home.

Next day the three storks left the steppes forever. The hunter did not follow them, and the storks settled down happily in the marshes.

But the frogs were less fortunate. As there were no mice in the marshes, the storks began to catch and eat the frogs.

To this day storks catch and eat frogs, and the frogs have learned what death is.

The Centipede
and
Its Legs

Long, long ago, the centipede made a living by making and selling legs. And because neither people nor animals were yet quite whole, the centipede prospered.

Anyone who needed a leg or two came to the market, chose what he needed and paid the centipede well.

But she did not flourish long. People and animals soon had all the legs they needed and they stopped buying from the centipede. When she brought her goods to the market no one would even stop at her stall.

'Buy some legs!' called the centipede to a man who was passing by. But he did not even notice her and went off.

'Buy some legs!' shouted the centipede to a dog. But he only barked and ran off.

'Buy some new legs!' the centipede begged of a horse. But the horse only neighed and galloped off.

The centipede was angry. 'No one wants my beautiful legs.' she cried. 'Am I to throw them on the rubbish heap? Am I to throw away a whole month's work? Indeed I shall not. I would rather keep them for myself, even if there were a hundred of them!'

And since that time the centipede has neither made nor sold legs. But she herself walks on a hundred legs that no one wanted to buy.

The Princess and the Cat Kingdom

There was once a king who had three sons. The two older sons were sure that no one was cleverer than they. The third and youngest brother, they thought, was a fool and they never lost an opportunity to tell him so. This worried the old king. He was afraid that after his death there would be strife between the brothers and that this would harm the whole kingdom.

For a long time he wondered which of his sons should succeed him on the throne. Finally he called them together.

'It is time you went out into the world,' he said. 'I shall set you a task. The son who after a year and a day returns with the most beautiful suit of clothes will inherit my throne and my crown.'

The princes agreed at once to go out into the world — particularly the two older ones. Each of them could already picture himself on the throne with the royal crown on his head. They each chose a fine horse and, clad in shining armour, they set out, the two older brothers in front, the youngest following behind. When they came to the first crossroads, each went his own way, the two older princes along wide, straight paths, and the youngest up a steep overgrown route with many bends.

The straight paths led to royal castles in neighbouring countries. There the princes became pages and were well thought of at the royal courts where they served.

The steep route, on the other hand, led through a dense forest, across mountains and valleys to a wilderness where not a living soul could be seen. The youngest prince was sure he was completely lost when suddenly a black cat appeared before him.

The cat ran up to him, rubbed itself against his legs, then ran on as if it were telling the young man to follow. So the prince followed. Leading his tired horse by the bridle he slowly walked after the black cat until he came to a beautiful castle.

The prince passed through the courtyard, and leaving his horse, entered a great hall. There, everything was so magnificent that the prince thought it must all be a dream. But it was no dream. The castle was real enough, but it was completely deserted. There was not a living person to be seen anywhere, not a servant, not a nobleman, not a king. Instead of people black cats stole about silently.

The prince came next to the dining hall, in the middle of which stood a table and a single armchair. On the table there was one set of cutlery, one plate and one goblet.

The prince was hungry and shyly he approached the able. Scarcely had he sat down than the goblet was full of wine, on the plate was roast meat and on the white table cloth a slice of bread. The prince ate hungrily and drank the wine. Then aloud he said, 'Thank you'.

Next moment a door on the other side of the dining hall opened and a large white cat appeared. She jumped onto the table, sat down as if on a throne and spoke.

'Welcome, Prince, and fear nothing! I know why you have come and if you serve me loyally for a year in this castle you will have what you need. Your service will not be easy, but if you persevere, you will be satisfied.'

The prince was full of amazement, but he promised to remain with the cat ruler and obey her commands.

And so the young prince's year of service began. He had to get up early in the morning, sweep the whole castle, carry out the ashes, chop firewood and bring it in — in fact he worked as a servant and not as a prince. But the prince did not complain. He worked hard and he worked well, and the cat ruler was pleased with him.

The months passed like lightning and one day the cat ruler herself came to tell the prince that his year's service was over. She brought an old, shabby rucksack and gave it to the prince saying.

'This is your reward for loyal service. Do not be surprised that the rucksack is shabby. Open it when you arrive home and you will see that it has in it what you desire!' With that she said goodbye to the prince.

The prince set out on his return journey. At the crossroads he met his brothers. They were riding proudly, wearing beautiful suits of clothes given to them by their masters, the kings of the neighbouring countries. When they saw their youngest brother carrying his shabby rucksack, they burst into laughter. And so they all three arrived home and at once presented themselves to their father.

The old king was pleased at the sight of the fine clothes worn by his older sons. But his youngest son angered and disappointed him, for he had with him only a shabby rucksack.

'Get out of my sight, you good for nothing,' he cried. 'How dare you come home with such rubbish.'

But the youngest prince was not put out. He opened the rucksack, and emptied it before the

astonished eyes of his father and brothers. Never had they seen clothes so magnificent. They fitted the youngest prince perfectly. The old king had to admit that the youngest prince had brought home the most beautiful suit of clothes. The throne and the crown must be his.

But the older brothers would not agree to this. 'Who knows where he got them or where he found them,' they grumbled. And they continued to grumble until finally the old king changed his mind and said.

'Very well, go out all three of you into the world again, and the son who after a year and a day brings back the finest horse will have my throne and my royal crown!'

The princes agreed, and without delay set out on their journey. At the first crossroads they separated, the two older brothers taking wide straight paths leading to neighbouring kingdoms, while the youngest took the same steep path leading to the castle of the cat ruler.

There he was awaited. The young prince again found himself in the dining hall of the castle where the table was laid for one and the single chair invited him to sit.

Scarcely had the prince sat down than his goblet was full of wine, on the plate was roast meat and on the white cloth a slice of bread. The prince ate hungrily, drank the wine, then aloud he said, 'Thank you'.

Next moment, the door on the other side of the dining hall opened and the large white cat — the mistress of the castle — appeared. She spoke.

'Welcome, Prince, and fear nothing! I know why you have come and if you serve me loyally in my stables you shall have what you need.'

The prince joyfully promised to serve the cat as best as he could, and the same day he set to work.

The work was not easy. He had to get up early in the morning, sweep the yard, clean out the stables and sheds, spread new straw for the horses and work as if he were not a prince but an ordinary groom or stable lad. But the prince did not complain. He worked as best as he could and the cat ruler was satisfied with him.

Again the months flew past and one day the cat ruler came to tell the prince that his year's service was over. Then she led him to an old ungroomed horse and said.

'This is your reward for loyal service. Do not worry that this horse looks old and ungroomed. Take him home with you, and when you arrive give him three taps on the shoulder. You will not be disappointed.'

With that she bade him farewell.

The prince set out on his return journey. At the crossroads where the three paths met he came upon his brothers. They were riding proudly on splendid horses which they had earned at the courts of their masters — the

neighbouring kings. When they saw their youngest brother on his old, ungroomed horse they just laughed aloud. And so they all three arrived home and at once presented themselves to their father.

The old king admired the horses of his older sons, but again he was angry and disappointed with his youngest son.

'Get out of my sight, you good for nothing!' he cried. 'How dare you come home with such a horse!'

The youngest prince was not put out, but tapped his horse three times on the shoulder. The old king could not believe his eyes. Never in his life had he seen such a beautiful horse. He had to admit that it was his youngest son who had brought back the finest horse. The throne and the crown must be his.

But the two older brothers again would not agree. 'Who knows where he got it or from whom he stole it,' they grumbled. And they continued to grumble until finally the old king cried.

'Very well, go out all three of you into the world again. The son who brings home the most

beautiful bride shall inherit my throne and the royal crown.'

The princes agreed, and the very same day set out into the world again. When they came to the first crossroads, they separated as before, the two older princes taking the wide, straight paths leading to neighbouring kingdoms, while the youngest took the same steep path leading to the castle of the cat ruler.

There he was awaited. He had hardly sat down at the table in the dining hall, and scarcely had time to eat and drink and say 'thank you', then the white cat appeared, sat down on the table as if on a throne and said.

'Welcome, Prince, and fear nothing! If once again you serve me loyally you shall have what you desire.' And she ordered him to work for a year in the castle garden.

It was not easy work. The prince had to get up early in the morning, sweep up leaves, weed the flowerbeds and prune the shrubs and trees, and work as if he was not a prince at all but an ordinary gardener. But the prince did not

complain. He worked as best as he could and the cat ruler was satisfied with him.

The months flew past and once again the ruler came to tell the prince that his year's service was over. Then she led him into the courtyard. There stood an ancient carriage.

'It is time to be off,' she said. 'And do not be surprised if you find in the carriage a bride wearing a white veil and a cat-skin coat! When you get home and kiss her, you will regret nothing.'

The prince climbed into the ancient carriage and next moment a bride sat down beside him. She had a wreath on her head and a thick white veil, but he could see that beneath the veil was a large cat. The prince was startled but he trusted the words of the cat ruler and set out for home.

At the crossroads he met his two brothers. They were riding proudly in golden carriages and at their sides sat the daughters of neighbouring kings. When they saw their youngest brother in the old and shabby coach and sitting next to him a bride wearing the coat of a cat, they laughed. And so all three arrived home and at once presented themselves to the king. The old king admired the brides of his two older sons, but again was angry and disappointed with his youngest son.

'Get out of my sight, you good for nothing!' he cried. 'How dare you come home with such a creature as a bride!'

But once again the youngest prince was not put out. He lifted the veil of his bride and kissed her, and there before the old king stood a princess such as he had never seen in his life. The old king had to admit that it was his youngest son who had brought home the most beautiful bride. The throne and the crown should be his.

But the older brothers would not hear of such a thing and again set up an outcry.

And at this point Princess Cat approached the old king.

'Your youngest son, Your Majesty, has no need of a throne and a crown,' she said. 'He has freed me from a wicked spell by his loyal service, and not only my hand is his but the whole of my kingdom. I invite you most respectfully to attend our wedding.'

The wedding took place within three days and was so splendid and so joyful that all remembered it to their dying day.

And to their dying day, everyone present told their children and grandchildren how the youngest prince by his loyal service freed the white cat and her cat kingdom from the spell that bound them.

The Cat, the Tiger and Human Strength

A man one day rode off to his fields. With him he took a cat to catch mice in the fields. But the cat ran off to the woods and there he met a tiger.

The tiger looked at the cat, shook his head in wonder and said. 'You look as if you are my cousin. But why are you so weak and tiny?'

'You would be weak and tiny too if you lived with man,' answered the cat. 'Man has great strength and does not allow me to grow bigger and stronger.'

'Is that what man is like?' asked the tiger.

'If you do not believe me, come and look. He is ploughing that field over there,' urged the cat.

So the tiger approached the man. 'I hear that you are very strong, man,' he said, 'and do not allow my cousin the cat to grow bigger and stronger. Show me this strength of yours.'

'I do not always bring my strength with me,' the man replied. 'Today I left it at home.'

'I shall wait for you here. Go and fetch it now,' the tiger commanded.

'I know what will happen,' said the man, 'I shall go home and you will run away. I will have to tie you to this tree to make sure you will stay here until I return.'

The tiger agreed to this proposal. The man tied him to the tree and went home to fetch a heavy stick. When he came back, he began to beat the tiger with his stick.

'Now you know how strong I am, tiger,' he shouted, and beat the tiger still harder.

The tiger howled and begged the man to let him go. 'I knew all along how strong man is,' he cried. 'I shall go now into the depths of the forest so that I shall never have to meet a man again.'

Then the man let him go, and the tiger hardly managed to crawl away.

'No wonder the cat is so small and weak,' he growled to himself. 'Even I who am large and strong barely escaped with my life.'

The Leopard,
the Stag
and the Snake

A stag was one day grazing in the forest, when suddenly he heard someone calling for help. He followed the voice and what did he see but a fallen tree lying across the path. Beneath it was a leopard. The tree had pinned him to the ground so that he could not move.

'How did this happen, Leopard?' he asked.

'The tree fell on me and caught me like a trap,' the leopard wailed. 'Lift it off quickly, or I'll die!'

The stag did not want to free the leopard. 'I don't know, Leopard, whether I'll be strong enough,' he said.

But the leopard went on moaning and begging and promising gratitude for ever, that in the end the stag relented. He pushed at the tree with his antlers once, twice and a third time and at last succeeded in rolling it off the leopard.

The leopard sprang up, shook himself, then bared his teeth. 'Thank you, Stag,' he said. 'Now I'm going to eat you.'

The stag was frightened. 'Is that the gratitude you promised me?' he asked.

'Gratitude, what's gratitude?' said the leopard. 'Surely you don't want me to die of hunger, do you? I am hungry. I've been lying here all day with nothing to eat.'

The stag pleaded. 'That's not just, Leopard,' he said. 'You promised me your gratitude and you must keep your word. What would the rest of the animals think of you? Come, let us ask someone to decide which of us is right.'

So the stag and the leopard at last agreed to put their case to the wise old snake.

The old snake listened attentively to the stag and the leopard. Then he said.

'The stag is right to demand gratitude from the leopard. After all he saved his life. But the

leopard is also right in wanting to eat the stag. After all, he doesn't want to die of hunger. It is a very difficult matter to judge. We must all go to the exact spot where everything happened. You will show me what took place and I will then decide between you.'

The stag and the leopard agreed to this. They took the snake to the fallen tree. The leopard lay down on the ground and the stag rolled the tree over him. The snake was satisfied.

'Good,' he said, 'and now, Stag, you must raise the tree again so that the leopard can get free.'

But the stag was not willing to do this. 'I've raised it already today and I'm not strong enough to do it again,' he said.

The snake shook his head. 'Well, if you're not strong enough, there's nothing to be done about it. But I can't pass judgment on you.'

The stag was not interested in judgment being passed. He thanked the snake and ran off to graze. The wise snake crawled after him.

And the leopard? Well, the leopard stayed where he was under the tree trunk and waited for someone else to come and help him.

195

The Young Herdsman and the Little Yellow Cow

There was once a poor boy who had no father or mother. His father died when he was a tiny baby and his mother when he was barely twelve years old.

So he stayed alone in the hut that had belonged to his parents with just a little yellow cow for company.

The boy took care of his yellow cow as best he could. He took her to graze on the slopes of the mountains and in the valleys, he took her to drink in the pure clear streams. He groomed her every evening and talked to her as if she were a human being, for he had no one else to talk to.

The cow rewarded him for his love. When the boy had grown up and become a fine upstanding young man, the cow suddenly spoke to him in a human voice.

'The time has come, my boy, for you to get married,' she said.

The young herdsman was astonished, partly because his yellow cow had spoken to him, and partly because she had spoken to him about marriage.

'Who would take such a poor lad as me for her husband?' he asked.

But the yellow cow replied.

'I know of such a girl. Listen! The ruler of the heavens, the Jasper Emperor, has nine daughters. They are all as beautiful as peach blossom but the youngest is the most beautiful of them all. But not only is she beautiful to look at, she is also a beautiful spinner. That is why she is called the Celestial Spinning Maid. She spins for the Celestial Emperor and Empress the finest silk for clouds. If you hurry you will have her for your wife. Today is the magic seventh day of the seventh month when she goes with her sisters to bathe in the celestial lake. If you take her by surprise and take her clothes when she is in the water, she will become your wife because it is so ordained.'

The young herdsman could scarcely believe his ears. 'But how can I reach that lake, little cow?' he asked. 'How can I get from the earth to the heavens?'

'That is for me to worry about!' said the cow.

'Just sit on my back and I shall take you there.'

She was as good as her word. As soon as the young herdsman climbed onto the back of the little yellow cow, she took off and flew straight to the heavens. She landed at last on the shore of a beautiful lake where nine beautiful girls were bathing. Their clothes were lying on the bank.

'Those garments made of red silk belong to the Celestial Spinning Maid. Quickly, take them, then hide in the undergrowth,' the cow told the young man. 'The Celestial Spinning Maid will ask you to give them back to her, but you must not until she promises to be your wife.'

The young herdsman did what the cow told him. He ran to the lake, took the red garments and hid in the undergrowth. But the girls in the lake saw him and set up a cry.

'Stop! What are you doing? Put those clothes back!'

But the herdsman ignored them. He held the red dress more closely to his breast and did not answer. At this the daughters of the Jasper Emperor swam to the bank. Eight of them put on their clothes, then called out.

'Ninth sister, your fore-ordained bridegroom has come for you. We shall leave you alone with him.'

The ninth princess could not come out of the water. She started to beg. 'Herdsman, give me back my clothes.'

But the herdsman replied. 'I shall give them to you,' he said, 'when you promise to be my wife.'

The Celestial Spinning Maid protested. 'How can I marry you without my father's permission?' she asked. 'If I married you against his will, he would punish us, for he is the Jasper Emperor and ruler of the heavens.'

The little herdsman would have perhaps given in, but the cow said.

'Do not be afraid of your father, Celestial Spinning Maid. I shall go and persuade him. You will discover that he will welcome your herdsman, for he is your fore-ordained bridgeroom. Just ask the grass, just ask the bushes, just ask the willow trees that grow here.'

What could the Celestial Spinning Maid do? She asked the grass as the cow had told her, and the grass answered. 'Today is the seventh day of the seventh month and this herdsman is your fore-ordained bridegroom.'

And when she asked the bushes, they gave the same answer. 'Today is the seventh day of the seventh mont and this herdsman is your fore-ordained bridegroom.'

And when she asked the green willow trees by the lake they gave the same answer. 'Never fear, Celestial Spinning Maid! Today is the seventh day of the seventh month and this herdsman is your fore-ordained bridegroom. Take him, he is yours!'

And so the Celestial Spinning Maid at last gave her promise to the herdsman. The herdsman gave her her beautiful clothes, the princess dressed and the yellow cow carried them back to earth.

There were happy days in store for the young man and the Celestial Spinning Maid. They loved each other dearly, their love was so strong that they could not bear to be apart even for a moment. The herdsman was so much in love that he forgot to take his little cow to graze and the Celestial Spinning Maid forgot to spin the fine silk for the Celestial Emperor.

In vain did the little yellow cow warn them, in vain did she tell them that they would anger

you like I shall fly after them. Bring your little boys and climb onto my back.'

The herdsman did as the cow told him and brought his two little sons and all three climbed onto the cow's back.

Like an arrow from a bow the cow shot into the air and very soon began to catch up with the envoys of the Jasper Emperor.

The herdsman cried out impatiently. 'There they are!' But he should have kept quiet. For as soon as the envoys of the Jasper Emperor heard him and saw that the little cow was on their heels, one of them pulled a pin from the Celestial Spinning Maid's hair and drew a line with it across the sky. The line turned into a silver river which people call the Milky Way, and the cow could not cross.

Nor could the envoys of the Celestial Emperor go further. The Celestial Spinning Maid with tears in her eyes gazed at her husband and children from afar.

Since that day to this, the herdsman seated on his little cow, with his small sons behind him have remained fixed in the heavens on one side of the Milky Way, and the Celestial Spinning Maid with the two envoys of the Jasper Emperor have remained fixed on the other. At least that is what they say in the far off Land of the Dragons.

All year round the herdsman and the Celestial Spinning Maid gaze across at each other, but once a year they are allowed to meet.

That is on the magic seventh day of the seventh month.

On that day all the crows in the world fly to the celestial river and form a bridge over which the Celestial Spinning Maid passes to visit her husband and her little sons. The faithful crows, it is said, have a bald patch on their heads worn down by the steps of the Celestial Spinning Maid as she walks over them. And in the evening when the herdsman and his Celestial Spinning Maid say goodbye to each other, they all shed so many tears that rain falls on the earth below.

the Jasper Emperor. The herdsman and his wife took no notice. And when a year later, twin boys were born to them, they forgot the world altogether. The little yellow cow had to graze by herself, the cloudy silk remained unspun and the Jasper Emperor in the heavens became more and more angry.

At last his patience was at an end. Angrily he sent to earth two of his terrible envoys to carry off the Celestial Spinning Maid. The herdsman was in the garden behind the house with the two little boys and saw nothing. But when in a few minutes he returned to the house, it was empty and his beautiful wife had gone. The herdsman ran to the yellow cow to ask what he should do.

'Tell me, little cow,' he said, 'where is the Celestial Spinning Maid? What has become of her?'

The little yellow cow replied. 'What I warned you of has come about. The Celestial Emperor was angry and sent two of his terrible envoys for your wife. They have carried her off, but if

The Jackal
and
the Partridge

A jackal went hunting one day and caught a partridge. He was just about to eat it when the partridge started to plead with him. 'Let me live, Jackal, and I shall fulfil all your wishes.'

The jackal let himself be persuaded. He said. 'All right, I shall let you go, but you must feed me, make me laugh and make me cry, otherwise I shall eat you.'

The partridge promised. 'Nothing could be easier,' it said. 'First I shall feed you. Come with me, Jackal!'

And the partridge led the jackal to a path near which they hid together in the undergrowth. After a time a countrywoman came along the path carrying a pot on her head. She was taking food to her husband who was working in the fields.

The partridge darted onto the path. Then it ran a few steps and fell down as if it had a broken wing. The countrywoman ran after it, but at the last moment the partridge flew a little further. The woman set down the pot at the side of the path and ran after the partridge again. But again the partridge flew on a little further and again the woman ran after it.

In the meantime, the jackal came out of the undergrowth, jumped on the pot and in a trice gobbled up the meat.

When he had finished he called out. 'Thank you, Partridge, I have had a good meal!'

'That is good!' replied the partridge and spread its wings and flew off. The countrywoman had not caught it and, in addition, she had lost her husband's dinner.

Beyond the wood the partridge and the jackal met again. The partridge said. 'And now, Jackal,

I shall make you laugh. Come with me!' And it led the jackal to a field where two brothers were ploughing. One brother was guiding the plough, the other was walking behind him breaking up the clods with a mattock.

The partridge told the jackal to hide in the undergrowth. Then it flew onto the ploughman's head and started pecking at his cap. The ploughman tried to dodge it, but the partridge only flew off for a moment and then came back to peck at his cap again. Soon the ploughman was red with rage.

'Brother, catch that partridge,' he yelled, 'or it will carry off my cap.'

The brother leaned forward and hit out at the partridge with his mattock. But the partridge did not wait. At the last moment it flew off and the mattock landed on the ploughman's head. The ploughman fell flat on his face. It was lucky for him that he was wearing his cap, otherwise his brother might have killed him.

When the jackal saw all this he started to laugh and he laughed so long he nearly split his sides. 'Thank you, Partridge,' he said. 'Now I have had a good laugh.'

'That is good,' answered the partridge and flew off.

Beyond the wood the partridge and the jackal met for the third time.

The partridge said. 'And now, Jackal, I shall make you cry. Come with me!' And it led the jackal to a tall tree. It perched itself on a twig and said. 'Look, Jackal, there is a nice piece of lamb lying on the ground. Help yourself!'

And there really was a piece of meat lying

under the tree. The jackal did not need to be told twice and he scratched at it with his paw. But the meat was the bait in a trap. The trap closed and caught the jackal by his tail. The jackal began to howl. He howled all night. The partridge was surprised.

'Why are you making such a fuss, Jackal,' it said. 'You wanted me to make you cry and I have. But you can stop crying now. Be glad that I have fulfilled all your wishes. That does not happen to everyone.'

This did not console the jackal at all. He grew angry, and jerked his tail so hard that he pulled it out of the trap. Then he took to his heels and was off. Since then he has never wanted anyone to make him cry.

The Wolf, the Hare and the Leverets

It was winter, the animals in the woods were hungry and one of the hungriest was the wolf. He was searching for something good to eat when he met the hare. With a growl he leapt at him and said.

'I am so hungry, I am going to eat you!'

But the hare did not flinch.

'You wouldn't get much of a meal out of me,' he replied. 'I'm all skin and bone. Just look! Wait till autumn and I'll bring you my children. They'll have more meat on them. Go to the village for food today. They've just killed a pig there.'

The wolf agreed. 'All right,' he said. 'I'll go to the village since you say there's been a pig killed. But don't forget what you've promised me! You bring me your young ones in the autumn or it'll be the worse for you!'

Winter passed and spring and summer. Then at last it was autumn and the wolf again met the hare.

'You haven't forgotten what you promised me in the winter?' he asked.

And the hare said. 'No, I haven't forgotten, Wolf! Tomorrow I'll bring you my young ones. There are six of them.'

The wolf went off, satisfied, and the hare hurried to his children.

Next morning he took them to a field of corn. There he broke off some ears of corn and pushed them into the mouths of all his leverets, in such a way that a little bit was peeping out.

Then he took them to the wolf. 'Here are my leverets,' he said. 'But take care! Since they've eaten up that lion, there's nothing I can do with them.'

The wolf was startled. 'What's that sticking out of their mouths?' he asked.

The hare replied. 'Oh, that's nothing! On the way here we met six wolves and now they're playing with their tails!'

The wolf was now very frightened. He did not want to lose his tail. Without a word he took to his heels and vanished into the undergrowth.

And so the hare and his leverets went home, taking with them six plump ears of corn for supper.

The Brave Half-a-Cockerel and the King

Once upon a time there were two old women who between them had one possession — a little cockerel. One day the first old woman said. 'What are we going to eat today? We have no milk, we have no flour. All we have is our little cockerel. Let us make soup with it!'

'No, no,' cried the other old woman. 'I like to see our little cockerel running around the yard.'

'The cockerel belongs to us both. I shall make soup from my half of the cockerel,' said the first old woman.

'Very well,' said the second old woman. 'But you must leave my half to run about in the yard.'

And the first old woman made soup out of her half of the cockerel and left the other half running about in the yard.

Half-a-Cockerel ran about the yard, waved one wing, scratched with one claw and pecked with half a beak. And as it ran and scratched and pecked, it found on the dunghill a purse full of gold sovereigns. Half-a-Cockerel rejoiced.

'Cock-a-doodle-do, cock-a-doodle-do, I have a purse full of gold sovereigns. I found it in the yard. I shall give it to my old woman!' And it ran towards the old woman's room to give her the purse of gold sovereigns.

But just at that moment the king himself drove past in a golden coach. When he saw Half-a-Cockerel carrying a large purse in his beak, he ordered his coachmen to halt the horses.

'What is that creature holding in its beak?' he asked his lackeys.

'A purse full of money, Sire,' they said.

'Then bring it to me!' the king commanded.

The lackeys grabbed Half-a-Cockerel, took the purse from him and drove off.

The little Half-a-Cockerel was angry.

'Cock-a-doodle-do, cock-a-doodle-do,' he crowed. 'I had a purse full of gold sovereigns. I scratched it up myself, but the king has stolen it from me. I will go to the king's castle and get it back!'

And he set off for the royal castle. He walked on and on, until he met a fox.

'Where are you going, Half-a-Cockerel?' asked the fox.

'I am going to fetch a purse of money the king has taken from me,' he said.

'I shall come with you,' said the fox.

'Very well!' said Half-a-Cockerel. 'Let us be on our way!'

And they set off together for the royal castle. They walked on and on, but soon the fox grew tired.

'Half-a-Cockerel, I cannot go on,' he gasped.

'Climb under my wing, then,' said Half-a-Cockerel.

And the fox climbed under Half-a-Cockerel's wing and little Half-a-Cockerel walked bravely on. He walked and walked, until he met a swarm of wasps.

'Where are you going, Half-a-Cockerel?' they asked.

'To fetch a purse of gold sovereigns the king has taken away from me,' said Half-a-Cockerel.

'We shall come with you!' said the wasps.

And they all set off for the royal castle. They walked on and on, but soon the wasps grew tired.

'Half-a-Cockerel, we cannot go on,' they said.

'Climb under my wing then,' said Half-a-Cockerel.

The wasps climbed under Half-a-Cockerel's wing and little Half-a-Cockerel walked bravely on. He went on and on, until he reached the river.

'Where are you going, Half-a-Cockerel?' asked the river.

'To fetch a purse of gold sovereigns the king has taken away from me,' Half-a-Cockerel replied.

'I am coming with you,' said the river.

And they set off for the royal castle. They walked on and on, but soon the river grew tired.

'Half-a-Cockerel, I cannot go on,' said the river.

'Climb under my wing then!' said Half-a-Cockerel.

The river climbed under Half-a-Cockerel's wing and little Half-a-Cockerel walked bravely on. He went on and on, until at last he arrived at the royal castle.

'Good morning, Sire,' said Half-a-Cockerel to the king. 'Please give me back my purse of gold sovereigns!'

'You will get it tomorrow!' said the king. 'Servants, take this Half-a-Cockerel to the chicken coop and put him with the other chickens!'

The king thought that his chickens would peck Half-a-Cockerel to death overnight. And sure enough, as soon as it got dark, the king's chickens began to peck, until they had nearly pecked Half-a-Cockerel to death.

But Half-a-Cockerel cried. 'Fox, come out at once before these chickens peck me to death!'

And the fox jumped out from under Half-a-Cockerel's wing, ate half of the king's chickens and killed the other half. Then he ran off.

Next morning the king visited the chicken coop.

'Good morning, Sire. Please give me back my purse of gold sovereigns!' crowed Half-a-Cockerel.

'You will get it tomorrow,' said the king. 'Servants, take Half-a-Cockerel to my room.'

The king thought that he himself would put an end to Half-a-Cockerel's life. And sure enough, as soon as it grew dark and Half-a-Cockerel had fallen asleep on the king's throne, the king came and sat down on top of him until he was nearly stifled to death!

But Half-a-Cockerel cried. 'Wasps, come out at once before I am stifled to death!'

And the wasps flew out from under Half-a-Cockerel's wing and stung the king so badly that he crawled off to bed crying with pain. Then the wasps flew away. When the king woke up in the morning, he was swollen all over and looked like a barrel.

And Half-a-Cockerel called. 'Good morning, Sire! Please give me back my purse of gold sovereigns!'

'You will get it tomorrow morning!' said the king. 'Wife, put Half-a-Cockerel into the oven tonight.'

The king thought that the servants would light the fire under the oven in the morning and so would roast Half-a-Cockerel. And sure enough, as soon as day dawned, the servants lit the fire and Half-a-Cockerel was nearly roasted.

But Half-a-Cockerel called out. 'River, river,

come out at once or I shall be roasted alive!'

And the river flowed out from under Half-a-Cockerel's wing and began to flood first the oven, then the kitchen and soon the whole castle was awash. The king first climbed onto his throne, then onto a wardrobe, and finally onto the roof. Half-a-Cockerel flew after him.

'Good morning, Sire!' he crowed. 'Please give me back my purse of gold sovereigns. If you do not give it to me, you will drown!'

The king saw that Half-a-Cockerel was too clever for him. He took the purse of gold sovereigns out of his pocket and threw it at Half-a-Cockerel.

'Here it is,' he cried angrily.

Only then did the river fall back and flow away. And little Half-a-Cockerel took in his beak the purse of gold sovereigns and with all speed ran back to his old woman.

And to the end of his days little Half-a-Cockerel ran happily round the yard pecking and scratching and crowing, 'Once I had a purse of gold sovereigns. The king stole that purse, but I was too clever for him. And my old woman is rich and happy, and I am happy too running round my yard.'

How Fairy Tales Reached the Earth

Long, long ago all the animals lived together in heaven. One day, the Good Spirit called them together and showed them a grain of corn.

'Which of you,' he said 'will bring me a bullock in exchange for this grain of corn?'

'A bullock for a grain of corn?' cried the animals in dismay. And none of them wanted to try. None of them except the wily hare who said. 'Good Spirit, give me the grain of corn and I shall try to exchange it for a bullock!'

And the hare set out into the world carrying the grain of corn. In the first village he came to, he sat down on the village green and dropped the grain of corn on the grass. Soon a hen came running from a nearby farm yard and gobbled up the grain. The wily hare grabbed the hen by a wing and ran with it into the farm yard to complain.

'Look,' he cried, 'your hen has swallowed my grain of corn!'

'That's easily settled,' said the owner of the hen soothingly. 'I have plenty of corn and will give you a whole ear if you like.'

'But that grain of corn was given to me by the Good Spirit himself,' answered the hare. 'Even a whole ear of corn would be too little for that one grain. You must give me the hen!'

And so the wily hare became the owner of a hen. The next evening he arrived with the hen at another village. At the first cottage he asked for a night's lodging.

'But do not put this hen in your hen house,' he said to the cottager. 'It's too big. You must put it with your goats.'

In the morning when the hare went to fetch the hen, he found she had been trampled to death by the goats. Loudly the hare lamented his loss.

'Do not worry about the loss of one hen. I have many hens,' said the good cottager. 'I shall give you another one.'

'But that hen was from the Good Spirit himself,' moaned the hare. 'No other hen could take her place. You must give me a goat instead!'

So the hare became the owner of a goat. And on the third day he arrived with his goat at the last village. At the outskirts of the village the hare asked for a night's lodging at one of the cottages.

'But do not put my goat in with yours,' he said. 'For she is strong and fierce. You must house her with your bullocks.'

In the morning the hare went for his goat. She was dead. A bullock had pushed her against the wall and crushed her. Loudly the hare lamented the loss of his goat.

'Do not worry about the loss of one goat,' said the master of the house. 'I have many goats. I shall give you one of them.'

'But mine came from the Good Spirit himself,' moaned the hare. 'No other would be her equal! You must give me a bullock in her place.'

So in the end the hare got a fine bullock in exchange for a grain of corn. When he took it up to heaven, the Good Spirit could not believe his eyes.

'You certainly deserve a reward, Master Hare,' he said. 'Tell me what you would like, a crock of gold, a crock of silver or a bowl of pearls?'

But the wily hare wanted neither gold nor silver nor pearls. He had caught sight of a big old gourd which lay at the feet of the Good Spirit. Hidden in it were all the fables of the world. When the Good Spirit wanted to tell one of these to his animals, he would pull the gourd towards him and out would come a fable of its own accord.

'Good Spirit,' said the hare, 'most of all I should like your gourd filled with fables.'

'And you shall have it,' said the Good Spirit.

'But you must always be careful not to upset the gourd. Otherwise the fables will be lost to you forever.'

'I shall be very careful,' promised the hare as he took up the gourd. But he had scarcely taken a few steps when he tripped over a heavenly stone. He dropped the gourd and it rolled over and over down the hill, and as it rolled the fables spilled out and were scattered to the four corners of the earth.

All that was left for the hare was an old and empty gourd.

And ever since then there have been fables all over the world about every animal that inhabits the earth.